SECRETS MY MOTHERS KEPT

Rebecca Tucker

The characters and events in this book are fictitious. Any similarity to real persons, living or dead, is coincidental and not intended by the author.

Copyright © 2020 by Rebecca Tucker
All rights reserved.
ISBN: 9798551020271

The purpose of copyright is to encourage writers and artists to produce the creative works that enrich our culture. In accordance with the U.S. Copyright Act of 1976, the scanning, uploading, and electronic distribution of this book without permission constitutes theft of the author's intellectual property. To use material from the book (other than for review), prior written permission must be obtained by writing RTucker@RebeccaTuckerBooks.com. Thank you for supporting the author's rights.

For more information, click or visit:

RebeccaTuckerBooks.com

For Deborah Kay Lane.
When I look at the stars, I think of you.

Table of Contents

Chapter 1	1
Chapter 2	12
Chapter 3	22
Chapter 4	39
Chapter 5	44
Chapter 6	55
Chapter 7	69
Chapter 8	78
Chapter 9	93
Chapter 10	107
Chapter 11	119
Chapter 12	136
Chapter 13	146
Chapter 14	160

Chapter 15	177
Chapter 16	189
Chapter 17	199
Chapter 18	212
Chapter 19	221
Chapter 20	230
Chapter 21	244
Chapter 22	259
Chapter 23	266
Chapter 24	273
Epiloque	277
Acknowledgements	279
About the Author	281
Book Club Discussion Guide	282

1

Austin glanced at the dashboard clock. She was seven minutes late (and counting) for her rendezvous with Gil and his crew. That it was her fault only increased her pique. Had she checked her mail yesterday rather than belatedly remembering it this morning as she hurried out the door, she could have taken care of the Commonwealth of Virginia's idiotic mistake then. Instead, she would have to interrupt her morning to call the Office of Vital Records before they closed at one. The state office had managed, in the six weeks she had been waiting, to screw up the seemingly simple task of sending her the correct birth certificate. One that actually had her name on it. Austin had no idea who Kaitland Emily Brouchard was, nor did she care. What she did care about was that, only three months before her Paris trip, she was still sans passport.

Austin pulled into the dirt parking lot next to the James River near Shockoe Bottom at seventeen minutes past the hour. She considered a moment, then left her zippered sweatshirt in the car. The late March weather had been unseasonably warm, with temperatures already in the low seventies, but her weather app indicated a cold front would move through by late morning. Cold fronts meant wind.

Wind swirled sediments in the air that could work their way into gears and joints. She told Gil yesterday that she'd stay until one, but if it hit earlier, she'd be done for the day.

On the other side of the parking lot, Gil paused long enough in his consultation with a bug-eyed, antennae-twitching student actor to glance Austin's way and offer a quick wave. She waved back. She opened the back door as wide as allowed to carefully remove her robotic rover from the back seat to the side of her car. The eighty-two-pound mechanical marvel represented over one-hundred sixty sweaty bloody hours of her time and she'd be damned if she broke it on its inaugural run. First, she would evaluate how it traveled over the dirt path and pebbles before testing it on the stones and rocks littering the paths closer to the water. She'd told Gil she wasn't driving her rover right along the water, though, and hoped he remembered that. It had to be in perfect working order when she turned it in during finals week.

She glanced downstream, toward the bridge with the now-defunct train tracks spanning the water. When she first moved to Richmond and knew no one but Rivka in town, she used to walk down to the river after class sometimes. Her first real memory of Richmond would always be of oak and maple trees lining the banks, broken up by the numerous rocks and larger boulders. The leaves, in vibrant reds, yellows, and oranges, fluttered on spindly twigs overhanging the whitewater rush of the James as it wound its way through downtown. As fall progressed, the leaves first littered the surface of the water, carrying its bounty of color downstream, then later, they sank to the river bottom, blending into murky muddiness thrown into turbulence each time it rained. She'd gone fishing beneath the bridge a few times, using a stick with fishing wire, a hook, and a wine cork for a bobber. She caught fish with that stupid contraption, much to her surprise. Bluegill mostly, but she always threw them back.

Someone called out a greeting. She looked toward the voice and saw Monica, a casual friend of hers since they shared a dorm floor four years back. She sat on an upside-down Home Depot bucket, painting some poor girl's face a saccharine shade of lavender. "Hey, Monica."

Monica waved the paintbrush at her, inadvertently getting it tangled up in the earbud wire dangling down her neck, disappearing beneath the collar of her t-shirt, and dislodging her cellphone from her bra. Monica cursed and handed the paintbrush to her hapless subject so she could reach in to adjust it. "Bluetooth, Monica," Austin called out. "Join the twenty-first century." Monica flipped her the bird.

Austin knelt by her rover as another voice, this one much closer, spoke behind her. "Hi. Austin, right?"

Austin looked over her shoulder at the silhouette standing behind her. She stood, but still found herself looking up. "Hi. Yes."

The woman, vaguely familiar, smiled and extended her hand. "Claire. Gil told me you were the monster's creator."

"Does he really call it a monster? So rude!" Austin tried to glare in Gil's direction, not that he'd notice, but ended up laughing instead. "Well, it is his monster, my baby, though."

"Both of you anthropomorphizing robots. Nice." Claire glanced over Austin's shoulder at the rover.

Austin stepped back so Claire could get the full view. The robotic crawler appeared small against the backdrop of the parking lot and rocky shoreline of the river and expansive gray-blanketed sky. As Claire knelt next to it, Austin said, "Careful. It's a terror."

"It reminds me of something." Claire tilted her head back, scrunching her eyes closed. Austin waited patiently, though she couldn't help but notice Claire's ponytail had bunched up behind her neck. She resisted the compulsion to straighten it out. When she was young and went shopping with her mom, she always stood at the counter, straightening the flyers and business cards stacked near the cash register. Her mom finally instructed her to keep her hands in her pockets whenever they went out. She turned her attention away from Claire's rumpled hair and looked instead at the multiple mini-rapids in the river, grown in number since the drought had started last fall and the water level dropped. Finally, Claire gave up trying to remember with a hand wave. "You know, the robot they have on Mars."

"Curiosity," Austin said. "You have a good eye. Mine's a replica of it. Miniaturized, though. Obviously."

"Of course you'd know. I should've just asked."

Austin silently agreed as Claire laughed, brushing her hands off on her jeans as she stood.

Austin took over Claire's spot on the ground. She finger-checked the fastness of the locknuts on the articulated joints connecting the body to the wheels. "Did Gil recruit you too?"

"A friend recommended he call me. I'm a sucker for helping student filmmakers."

Austin glanced her over. "Yeah, you don't look like a student."

"God, I already look that old?" Claire laughed again. Austin wondered if this odd cheerful state was the norm for her. It wasn't unpleasant, her laugh or demeanor. It was just alien to the type of people she hung around. The stereotype of boring engineering students held some truth. She remembered her last class project group. They were totally boring. She supposed she probably was too.

Austin tuned back in as Claire was saying, "—graduated with a master's degree in Fine Arts, photography, obviously." Claire tapped the camera dangling from a sparkly rainbow-colored strap looped around her neck. "I did start in film, but no passion, at least not after I discovered photography."

"Cool. My brother's a photographer. He has a studio here."

"Yeah, I..." Claire trailed off as Austin stood abruptly and walked past her to her car. "Something wrong?"

"Loose nuts." Austin opened the passenger-side door and unlatched the toolbox sitting on the floorboards. She pulled out a flat hook wrench. After a pause, she tucked a mini-socket wrench in her back pocket. "Nothing these won't solve."

She returned to her spot by the rover and got to work tightening the locknuts, starting with the right rear joint and methodically working her way through all the joints. "Sorry. You were saying?"

She glanced up, but Claire shook her head. "Nothing."

Austin scooted up to work the front-end joints. "So, you're here to take pictures, like behind the scene shots?"

"Among other things." When Austin raised her eyebrows and shook her head, Claire frowned. "Guess Gil didn't mention it. I have the camera that's going in your rover."

"Right, yeah, sorry I'm dense." Austin looked at Claire's camera and grimaced. It rivaled a coconut in size. "That's not the one you want to use, is it? It'll never work, too heavy."

"God, no. This thing costs three months' salary. I like Gil, but not that much."

"I don't blame you. But apparently, I do like Gil that much. The rover is also my final project for my engineering robotics class."

"So, your anxiety is about here?" Claire motioned in the space a foot above her head.

"Higher. Although I'm not being entirely altruistic. I'm dying to see what it can do. How much is truly functional. Plus, maybe I can use some footage to turn in with my project. Where's the camera you want to use?"

Claire opened up the brown canvas camera bag by her feet and pulled out a much smaller camera. "GoPro. I don't think it'll throw off your monster too much."

"Again with the monster." Austin removed the casing cover and eyeballed the space.

"Sorry. Do you have a name for it?"

"Inquiry." Austin held out her hand.

Claire handed her the camera. "Cute. A little more gravitas than Curiosity, huh?"

"A little more tongue in cheek, I'd hoped."

She felt Claire watching as she tested the camera's fit in the casing, which protruded above the body of the rover, much like a head. She'd built it before Gil asked for her help, designing it more for balance and aesthetics than functional usage. She had a dummy camera made of cardboard to put in the head for her class presentation.

"What're you thinking?" Claire asked.

"The casing's too big." Austin handed the camera back to Claire. "We're not going to be able to test it today. Even if I tack it in place, it'll slide. I'll need to fabricate a better cage for it." Austin popped open the car trunk, rooting through a sparse collection of loose tools. She kept her measuring tools in a separate bag, which was unhelpfully sitting on her work table at home. Finally, she found a simple pair of calipers. "Not as precise as I normally use, but it'll do. Can I see the camera again?"

Claire handed it over. "It's cool that you're in engineering. I always see these articles on how there still aren't that many women in science."

Austin sketched out the camera's general shape in her composition notebook, then made measurements for each specific section of the camera. Claire said something. Austin shook her head. "Sorry, what?"

Claire waited until Austin looked up from her notebook to repeat herself. "Are there many women in your program?"

"Not really, no." Austin handed the camera back to her.

Austin tucked the notebook in the back of her waistband. "Okay, we can't test the camera, but we can run Inquiry around, see how it does off-road. Not close to the water, though."

Claire moved deftly out of her way as she bent to check the connections on the suspension system. "It must be hard, being in a mostly male field," Claire said.

Austin used the controller to move the rover toward an area of heavy gravel at the edge of the parking lot, walking behind it. "I'm not in the field. Student, remember?"

In a couple of long strides, Claire caught up to her. "Pretty sure you know what I meant."

Austin blushed. "Sorry. I didn't mean to sound like an ass."

Claire laughed. "No worries."

Austin frowned as the crawler's rear wheels lost traction over sand and spun deeper into the soft ground. "Steering mechanism's too loose. Maybe it's the tread."

"What's that you're using to operate it?"

Austin showed her the controller. "It's a standard controller for remote-controlled cars. I'm in manual mode right now. I also cannibalized the car motor, a 12v, but reconfigured the wiring so I could adjust the speed and direction to match the bulk. Otherwise, it would just tip over or spin in circles."

Austin stretched on her side and used the mini-socket wrench to tighten the nuts on the inner portion of the wheels. "That should help."

Austin tried the crawler again over the sand and gravel. Success. If you can't level the foundation, the traveler must adapt. Satisfied, she directed it toward dirt footpath heading toward the river's edge. "Alright! Let's move on to something bigger."

Claire watched Austin maneuver the robot further along the dirt path. The moment it hit rockier ground, it stalled, trying to gain traction over the larger stones. She jumped ahead to catch it before it toppled to its side.

"Ugh, defeat snatched from the jaws of victory." Austin trotted to Claire's side. "Can you use that camera as video?"

"Of course. What am I filming, exactly?"

"Inquiry's complete failure to crawl over this row of rocks. I'm not sure if it's a suspension system problem or the differential pivot." Austin reset the rover. "That's what allows for a shifting balance. If you could get close-ups of the wheels as well as a wide shot, that'd be great."

Claire filmed from several angles and over different paths. After half an hour, Gil finally made his way over to them. His omnipresent peppermint scent wafted over her as Austin explained the issues, asking, "Where's the path you want the rover to run?"

He walked her along a five-foot stretch between two boulders. Austin shook her head. "It's not going work there, Gil. It's not big enough to handle these rocks."

Eventually, they agreed on a different location that, once Austin made some modifications to both the path and the rover, she thought would work. The wind picked up. Austin turned to Gil. "I'm done. I can't afford to gook up the joints. Not much more we can do today, anyway. Not until I adjust the casing for the camera."

Austin turned to Claire. "Can you send that footage to my dropbox?"

"No problem. Probably be in a couple of bite-size files, though, to make it easier to download. I'm heading out, too, so I'll send it when I get home."

"Thanks." Austin maneuvered Inquiry to her car, both Gil and Claire walking beside her. Claire helped her lift the rover into the backseat. Austin used the middle seat belt to hold it in place. Monica wandered over to them.

Gil gave Austin a quick hug. "Thanks for the help, Austin.

Don't forget next film session is in two weeks, same time." With that, he was back with his camera across the lot.

"No lunch? I feel so used," she called out to his retreating back.

Monica slung an arm around Austin's shoulders. "He's treating for beer later. Coming?"

"Where?"

"The Village, duh." Monica rolled her eyes. "Seven, I think. We'll probably wrap up here about four."

"Can't tonight. Date night."

Monica grinned and winked at her. "Lauren?"

Austin blushed. Monica had made no secret that she thought Lauren was hot. "Who else?"

Claire looked at her expectantly. "You need my phone number."

Her statement threw Austin off-guard. "What?"

"To text me the dropbox info. Also, we'll need to meet up to work on your rover."

"Oh, right." Austin handed over her phone.

"You can tell Lauren it's just school stuff," Claire said as she typed.

Austin shrugged. "I don't think she's the type to care." She texted Claire as soon as she got the phone back. "Got it?"

Claire glanced at her screen. "Yup."

Austin got in her car, waving to both of them as she drove off the lot. Should it bother her that Lauren never asked how she spent her time, or with whom? Probably not. After all, Austin never asked the same of Lauren either. Was that odd?

***

Austin got home with fifteen minutes to spare before the records office closed. She pulled the payment receipt from the envelope she'd left on her work table and dialed the number on it.

"Virginia DoH, Vital Records. This is Sandra. Can I help

you?"

"Yes. I got the birth certificate that I ordered from you, but it's the wrong one."

"The wrong one?" The clerk sounded perplexed.

Austin walked into the kitchen and emptied a red Solo cup filled with stale water into the sink. "Yeah, it's someone else's certificate, some person named Kaitland. Definitely not me."

"I see." There was a long pause and then she said, "I apologize for the error."

"If I stop by Monday morning, like at nine, can I pick up the long copy in person? It's kinda urgent." She filled the cup with tap water and wandered into the living room.

"Of course. What is your name?"

Austin told her and confirmed her birthdate. She could hear the lady typing for what felt like long minutes.

The clerk said, "I'll mark down an early appointment for you and have this expedited."

"Thanks." Austin was about to hang up when she heard the clerk speak again. "Just a moment. You said Austin Nobel, born April nineteenth?"

"Yeah, ninety-three."

"Make sure you bring in the incorrect copy when you come in. I'll make a note of it in your file. We need to account for the certificate that was sent in error."

Austin wasn't sure, but the clerk's voice sounded sharper. "Sure."

"Have you made any copies of that birth certificate?"

"No." She replied.

The clerk thanked her and ended the call.

Austin added a note about early morning appointment in her calendar app.

With a few hours to kill before her date, she worked on the rover. Claire had already uploaded the files for her, so she looked at those first, but couldn't glean much from it. She checked all the easy stuff, the brackets and locking hex nuts, along with the clamp hubs on the wheels, but couldn't find any connection errors. That probably meant it was the pivot. Taking the body apart, even on one side, would take more time than she had today. Plus, she might need the welding shop on campus. She'd have to take it with her to campus Monday.

At three-fifteen, Austin tucked her tools away and set the rover beneath the work table. Lauren had texted her yesterday afternoon to show up at four, so she jumped in the shower and got dressed. Nothing fancy. They never did anything fancy, and Austin had long gotten over the fact that Lauren would always look gorgeous, while Austin would always be in some boring variation of jeans and a collared button-down for their dates. If she didn't mind, and Austin suspected she liked being the one who caught all the attention, then Austin didn't mind either.

~

2

Austin bounded up the stairs to reach the second-floor landing of Lauren's apartment building. She tucked her hair behind her ears, then knocked on the door.

A couple of minutes went by. She pressed her ear against the door. She couldn't hear anything inside. She knocked again.

"Hey! You're early."

Austin looked behind her. Lauren's neighbor, a lanky guy with tribal tattoos covering both forearms, took two steps at a time to reach the landing. Austin looked at her phone. Three-forty-five. "I am, but why do you know that?"

He tucked his skateboard under an arm. "Lauren said you were coming today around four. You here for your box?"

Austin remembered he was a grad student though she blanked on his name. He took out his apartment keys from a jacket pocket. She read the tacky silver name tag swinging on his keychain. Dylan. "Box?"

He unlocked his door. "Lauren left it with me last night. Said you'd need it today."

Austin brushed the hair from her eyes. Wouldn't be the first time Lauren got a last-minute gig and had to bail. She usually sent a text, though. Austin checked her phone. The last text she got from Lauren was from yesterday morning, confirming today.

Dylan pushed his door open. The entryway led directly into the kitchen. Austin leaned against the doorframe, aiming for casual. "Any chance she mentioned where she was going?"

He set his skateboard in the corner. "California. I saw her this morning while she was waiting for her Uber to the airport."

Dylan pointed at one of the iron-barred, yellow-padded kitchen chairs that looked like her grandparents had delivered it straight from their outdoor patio. Austin perched on the edge of the seat next to the small round kitchen table. California? Must've been a helluva gig offer.

Then, she heard Dylan say something about a moving van leaving last night and she caught on. This wasn't a gig; it was a move. And Lauren had not only ditched her without a word but had actively deceived her about it. She slid back in the chair. Her mouth tasted like sawdust.

Dylan looked at her, then opened the refrigerator and pulled out two bottles of beer, twisting the tops of both before setting one in front of her. "Wow. She didn't tell you, did she?"

Austin shook her head and took a swig of the beer. It did nothing to alleviate the drought in her mouth. It tasted like shit, too. She peeled down a corner of the label. He should've asked and saved himself a beer.

"That sucks, man. Who the hell does that?" Dylan dropped into the seat across from her.

She ignored him as she turned on her phone, thumb hovering over the messaging app. What could she say?

She slid the phone in the front pocket of her jeans. She looked at Dylan. "Thanks for letting me know."

"Well, you're handling it better than I would, that's for

sure." Dylan drained most of his beer, glancing at Austin's barely touched bottle.

Austin shrugged. She didn't know Dylan and anything she might feel was none of his business. It was bad enough that she sat in his kitchen, rejected and discarded by her now apparently ex-girlfriend. She knew Lauren was impulsive, but this wasn't an impulsive thing, not with moving vans and a probable morning flight. How long had Lauren been planning this? And why didn't Lauren tell her?

Austin drummed her fingers on the table. She needed to bail. She drank a little more of the beer so she didn't feel like she was wasting his generosity. "So, the box?"

"Right." He jumped up and opened the hall closet door, pulling out a shipping box, neatly closed with overlapping tucked-in flaps. He set it on the table, which wobbled precariously. Austin barely caught both beer bottles before they toppled over. She watched Dylan maneuver a tattered square of folded paper with his foot beneath one of the metal table legs. "I gotta get a new table."

Austin glanced at the offending table. "It's probably your foundation, not the table."

Dylan took the two beers she handed him. She lifted the edge of the table, turned it an inch, tested the wobble, and repeated the turn and test action until the table rested firmly on the floor.

"Right. Thanks." He handed her beer back, which she set on the table before picking up the box. "Oh, you gotta go?"

"Yeah. Thanks for keeping the box for me. And for the info, I guess."

"You bet." Dylan stood to the side of the door as she moved out into the hallway, leaning against the frame after she passed. He followed her to the top of the stairs. "Hey. You sure you're okay? Need a hand downstairs with the door?"

"I'm good, thanks." She felt Dylan watching her as she

went down the stairs, heard the wooden floor creak as he lingered to watch the newly abandoned step away from his world.

As she got the door open, he called down, "Don't be a stranger." Very polite. Unlike her, as she said nothing while she went through the door and shuffled to her car, box in hand. Once in the car, she thought for a moment, then texted Claire. Damned if she was going to sit around all night, dwelling on this.

***

To her surprise, Claire had offered to pick her up at six-thirty, which suited Austin fine. Parking near The Village on a Saturday night was an exercise in torture.

Austin settled on her couch and opened the box from Lauren. She had expected to see a note offering an explanation, or at least an apology, for her flight from Richmond. There was nothing. Just three t-shirts, one pair of sweatpants, and a small memo pad. Austin flipped through it. It was filled with her original calculations for her robotic engineering finals project. "Totally helpful now." She tossed it on the coffee table. It had taken her three hours and twenty minutes to redo all the numbers the night she couldn't find those damned notes. She pushed the box away with her feet.

What the hell? She thought it unbelievable that Lauren hadn't contacted her, had left her in this state of suspended confusion. Truthfully, though, she felt like that a lot even when Lauren was here. She wished she felt more surprised at this turn of events, but she'd always expected something to happen. She just didn't know what.

She was pacing by the door, waiting for Claire, when her phone rang. She glanced at the caller ID and felt a twinge of disappointment. "Hey, Mom."

"Hi, darling. Am I catching you at a good time?"

"I may bail quickly. A friend's picking me up for dinner."

"A date?"

Austin hadn't mentioned Lauren to her. It seemed too early and too casual. Now, she was glad she hadn't. "No, a group of us."

"It's late for dinner, isn't it?" Her mom ate dinner at the ridiculous hour of four-thirty.

"You're right, Mom, forget dinner. I'll stick with beer."

"Keep the dinner. Drinking on an empty stomach never turns out well." Her mother laughed.

"Personal experience talking?" Austin laughed too. Her mom enjoyed a glass, or three, of wine with dinner. Not every night, but often enough. "They may have other plans, but I'm having coffee. And no, it's not too late for that."

"Well, you're young. I'm sure you can drink coffee at eleven and be asleep by midnight."

"Interesting hypothesis. I'll test it."

"I don't want to keep you. I just thought I'd call and see if you received the itinerary for your Paris program. I'm so excited for you, darling. And so proud."

"Mom, are you still boring your students about it?" Austin glanced down the street. She didn't want to try to extricate herself from the call once Claire got there.

"It's an elite program, Austin. I'm encouraging them to pursue their dreams with stories of your success."

"Good spin, Mom, and yes, I got the info today. Very exciting."

"And your birth certificate? Did you remember to send off for that?"

Austin groaned. "Yeah, about that. I got it in the mail yesterday, but they screwed up and sent me the wrong one."

"What do you mean?"

"Just that. It belonged to someone else. Don't worry. I called and got it cleared up. I'll be able to pick it up Monday morning."

"Good." Her mother took a sharp breath as if to say something else, but she didn't.

A green Chevy Malibu turned down her street, moving slowly. She'd seen the same car in the river lot this morning, so it had to be Claire. "Gotta go, Mom. My ride's here."

"Okay. Have a good night, darling."

"You too, Mom."

"Oh, and Austin? Let me know when you've taken care of that birth certificate issue. Identity security is no joke. It behooves us to stay on top of any issues."

"Yes, it definitely behooves us to do so." Austin was still chuckling after she hung up and slipped into the passenger seat of Claire's car.

***

At the diner, Austin shared one side of the booth with Monica, who took the outside seat. Austin leaned against the wall, thankful for the space, unlike across from her where poor Claire was sandwiched between Gil and the bug-eyed antenna girl from this morning. Austin couldn't remember her name, maybe she'd never been told it, but she could still see the remnants of green paint and glitter around the girl's ears.

Monica snagged a few fries off of Gil's plate. "Where's Lauren?"

"Sorry to disappoint," Austin said, pushing her plate toward Monica. She'd eaten a bacon cheeseburger and could only manage to down a couple of fries after that. "but I don't think she'll be able to make it, being all the way in California."

Monica raised her eyebrows, pulling the plate closer to her. "But what about date night? What'd she do, take a vacation without you? Bad girlfriend."

"More like a permanent move." Though Austin kept her eyes on the table, she saw everyone's heads swivel toward her. Expecting the story, she supposed. What the hell. She didn't want to have to avoid the subject of Lauren if Monica was going to keep bringing her up.

Austin explained what happened earlier at Lauren's apartment, answering a few questions with 'I don't knows' before distracting them from the subject by mentioning the screw-up with her birth certificate. It was a terrible segue, but no one called her on it. While Gil and others commiserated with the irritations of dealing with bureaucracy, Claire seemed intrigued, suggesting she make a copy of the wrong form before returning it.

"The clerk specifically prohibited me from doing that," Austin said.

"Well, then you certainly can't, of course." Claire offered a bland smile.

"Troublemaker," Austin muttered.

Allison, their server, arrived at the table, setting six shots on the table before taking their dishes back to the kitchen. Austin watched her disappear through the swinging double-doors. Allison had been a fixture in this place for the past twenty years, an eternity, to hear her tell it, though she always said it with a smile. Austin couldn't imagine.

Gil slid the shots around the table, winking at Austin as he set one in front of her. Monica picked up her shot and everyone but Austin followed suit. Five pairs of eyes stared at her.

"Guys, you know I don't drink much. Go ahead."

"To not drink much, you have to drink a little. This is your little." Monica slung an arm around her shoulder and squeezed. "Don't think, just because we're a mature group of almost college-graduates except Claire, that we're not above peer pressure. Pick up the shot."

Austin sniffed at the liquid. "What is this stuff?"

"Fireball whiskey."

"Smells like Halloween." She saluted the others at the table with the shot glass. "L'chaim!"

The liquid burned going down but tasted like atomic fireball candy she thought it might. Tasty. She didn't resist getting a second one when Allison came around again. She noticed Claire ordering coffee, which was great because Austin didn't feel like walking the two miles home.

An hour later, Claire let Austin know she was planning on leaving. Monica piped up, offering to give her a lift home later, but Austin declined. She was more than happy to call it a night. She counted out cash to cover her bill and a tip, while Claire did the same. She waved to the three left in the booth as she and Claire slipped out the back door.

"Why do you keep looking at me?" Claire asked once they got into her car.

"You look familiar. I thought so this morning, too, but I can't figure out why."

"We've met before, a few months ago."

Austin couldn't think of a good response. To not remember someone who remembers you. Embarrassing. For her, not Claire. She looked out her side window. "Sorry."

Claire waved her hand. "You were busy at the time. On a ten-foot ladder, stringing wired lights between trees, I think."

Austin knew the night she was talking about. It was the night she'd met Lauren. "That was the night I was helping Brian, my brother, with an outdoor photo shoot. You were there?"

Claire didn't respond. Suddenly, Austin connected Claire with the name her brother often mentioned. "You work with Brian. God, you must think I'm so stupid. You're, like, his number one photographer. I knew your name, but it never clicked."

"Work for Brian." Claire corrected, looking happier, perhaps because she wasn't as forgettable as Austin had made it seem.

"That was an awful night. It was six o'clock on a February evening."

"It wasn't fun. Whose bright idea do you think that was, anyway? Not Brian's. Lauren's?"

The thought of Lauren reminded Austin how forgettable Austin was. She shook her head. "I don't think the models have much say in those things. Probably the ad agency that hired her. Do you know Lauren?"

"She was the model at the photo shoot." Claire looked at her like she'd hit her head.

"I meant—it sounded like you knew her."

"I did some shoots with her late last year." Claire glanced at her. "Monica mentioned you guys are dating."

"Were. Monica did?"

"This morning, before you got there. I don't remember how it came up," Claire came to a stop sign. "I've forgotten. Which way?"

"Right here, left on North Meadow, right on West Main." Austin felt caught off guard, exposed by Claire knowing things about her when she knew so little of Claire.

They spoke little the rest of the ride home, but as Claire pulled in front of Austin's apartment, she said, "I'm sorry for what happened with Lauren."

Austin paused, hand on the door latch. If Claire, or anyone for that matter, could explain to her what actually had happened with Lauren, that'd be great. Because she didn't have a clue. Of course, she thought, that may be why something had happened.

Austin didn't know how to respond to Claire. She was being nice, though, so Austin, with a half-grimace that meant to be a smile, said, "Thanks," before sliding out of the car.

She stopped in the lobby to check the mail, thinking perhaps Lauren had sent her a letter before she left, but there was nothing. Lauren's silence, more than anything, grated on her. She'd never been ghosted before. It sucked.

~

3

First thing Monday morning, Austin drove to the records office. She got out of the car, then remembered what Claire had said about making a copy of the form. Even though she had no real reason to do it, it could be interesting to compare the two. Maybe she could work out how they got mixed up.

She scanned a copy to her iPad and saved it to her Google drive. She felt a twinge of guilt, but shook it off. She'd probably delete it as soon as intrepid Claire had a look.

The errand only took a few minutes, but Austin was still late for her morning class. It took her forever to find a parking spot on campus. That's why she preferred to walk most days. The two-mile walk, done twice a day, constituted the entirety of her exercise regime. More than enough, as far as she was concerned. It was also the only type of exercise she could do with a feeling of basic assurance that she wouldn't get hurt.

After class, she considered going home for lunch before her one o'clock class but thinking of her birth certificate led to thoughts of traveling, which made her think of boxes. Rivka, her best friend and associate rabbi at Beth Israel, had never replied to her email about some boxes the local UPS store was donating for Mitzvah Day. She could have called but dropping in on Rivka at the synagogue and disrupting her orderly day was so much more fun.

Austin found Rivka's office door open and the woman herself hunched over her desk, scribbling on a notepad with a pencil the size of a nail. A small nail. All of Rivka's pencils were little nubs. They were presumably full-sized pencils once, but Austin had never witnessed Rivka using one at that stage. It was a minor mystery.

"Are you going to stand in my doorway all day? Or were you planning on coming in?" Rivka looked up from her desk.

Austin stepped into the room. "I was mentally making fun of your pencils."

Rivka held up her pencil nub. "Holly Davidson—she's a sixth-grader now—wanted to do something for the synagogue a few years ago. Something she could do without help. I asked her to collect pencils teachers were finished with and bring them to me. I told her it would be donating to the synagogue and I'd use all the pencils she brought so we wouldn't have to buy them."

"And she's been bringing them to you ever since, right?"

"Yup." Rivka dropped the pencil on her desk. She motioned Austin over to where she sat, pulling out her bottom desk drawer. It took some effort because every nook and cranny of that drawer was filled with pencil nubs.

"Wow, Rivka. That's a lot of pencils."

"I'm thinking of coming up with something new for her to do, honestly. I've got shoeboxes filled with them at my home office, too." She shut the drawer. "What brings you here?"

Austin lifted her eyebrows and waited. Three, two—

Rivka snapped her fingers. "UPS addresses. I forgot to email them."

She plucked a pink sticky note stuck to the side of her laptop, glanced at it, then handed it over to Austin. "These three. Sorry to drag you out here."

"I was in the area anyway. Had to swing by vital records."

"Birth certificate?"

"How'd you know?"

"Your mom mentioned something about a mix-up in an email yesterday."

"They sent the wrong one. How inept is that? I got the right one this morning. I texted her that. She's so tweaked about it. You'd think she was the one going to Paris."

Rivka laughed. "She also keeps emailing me articles on ways to stay safe while traveling abroad. She didn't think you'd read them if they came from her."

"I haven't gotten anything from you."

"Of course not," Rivka said. "I can't even remember to send you UPS addresses."

Austin chuckled and wandered by the bookshelves built into one side of the office. "Hey, where's Rabbi Adler these days? I usually see his car in the lot if I drive to school, but last week, nada."

"His mother passed away last week. He's in Louisiana, taking care of things."

"Oh no. I'm sorry to hear that." His mother? Rabbi Adler had to be pushing seventy-five easily. "Anything we can do?"

"I spoke with him this morning. Thoughts and prayers are all he asked for." Rivka gave a weak smile. An overused phrase these days, but still heartfelt in the right circumstance.

"How's he doing?"

"All right, given the circumstances. He needs to stay a couple more weeks to help take care of estate things. I think he's feeling overwhelmed."

"Even if you do the estate planning and paperwork in advance, I can't imagine you can prepare for how that loss feels." Austin knew her parents would, one day, pass away. She preferred to ignore the knowledge. "What else did he say? The rabbi thing, I bet."

Rivka sighed. "How you'd know?"

Austin dropped into the chair across from Rivka's desk. "You'd be a stellar senior rabbi, Rivka. I can't imagine anyone else taking over for Rabbi Adler. Why the doubt?"

"It's a huge responsibility, Austin." Rivka ran a hand through her hair, then rubbed her eyes. "And we just had a baby."

"Yeah, that thing's getting cuter by the day, too. When I first saw him, I confess I had my doubts, but he's a good raisin."

"I'm glad you approve." Rivka stood, grabbing her purse off her desk. "Speaking of which, I have to get home. Walk out with me."

Austin followed her down the hallway and out the side door into the parking lot. "I'm just saying you deserve us. And we would be lucky to have you."

Rivka squeezed Austin in a one-armed hug. "Thank you. You're biased, but thank you. If you want to offer your support, I'm leading Passover services this Friday evening. Try to make it?"

"I'll see you there."

***

The next day, Claire texted her during Philosophy in Science class, asking if Austin wanted to come over that night to work on the casing for the Go Pro. Austin arrived at Claire's first-floor apartment promptly at five, a canvas tool kit slung over her shoulder and the rover's head in her hands.

She could smell something cooking from the lobby that made her mouth water. Claire opened the door and Austin followed her nose directly into the kitchen, where Claire had a rack of meat pastries cooling on the counter. Claire offered her a bottle of water and told Austin to help herself to the food.

They didn't look like much, like tacos pinched closed, but the taste was delicious; ground beef, carrots, and potatoes mixed with a ton of spices—Austin had no idea what kind—without being too spicy and a thin crispy dough that crunched with each bite.

"These are really good. You made these?" Austin polished off another one.

"Yeah, it's my grandma's recipe. She's from Columbia. Dad's side. I don't make them half as good as she does, though."

"I don't believe that. Have you counted how many I've eaten?" Austin had lost count after the fourth one, but they were small, she told herself, reaching for another one. "What are these called again?"

"Empanadas. You've never had them before?" When Austin shook her head, Claire pushed the plate of empanadas in front of her. "Help yourself. I make dozens at a time and just keep them in the freezer. Easy meals."

"When you invited me over, I figured we'd just order takeout. I brought menus." Austin whipped three take-out brochures from her back pocket.

"You don't cook much, huh?"

"Not so much, but these are healthy places." Austin looked at the menus—pizza, deli sandwiches, and Chinese food. "Mostly."

"We can still order in if you want."

Austin glanced at her. She was teasing. Claire's phone rang. She held up a finger and turned left down a short hallway, into what Austin presumed was her bedroom, apologizing before shutting the door.

She let her eyes roam as she ate, taking in the space. The kitchen opened up into the living room, with a bar countertop substituting for a kitchen table. The living room held a single floor lamp parked next to a worn but still intact brown leather sofa. A flat-screen TV, fifty-two-inch, Austin gauged from her perch, was centered on a metal frame jutting out from the off-white painted wall across from the sofa.

Claire walked back into the kitchen and regained her stool. "My father, just checking in," she said as she set the phone down.

"Is he here in the state?"

"Fredericksburg." She waved her hand around the apartment. "Do you approve?"

"Very minimalist. For some reason, I thought you'd have lots of stuff around."

"What kind of stuff?"

"I don't know." Austin looked around again at the empty floor space and bare walls. "Art stuff, I guess. At least on your walls."

"You're not wrong. I do usually have some pictures on the wall. Can't you smell the paint?"

Austin shook her head. She could smell the mouthwatering spices emanating from the plate of food in front of her although if she ate anymore, she would need to unbutton her jeans. That would be embarrassing.

"I repainted the walls over the last couple of days. They were a light brown, like a brown egg color. Awful."

"Oh." Austin pushed the plate of food away and gathered up her dirty plate, taking it to the sink.

"I got it." Claire brushed her out of the way. With an economy of motion Austin's engineering mind appreciated, Claire scraped the plates and dropped them in the dishwasher. "Silly to have one when it's only me here, but it came with the place." Claire pointed to Austin's tool bag. "You wanna get to it?"

Austin shrugged, looking around. Nothing about the place told her anything about Claire. Curious, she asked, "Can I see some of your work? Photography, I mean."

"Really?"

"Yeah. I don't know a damn thing about photography, but if you work for my brother, you must be very good."

"Thanks." Claire stood silent a moment, tapping a fingernail against her front teeth. "Yeah, okay. C'mon, I'll show you the workroom."

Austin trailed behind Claire through the short hallway and an immediate left into a bedroom that had been transformed into a workroom. Two large drafting tables took up much of the room, one across the other on opposite walls. A clothesline ran along the far wall, attached to an eyehook on each end. A row of photographs faced her, attached to the line with clothespins.

"Aren't you worried the clothespins will damage the paper?" Austin asked, moving closer to the hanging pictures.

"Those are working copies, not final prints. You'll see I've marked them up. But don't bother with those. They're test runs for lighting."

Austin glanced back at her. Claire hadn't entered the room. She'd stopped just inside and was now leaning back against the doorframe, hands hidden behind her back. She looked back at the photos. "I feel like I'm intruding."

"You're not. Just remember they're works-in-progress. I'm trying to decide which ones to include for my gallery show in a few weeks."

"A show? That's impressive." And Austin was impressed. She remembered the days when her brother labored and dreamed of getting a gallery show. Then, he did, more than once, and he began to dream of starting his own business. And he did that too. She wondered if she'd ever have his kind of gumption.

"I'm a little nervous. It's my first show at a bigger gallery." Claire blushed.

"I'm sure you'll be fine. Where do I start?"

Claire nodded toward a portfolio on the desk to Austin's left. She flipped open the cover and picked up the top photo.

The woman in the photograph was a skin-covered skeleton, with a purple knit cap fit snugly over a bald scalp. She sat, slumped, in a wheelchair, sharp ankles the color of bone emerging from the tasseled edge of a plum-colored afghan spread over her lap and legs. An IV pole stood to the right of the woman, the plastic tube drooping down then snaking around the wheelchair armrest, disappearing beneath the throw.

What struck Austin, and she supposed it was deliberate, was the captured lack of expression on the woman's gaunt face. There was no attempt to smile or acknowledge the photographer; the sunken eyes reflected no light from the nearby window. The overall impression of stillness, living death, was absolute.

Disturbed, Austin replaced the photo, hesitated, then picked it up and turned around to show Claire as she asked, "Do you know her?"

"She was my mother."

Austin had thought that likely, could see the resemblance, despite the dilapidated state, in the thin upper and full lower lips, the high cheekbones, the slightly downturned shape of the eyes. "What happened?"

"Ovarian cancer caught late. Too late. She died four years ago, within a year of being diagnosed." Claire stepped over to the other work desk, flipping open a portfolio cover. "That was the wrong portfolio. I meant for you to look at this one. Those are, well, I'm not sure what I'm doing with them yet."

"I'm sorry about your mother." Claire didn't appear upset, but Austin wondered if she hid things, the way Austin often did. They knew so little of each other. Acquaintances, really. She couldn't tell if questions were okay to ask. She claimed Claire's previous spot against the doorframe.

As if she read her mind, Claire looked up from the portfolio and smiled at her. "You can ask about it. I don't mind."

"How old were you?"

"Twenty-two. Old enough."

"Old enough for what?"

"To handle it, I suppose."

Austin tried to imagine her own mother, tiny but fierce from years of cajoling, admonishing, comforting scattered teens in high school hallways as the principal, slowly fading away, diminishing into an absent skin-covered skeleton in a wheelchair. She couldn't. "What was her name?"

"Beth. I took care of her during her last year. She came to live with me from Annapolis, which didn't go over well with my then-girlfriend, but Mom was adamant about not spending her last months in a hospice."

"That must have been difficult." Austin had meant to say 'painful' but for some reason, that word seemed too intimate to ask a stranger to admit to.

"At times. We had a home nurse who took care of most of the medical stuff."

"Were you very close?"

Claire looked surprised, then thoughtful. "We weren't, actually. No one's ever asked me that. Most people just assumed we were because she moved in with me. Truth is, we hadn't spoken for three years."

She waved Austin over to where she stood. Austin moved closer to the stack of photos on the desk. She tapped the stack. "Look at these if you want. I hate the idea of you being depressed every time you think of my work. There are some fun ones here, I think."

There were. Austin laughed at a teenage boy in a kiddie pool, long legs dangling over the edge, while a huge dog—a mastiff Claire told her—stood by the boy. Claire had captured the dog shaking off, fur and water caught frozen in mid-spray, a dazzling prism as the sun's rays bent and twisted through the water droplets.

"I'm having a glass of wine, white. Would you like one? Something else?"

"Wine's good, thanks. Only half a glass, though."

Glass in hand, Austin perused the portfolio contents, asking questions here and there, hoping she didn't sound as ignorant as she felt. If she did, Claire didn't remark on it, for which Austin was grateful. It was embarrassing, considering her brother was an award-winning photographer and a photography studio owner.

More comfortable now, Austin wandered across the room to look at a smaller stack of pictures scattered on the desk there. She flipped through a few. "You do mostly portraits?"

"Yep," Claire answered from the bathroom across the hall.

"These are, wow. I like the sepia, uh, what do you call it?"

"Tones? Is that what you're thinking of?"

"Probably." Austin looked down at the next picture in the stack and caught her breath as Lauren's glossy face stared back up at her. "There's a familiar face."

Claire entered the room and blanched when she saw the picture. "Oh! I guess I should've warned you. I forgot those were there."

"I don't require a warning. It's fine." And it was fine after the surprise faded and an odd sense of curiosity replaced it. Austin lifted the picture to study it more closely. "Is this from the studio, or on the side?"

"It wasn't part of her modeling work. I just asked her when she was there one day if she would mind doing some portraits for me."

Austin heard tentativeness in Claire's voice and wondered why. Had she been seeing Lauren before they met? Richmond had a small dating pool, she knew, so it wouldn't be that strange. She considered it. Claire didn't come across as deceptive, though, and Austin felt sure she would have mentioned it had that been the case. What, then? A crush on Lauren, perhaps? Austin slid her gaze to Claire, who was busying herself with straightening supplies and scraps of paper and anything else her hands landed on. No, Claire was the type people had a crush on, not the other way around.

Austin looked at the picture and the several behind it in the stack. Lauren was beautiful of course, but the way Claire captured her didn't seem intended to focus on her beauty but rather her expression, similar to the picture of her mother. "You've caught something in these that I can't put my finger on. These expressions, I've never seen them on her. She looks not exactly vulnerable but–" Austin searched for words and failed.

Claire held her hand out for the sheets and studied them a moment. "When I saw her in the modeling shoots, she seemed self-assured, confident, you know? But it didn't seem real at all. When I took these, I realized why."

Austin waited but Claire didn't say anything until she prompted her with a gesture.

"It's just that she seems so uncomfortable in her skin. Like if she could shed it, she would in a heartbeat."

"I think you may have known her better than I did," Austin mused.

Claire set the photos down. "Can I ask you a question about her?"

"Sure."

"Why doesn't it bother you that she just took off like that?"

Austin bristled. She didn't say anything about how she felt about Lauren or her departure. Why did everyone assume that, because Austin wasn't shuffling around broken-hearted and weeping, she didn't care? She wasn't at all clear on what her feelings were toward Lauren when they were together.

Now, she was equally uncertain about how to feel about her departure. Did this uncertainty, unknowingness of feelings, mean there weren't any? You didn't have to love someone to feel abandoned by them.

Claire was still looking at her expectantly. Austin shrugged. She didn't want to talk about Lauren anymore, or death and loss and wanting to slither out of one's skin.

"Did you ask her out?" Claire asked suddenly.

"Who?"

"Lauren."

Austin shook her head, dropping the photos back on the desk. "No."

"She asked you?"

"Why is that so surprising?"

Claire shrugged. "She didn't strike me as having that much courage."

Austin wandered to the back of the room, along the row of hanging photographs. "I suppose it does take some courage, in general. I've actually never asked anyone out."

"Really? Why?"

Austin shrugged, sorry she mentioned it. She didn't know why, had never thought about it in-depth. She did have some social skills, but there was something about going up to someone she didn't know, with purposeful straightforward intent, that did scare her. Not the idea of rejection. That's life at its most common. Maybe it was fear of someone she wanted looking back at her and telling her yes. The thought of it made her legs itch to flee. Absolutely not courageous enough for that. It was idiotic. No wonder she never thought about it. She bit her lip to stop from saying anything. She might not be interested in impressing Claire, but she didn't need to make herself look like a total disaster. Lauren had done enough in that department.

She glanced at her phone. "It's eight already. Do you want

to look at the container I made for the camera?"

"Yes. I'm sorry. I totally hijacked our work plans for the evening."

It was Austin's fault they got sidetracked, but Claire didn't give her a chance to take the blame. Claire moved swiftly down the hallway and disappeared into the living room, but Austin stood a moment to readjust her mindset. This evening had been much more effort than she anticipated. She was exhausted. She wondered if she could bail. That bailing would be rude and Claire would take the blame for it stopped her from heading toward the front door.

The case Austin had constructed for Claire's camera left an inch of space free on all sides. She told Claire she could use foam pads with adhesive backs to keep the camera from sliding when the rover was moving, as well as protect it from the bumps and jostles that could also be expected as it traversed the rocky path Gil had showed her during their walkthrough.

Claire looked unconvinced. She held the camera with both hands, cradling it against her like a baby.

"Tell you what," Austin finally said, "at the next trial run, I'll make sure the top of the casing is removable. On Saturday, we'll run it slowly over the paved parking lot first to see how it does. Then we do a test crawl over gravel so you can see if you're comfortable with how it's moving inside the box, okay?"

"I know I'm being stupid. You clearly know what you're doing."

"You're being protective. I get it." Austin rummaged through her tool kit, which held a various assortment of engineering must-haves—mechanical pencils, gridded notepads, measuring tools. She finally located a package of Blu Tack. "Oh, wait, we're not filming Saturday. I forgot it's Easter weekend. Are you free anyway?"

"Until noon. I'm driving up to spend the night at my dad's."

"Okay. We'll test run it before you go. We can do it at my place. The parking lot is half-paved and half-gravel."

"Sure."

Austin attached the Blu Tack to the bottom of the case and carefully placed the camera on top of it, ensuring it was exactly centered. "How do you control what the camera records remotely?"

Claire held up her phone. "App, of course. I can zoom in or out, do slo-mo, and other stuff."

"You and Gil will be recording what the camera sees while it's moving?"

"That's the plan. He'll take that footage and incorporate it into the film during editing."

Austin pulled out her vernier caliper to measure the spaces between the walls and the camera, including the corners. She jotted the numbers down in a memo pad while Claire peered over her shoulder. Her breath smelled of mint and sunflower seeds, which was odd because she and Austin just ate the same thing and Austin was sure her breath smelled nowhere near as pleasant.

"You are seriously methodical. I bet those are textbook notations," Claire said, pulling back.

Austin frowned at her notes. "Close." She erased a dot between two numbers. "Don't want to mistake that for a decimal point."

"Of course not. The horror." Claire finished the wine in her glass and set it down. "Anyway, you've eased my fear. I have no doubt my camera will be in safe hands."

Austin removed the camera from the casing and handed it back to Claire, who started down the hallway, then stopped. "I forgot to ask. Did you get that issue with your birth certificate cleared up? I've been thinking about that.

Curious."

Austin blinked, then remembered what Claire was talking about. "Yeah, I did, yesterday morning. They were super weird about it."

Claire disappeared from view then quickly made her way back to the kitchen. "Who was?"

"The lady at the office. She asked like three times whether I had made copies or written down any information from it. And then there was another guy working there, in the back, and he just kept staring at me. It was so weird."

"Did you break the rules and make a copy?"

"I scanned it but haven't had time to look at them both." Austin hadn't seen the point once she confirmed the second document she got was correct.

Claire didn't roll her eyes, but it looked like she wanted to as she asked, "Do you have them with you? Do you mind if I look?"

"Good God, Nancy Drew." Austin rummaged through her messenger bag, pulling out her iPad and a manila folder. "I had to apply for my passport this morning. Paper one is the correct one. Old one's on the tablet."

As Claire studied the paper, Austin opened the scanned copy on her tablet. Claire took both into the living room and sat on the couch. Austin followed.

"So, different baby name, different mother's name, father's name on the correct one, but not on the wrong one. Which is odd because she was married at the time."

"What?" Austin peered over Claire's arm at the paper.

"There's both a maiden and married name here."

"Huh." Married, but the father's name had been left blank.

Claire continued her comparisons. "Same date, same time—what are the odds?—same city, county, state. Oh look, you don't have a hospital listed on yours."

Austin looked at the paper Claire tilted toward her. "Is that unusual?"

"I don't know. Do you know what hospital you were born in?"

"No idea. For some crazy reason, it's never come up in conversation."

"Smartass." Claire continued looking between the two certificates, then sat up straight. "Look at this."

Austin looked where she was pointing at a sequence of numbers on the top right-hand corner of the paper. "File number, right?"

"Probably. Now, look at this one."

The number on the scanned copy was the same. Austin looked again carefully at the scanned one and then took the sheet from Claire's hand for a closer view. The numbers were identical. "That explains the clerk's error then. If the original clerk assigned the same number to two different certificates, I might keep getting hers and vice-versa. I don't want her getting mine. What if she's shady?"

"Shady? Unscrupulous, of poor character?"

"Are you making fun of me?"

"Absolutely." Claire plucked the paper from her hand before she could slide it back into her folder. "Seriously, though, that's a pretty big mistake. It's hard to believe."

"Maybe the clerk was new."

"Wouldn't that kind of thing be automated though, like the system would automatically assign the numbers as babies were born?"

"No idea."

Claire didn't speak for a bit as she looked between the paper and tablet.

"What?" Claire's interest was making her nerves jingle.

"What if," Claire hesitated, then said, "the first certificate was amended to the second one?"

"But why? It's computer-generated, right? So, if there's a

mistake, they can simply delete it."

"I was thinking more like, what if you were adopted. They amend birth certificates in cases like that, I'm pretty sure. I had a friend in high school…" Claire trailed off, handing the tablet back to her. "Well, I guess you would know, though."

"I would know." That came out sharper than she meant. Austin took the tablet and paper from Claire and put both in her bag. She wished she hadn't mentioned anything about this. It wasn't Claire's business and it wasn't a big deal. A simple clerical mistake. She checked her phone. "I better get going."

Claire walked with her to the door. "Hey. I'm just throwing random ideas out here. Don't listen to me, okay?"

"It's fine." Austin stepped out of the dimly lit lobby. It was raining outside. She pulled the bottom of her t-shirt over the top of her bag.

"You want to borrow an umbrella?" Claire asked.

"Thanks, no. It's just a couple of steps." Austin smiled. "I won't melt."

"What time Saturday did you want to meet?"

Austin had already forgotten she had invited Claire over. "Eight? That okay?"

"Fine." Claire opened the lobby door for her. "See you then."

Austin hurried to her car, trying to keep the bag covered. Stupid of her not to check the forecast. A gust of wind blew rain pellets hard against her as she struggled to open the car door against the rush of air. Once inside, she turned on the heater and headed home. What Claire had said about amended birth certificates turned over in her head. There had to be a simpler explanation for the file numbers because that was ridiculous. She resolved to go back to the office in the morning to clear this up once and for all.

~

4

When Austin returned to the records office Wednesday morning after going to the passport acceptance facility, the only clerk there was the creepy older guy, standing expectantly behind the counter. She considered leaving, but then she'd have to come back yet another day and she had already rehearsed what she needed to say. She approached the man and explained about getting the wrong birth certificate.

"Now, I didn't make a copy of the first one," she said quickly. Dead giveaway for a lie, right? But the clerk didn't say anything. "I do have a very good memory, though. I'm certain both of these documents had the same file number at the top." She tapped the number on the copy she had made from her original, correct one.

He didn't glance down at the paper but instead stared at her like he did the other day and unexpectedly said, "Of course they did. This is the amended one."

Austin found herself speechless. The door jingled and the clerk from Monday bustled into the room, followed by a couple.

"Good morning, Jeremy," she called as she walked past the counter toward the employee-only door. She frowned at

Austin. "You're back. Is there a problem?" She looked at Jeremy, as did Austin.

"She wanted to make sure this was the long form. I guess you were expecting it to be, well, longer, right?" He held the copy toward her. Austin thought she saw a touch of desperation in his eyes.

"Right. I'm dotting my 'i's and crossing my 't's for my passport." Austin tried to sound casual. "First time going overseas."

The clerk nodded knowingly and disappeared through the back-office door. As soon as she was out of sight, Jeremy leaned forward and spoke quietly. "I'm sorry. This is my fault. I sent you the other one. I thought you'd want it."

"Why? What're you talking about?" Austin heard ringing in her ears and took a deep breath to calm herself.

"I can't talk here." He grabbed a post-it pad and scribbled something down, then handed her the note. "Call me, okay? I'll explain it."

Austin took the note, not taking her eyes off him. Was she really going to call this strange guy and meet him somewhere? He didn't look as creepy now, more concerned, maybe even scared. "Somewhere public."

"Wherever you want."

She didn't want to call him, though, didn't want him to have her phone number. She could hear the couple behind her whispering to each other, impatiently shifting their feet. She leaned in over the counter. "How about tomorrow, five-thirty, at," she struggled to think of a place she never went to, "that restaurant on Grace street, Naara's Cafe?"

"I can do that. Just call if something comes up," Jeremy answered.

Austin stuck the Post-it on the copy she held and stepped away from the counter just as Sandra walked up, saying, "Thanks for covering, Jeremy." She looked at Austin. "Flat tire."

"I hate when that happens." Austin waved and left the office. What the hell, she thought, getting into her car. What the hell was that all about?

***

Later, a couple of minutes after getting home from morning class, Lauren called.

Austin debated not answering as her phone rang. She slung her bag on the couch and walked into the bedroom, discarding her shoes as she sat on the bed. Curiosity won. She answered on the fourth ring.

Lauren must've expected a fight. She came out swinging with the offense-is-the-best-defense approach. She had excuses for why she left without a word. It was a last-minute decision, she said. A chance for a national modeling contract. She wasn't sure how long she would be gone, and on and on. Austin wished she had started with a simple apology. 'Hello, I'm sorry I didn't tell you' would have sufficed. It would be over and done with and they could move on without antipathy.

"You could have told me. It's not like I'd have stopped you." Austin said when Lauren finally took a breath.

"I felt bad about taking off."

"If you had told me, it wouldn't be taking off. I'd have known and you wouldn't feel bad. See how that works?"

"I didn't want the drama, okay?"

That stung because it was so blatantly untrue. Austin silently counted to ten. "Drama, Lauren? Are you honestly going to say I'm the dramatic type?"

"No," Lauren finally said.

"I would've handled it fine. I just wish you had shown me some respect. It's your life, Lauren. Do what you want. Hell, I'd have helped you pack. You're acting like you were trapped in a relationship with me for years instead of a few weeks."

"It was at least two months, you know." Silence, and then she said, "Maybe I should have told you since it sounds like you obviously don't give a damn that I left."

There it was, the catch-22 that Lauren flung at her feet like a bola. Austin should've seen this coming. She knew Lauren was insecure, irrational at times. But she was tired and didn't feel like being baited into an argument. What did Lauren want her to say? When she sat in Dylan's kitchen last Friday, watching him wrangle a box of her things from his closet, she couldn't determine which feeling was greater, hurt at Lauren's unceremonious departure or humiliation at being so discarded. That Lauren had set Dylan up to bear witness to her abandonment only made it worse, but she had quickly wrapped those feelings up into a tight little ball that she tucked away and camouflaged with the tattered remnants of her dignity. Now, she had nothing to say.

She was, Austin realized, miffed that Lauren would call now. Days had passed. More than enough time for Austin to compartmentalize the situation and its attendant emotions. She had things on her mind more pressing than whatever Lauren wanted from her now. She had no intention of unraveling her insides for Lauren's ego or edification. "Why'd you call, Lauren?"

"I wanted to see how you were. Make sure you were okay." Lauren sounded small and anxious, childish.

"I'm fine." And then she gave a little, saying, "Look, I care about you, Lauren. It hurt that you left without saying goodbye. So, thanks for calling now, I guess."

Though it sounded flat and disinterested to her ears, it seemed to perk Lauren up, the knowledge that Austin did care for her in some way. She asked Austin a couple of questions about her upcoming Paris trip. Had she been in Austin's bedroom, rather than 3,000 miles away, Austin might have told her about the strange circumstances surrounding her birth certificate, the emerging questions, and the precipice Austin felt like she was standing on. But they didn't have their physical closeness now to masquerade as intimacy and Austin felt it would be wasted breath. Not that Lauren wouldn't care. She would. She might even be concerned enough to ask questions, but she was already gone. She was building something new on the other side of the country for reasons she didn't feel comfortable sharing with Austin, so Austin felt restrained now, in this awkward 'can't we still be friends' conversation.

They hung up a few minutes later, Lauren with a hesitant, vaguely uncertain air and Austin with a huff of impatience. The entire interaction left Austin feeling dissatisfied and irritated. She couldn't lay the blame on Lauren. Not entirely. She had been feeling disconcerted ever since she spoke with Jeremy this morning. Lauren had only exacerbated it. Austin wanted to reassure herself it probably was nothing; that whatever this man, Jeremy, had to tell her, it was a simple explanation for the errors she discovered with the birth certificates. As Austin heated leftover take-out spaghetti for lunch, she couldn't help feeling disquieted at the notion that Jeremy knew something about her, about this situation, and she wasn't sure she wanted to know.

~

5

Austin sat in an unadorned wooden booth at Naara's Cafe, facing the door, waiting. The cafe was located below ground, with shops above. The room was dim, with lighting resembling sunlight filtered through dust clouds. Two chandeliers hung from the ceiling, and candles were lit on every table. She found the smell of the food on the plates around her appealing, reminding her of the empanadas Claire had served the other night, but her stomach had twisted itself into knots, rendering her appetite nonexistent.

She drummed her fingers on the tabletop. Her breath was short, fast, shallow. She willed herself to draw in measured deep breaths to slow her heartbeat. All it did was make her light-headed. She'd spent last evening searching the Internet for why birth certificates might be amended. Reasons other than adoption did appear, but none made sense in her own context. In each case, name change, date or spelling errors, even gender reassignment, her parents' names would have been on the original certificate, unaltered.

A server stopped by. Austin ordered a decaf coffee. She could hardly sit still as it was. Jeremy came through the door, or at least she thought it was he. All she could see was his scraggly beard and the shiny dome atop his head. Austin lifted a hand until he spotted her.

He greeted her, then settled in across from her in the booth. He ran a hand through his beard several times. Austin tried not to watch, thinking about the inherent uncleanliness of beards. You had to be meticulous with cleaning them, she figured, which most guys definitely weren't. Jeremy cleared his throat. "After what you said yesterday, it's obvious you had no idea you were adopted."

"You say that with such certainty." Austin looked away from Jeremy's gaze. She crossed her arms. "Computers make mistakes, or at least they're programmed by people, who make mistakes. What's to say there wasn't a glitch that caused the system to assign the same file number to two people born the same day, the same time, in the same county? Rare, but I bet it happens."

Jeremy started to speak but the server appeared with her coffee. Jeremy ordered a coffee, but not decaf. He spoke after the server left. "No. Not in a case like this."

"Like what?"

"Where the only things amended are the baby's name and the mother's name, plus there's no father listed, no hospital. It's pretty clear from that alone, but there's something else." He looked down at the table, the overhead lamp reflecting off his pale freckled head. "There's a note in the file about the adoption. No information, just a note about the original certificate being sealed due to adoption."

Austin looked at him, then quickly down at the dark green carpet. She knew. She knew in her gut this wasn't a mix-up or an ill-conceived assumption on Jeremy's part. This was real. Bile rose in her throat, tasting of acid and coffee. She swallowed and flagged the server down, asking for a glass of water, then abruptly changing her mind before the woman stepped away.

She stood, shaking the table and sloshing coffee over the

sides of her mug. She dug into her pocket, pulled out a five-dollar bill and dropped it on the table. "I need to go," she mumbled, stumbling into the open space.

Jeremy attempted to stand, but his girth prevented any quick motion. "You still have my number, right? I have resources, people who can help if you need it."

"Yeah, still have it," Austin answered, not sure at all whether that was true. It didn't matter. She knew where he worked. She started toward the door, then glanced back at Jeremy. "I don't know if I want to thank you or tell you off for dumping this on me."

Jeremy said nothing.

Austin sighed and shook her head. "Thanks. I guess."

She didn't wait for a response, hurrying up the steps to the door, and then up the short flight of stairs until she stood on the sidewalk. The sunny sky from earlier had given way to a layer of thick, billowing clouds, with darker wisps of clouds scurrying below. She headed down the street, toward her car. A thin crackling of thunder sounded off in the distance. That seemed about right.

***

It was pouring by the time Austin returned home. She sat on the couch in the semi-darkness of dusk. Her thoughts, half-formed, tumbled over one another, nonsensical and overwhelming. Images of her parents, her mom mostly, flickered through her mind as a realization grew within her, rising from the pit of her stomach, finally forming the coherent thought that there were going to be repercussions for the conversation she'd just had with Jeremy. Her world would change—it had already, though she couldn't yet feel it and didn't understand what those changes would be. The foundation built of all she knew was shifting beneath her feet as she wobbled.

It had always fascinated Austin, the illusion of solidity.

That even the densest materials—osmium, basalt, the earth beneath her feet—was, at its smallest level, in continuous ontological motion. Subatomic particles in an ongoing state of becoming or, depending on its surrounding environment, unbecoming only to transform into a different state of becoming. It never terrified her, this concept of everything around her being in constant flux that defied immutability. All she ever saw, even with her limited understanding of physics, was an expanse of endless possibilities. Now, as she found herself tumbling down in the space between those particles, she realized it never occurred to her that she, too, was mutable.

And then there were her parents. She couldn't think of them yet. Couldn't bear the thought of what this meant, of how they knew something so fundamental, so key to her existence, and how they chose to keep it secret from her. She had never thought about, had never considered, the nature of betrayals. Now, she had her parents' long-told lies exposed and she would have to address them, regardless of her strengthening desire to bury this new unwanted information beneath her feet, stomp the soft dirt into a hard pack then walk away. Suddenly, it seemed so much more than she could handle. She curled up on the couch. She fell asleep within minutes.

It was half-past midnight when she awoke, stiff and disoriented. She checked her phone. Her mom had called at seven; Claire at just before eight. She used the light of her cellphone to stumble into the bedroom.

She would not call her mom back tomorrow, Austin resolved as she brushed her teeth. She couldn't be sure of keeping calm, maintaining control. If she was going to handle this without having a meltdown, she needed to stay rational. She needed a step-by-step action plan to stay upright now that her world had been turned upside down. And if she approached her mother without a plan, without an idea of what to ask, she would lose her best chance at getting the information she needed to start making sense of all this.

Anxiety pushed up from her chest into her throat as blood vessels pulsed in her neck. She gripped the edges of the sink, shut her eyes tightly, and willed herself to relax.

Returning to her bedroom, she sat at her desk and plucked a pen from the holder. She scribbled out a few items on a scratch pad she could pick up from Office Depot in the next day or two. She rubbed the back of her neck. There was more she could do right now. Outline her plan of action. Determine which steps she could do alone, and which required other people to cooperate. What might be free, and what might cost her money. She could do these things, but it was late, and she had class in the morning. It could wait for one night.

As she lay in bed, she thought drowsily of last Thanksgiving at her mom's. Her father hadn't been there, not unusual since his move to Arizona, but her brother was there, along with her Aunt Denise and Uncle Harry and their son, Paul, who was a year younger than she. She and Paul had been inseparable during the extended family's annual summer vacations at Rehoboth Beach in Delaware. Indistinguishable, too, when they were very young, both sporting a mess of short brownish hair turned almost blond from hours spent in the sun.

She wondered now if part of the closeness she felt with Paul had been their physical alikeness. No one questioned that they were related. In fact, many of the storekeepers had often thought them siblings, an inquiry that made Austin flush with pride. Paul thought it funny.

They were still in touch, superficially in any case, mostly through social media. At Thanksgiving, he had begged to see her Inquiry project, the building of which she had documented on her Instagram account. She, in turn, had congratulated him on his recent promotion at the bank. It wasn't the same, of course, as when they were children. He was at least six-feet tall now and his facial features had filled out, though his rounded chin and nose were now half-hidden by the bushy beard he grew two years ago. Even without the facial hair, it was hard to fathom they had actually looked so much alike as children. Nothing remained to indicate a resemblance now. That thought had occurred to her as she was hugging him hello that evening, and it had sent a pang through her of something ineffable lost.

The feeling had stayed with her through the meal, as she glanced at the faces seated around the dining room table. The familiarity of each only serving to emphasize their similarities to one another and the differences between them and herself. She hadn't thought much about it at the time, having grown accustomed to not seeing her own features in others' faces. She had stopped dissecting family members' faces in an attempt to find out where she belonged in their genetic spectrum. She had assumed, had told herself often, she must look like a great-grandparent somewhere along the line. She was unique only to these generations sitting before her.

And she certainly didn't want her father's long skinny nose or her mother's wildly untamable curly hair. Not when she already had his irritating habit of pacing a room when talking and her constant need to push the hair back from her forehead. Had she picked up all these mannerisms as substitution, so that she would finally have some visible connection to her parents? She also shared her mother's sense of humor and her father's disciplined approach to work. If nurture had provided her with the tools she used to navigate her world, was it really that important to discover what nature had to offer?

***

Austin slogged through her two classes on Friday,

spending the class time to search for adoption sites on her iPad, which turned out to be harder than she anticipated. So many websites were for couples looking to adopt, with large font ad-type pop-ups enticing women to give up their babies. Her stomach churned at the blatant commercial nature of it all. Other sites were huge repositories of information but too hard to navigate on her tablet. Finally, she stumbled into a website with easy-to-read FAQs that helped her understand at least a little more about the adoption triad, as everyone on the sites referred to it. She read a few forum posts, too. These people were information warriors, sharing tips and techniques for searching that astonished Austin. She had barely dipped a toe in the water and she felt overwhelmed.

When she came home that afternoon, she fell asleep on the couch, once again exhausted. She woke up at just before six, when her phone chirped. Rivka had messaged her, reminding her to come to services. Austin had completely forgotten that she'd promised to but getting out of the house, out of her head, sounded like a great idea.

It was a few minutes past seven when Austin slipped through the front door of the synagogue, wincing as a loud crack reverberated throughout the lobby. She really needed to remind Rivka to invest in some WD-40. The entry room was empty. She could hear children clamoring on the other side of the inner doors. She snagged a bookmark copy of the evening's selected prayer readings and slipped through the thankfully silent inner doors to take a seat in the back row of chairs.

Joy, one of Beth Israel's three cantors, and a gaggle of kids stood upfront on the bimah, next to the Shabbat table, singing the blessings for the candle. Only a few of the children could remember the words for the subsequent blessings said over the wine and bread. Austin recognized the loudest voice although she couldn't see its owner. Lizzie, a young girl of seven, had been a faithful attendee of the Hebrew class Austin taught last summer. She had been the loudest voice there, too.

Austin closed her eyes and drew a deep breath through her nose. The smell, a mixture of pine trees and warm vanilla, reminded her of a trip she had taken with her mom after high school graduation. They had flown up to Maine and traveled by train up the coastline, stopping to camp along the way. One of the campgrounds was nestled within a pine forest, ground so thick with littered needles that her feet sank an inch with every step. She had searched online and in every local shop for pine-scented candles, but none matched her memory, and all left her disappointed.

It quieted as the children sat on the rug in front of the pulpit where Rivka stood, patiently waiting to speak. Austin had not listened to Rivka's sermons before. As the associate rabbi, she often led the Shabbat for Tots service in late afternoon, as well as other prayer sessions during the week, but Rabbi Adler usually led the Shabbat evening and morning services. Austin thought about Rivka's ongoing resistance to taking on the mantle of senior rabbi. Last fall, Rabbi Adler had announced his imminent retirement for this coming summer. Rivka had told her that he had, in confidence, asked if she would consider filling his position, but she'd declined. When Austin asked why, Rivka shrugged and said she didn't feel ready yet to lead the community. Judging from their conversation the other day, Rivka hadn't budged much on her position, which was a damn pity. Austin had known Rivka long before she'd left for rabbinical school in Philadelphia, and couldn't imagine a better vocation for her. When Rivka returned from a year in Israel and applied to be assigned to Beth Israel during Austin's sophomore year at VCU, Austin was thrilled.

It seemed Rivka could hear Austin's thoughts. Her eyes

lighted upon her just as Austin looked at her, smile broadening as she dipped her head in greeting before leading the assembly in prayer.

It had been at least a month since Austin last made a Friday evening service. Lauren exhibited zero patience for anything to do with religion. Austin assumed her dislike of organized religion was a rebellion of sorts against her upbringing within a strict conservative Southern Baptist home. She rarely spoke of it, but Austin could hear the derision in Lauren's tone when she did and so hadn't pressed for more information. She wondered how Lauren's parents felt about Lauren's work. Somehow, she doubted a modeling career was something they dreamed of for their daughter, but Lauren's ambition, or perhaps need for attention, had overpowered her need for parental approval.

God, why was she even thinking about Lauren? She returned her attention to the service, soaking in Rivka's rhythmic intonation, the congregants' recitations. She loved being here. Being present in this refuge from her daily life of gridded paper, page-long differential equations, and crowded lecture halls. Austin felt at home in this synagogue, this community. She glanced around, recognizing many of the people here tonight. The long wavy brown tresses held with simple butterfly barrettes, paired with the salt and pepper crewcut, were the Wolfsons, who were expecting their first child any day now. The blonde pixie cut sitting alone next to two folded wind-jackets belonged to Meredith Beckman. Her two sons, aged six and eight, sat upfront with the other kids. Meredith's husband—Austin didn't know his name—had come to services only once, over a year ago. He had dark, short straight hair, with a shadow stubble. He had spent the entire service texting on his phone. She suspected he was only there at the behest of his wife. She remembered how Meredith had occasionally leaned into him, whispering in his ear, lowering his arm gently so she could bring over her prayer book to share even though he had one sitting right next to him. Not to mention the blessings were projected on two huge screens at the front. He would briefly run his eyes over the page, then return to his phone. With a silent sigh, she would edge away, returning the book to her own lap.

This evening, Austin was distracted herself, thoughts of her upcoming student-exchange program in Paris warring with Lauren and the recent adoption bomb. Lauren required no action except Austin shoving all thoughts of her into a little box, locking it up, and tossing it into a dark corner of her mind. But the bomb. She had no idea what to do about it. She was tempted to try the little box trick, but she doubted she'd succeed at compartmentalizing it away. She would need to speak to Jeremy again. He seemed knowledgeable. And Rivka, too. Just then, she heard Rivka say her name. She looked up to find Rivka pointing at her.

"Austin, wave your hand."

Obediently, Austin waved without a clue why she was doing it.

"Most of you know Austin. She's one of the organizers for this year's Mitzvah Day. If you have any questions, or if you're interested in volunteering, feel free to talk to either one of us during the Oneg Shabbat, which, as always, follows service tonight. Although perhaps I should ask Austin if she's staying." The audience chuckled and looked back at Austin expectantly.

She was planning on it, but she hated when Rivka put her on the spot like that. Austin nodded and Rivka beamed.

Service ended after a few member announcements. Austin hovered around the snack tables in the back of the sanctuary, munching on a small plate of grapes. Two teenagers, full of reluctance but spurred on by parental prodding, shuffled up to her and volunteered for Mitzvah Day food drive activities.

Austin dutifully recorded their names and numbers in her phone. She watched with some amusement as Rivka made her way to the back, her progress slowed to a crawl as people stopped her to chat. Finally, Rivka reached her and pulled her in for a bear hug. "Shabbat shalom!"

Austin returned the greeting as Rivka examined her face. "What happened?" Rivka asked.

Austin shrugged. Somehow, Rivka always knew when something bumped Austin off her track. An unexpected lump formed in her throat. "Long story. Do you have time this week to talk?"

Rivka checked on her phone. "I have Thursday night free. Would that work?"

"Yeah. Thanks."

Rivka frowned and looked at her phone again. "I could reschedule my Tuesday night call if that's better."

"Thursday's fine. It's not a hair-on-fire emergency."

Rivka moved closer and grasped both her shoulders. "Are you sure?"

Austin nodded. Her eyes watered and Rivka's face turned blurry. She looked up, over Rivka's head until her vision cleared. "Your house?"

"My house. Call me if you need me before then, okay?" She looked around at the crowd. "I ought to continue my rounds, but I'll see you Thursday."

Austin relaxed as Rivka pulled her in for one of her mama bear hugs. If anyone could help her navigate the chaos that threatened to envelop her, it was Rivka.

~

6

Claire knocked on her apartment door at exactly eight a.m., Saturday morning. She was so punctual that Austin wondered if she perhaps had been early and simply waited in her car. If so, too bad she hadn't knocked when she'd arrived. Austin had been up since three a.m., her second night filled with turning and tossing. As she hurried to the front door, she wondered if Claire would ask her about the birth certificates. What she would say if she did? Claire's enthusiasm about the birth certificate mystery concerned her. Almost as if Austin was a fun new project for Claire. She wasn't sure she wanted to talk about it yet. It was all still so jumbled in her mind. Her mother's calls had increased in frequency over the past two days, which she completely ignored. She did send her a text about how busy she was right now. That wasn't going to buy her much time.

On her way home from synagogue last night, she had stopped by an office supply store to pick up a three-ring binder, paper, dividers, and a paper-hole puncher. If she was going to create an action plan, she needed to be organized about it. When an engineering project overwhelmed her, like designing and building Inquiry, she'd break it down into smaller and smaller mini-projects until she felt confident she could do it. That's what she had to do with this.

She had the door open before Claire had even finished knocking. "Hey. Thanks for coming so early."

Claire hovered in the doorway. "I'm excited to see what you've done."

Austin stepped aside and pointed to a rectangular fold-up table pushed up against the wall across from the front door. "Go ahead and set your bag there, next to Inquiry. I've set everything up so it's ready to test once we get the camera in there."

"Great." Claire carefully set the bag down and took out her GoPro.

Austin held out a mini-flashlight. "Sorry, no overhead light in here." She handed the flashlight to Claire. "Would you mind holding it over the casing?"

Claire turned on the flashlight and held it up over the rover's center. "Here?"

"Yep." Austin glanced at her phone. "Oh, but I'm being kinda rude. You have a few hours before you need to leave, right?"

"Yeah. Why?"

"When I come over, you feed me, give me drinks. When you come over, I put you right to work."

Claire laughed. "It's fine."

"I'm out of coffee, but I have soda, water, iced tea?" Austin motioned for Claire to follow her through the extended living room into the kitchen.

"Water's fine." Claire stopped in the middle of the second living room, looking at the track running in an oval shape on the ceiling. Black curtains were bunched next to the wall at one end of the track. The couch lined the wall within the framed area. "I thought you said you don't do photography."

"I don't," Austin called back from the kitchen.

Claire fingered the sheets. "Aren't these darkroom

curtains?"

Austin reappeared with two bottles of water. "Close, but I don't use them for that. They're stiffer, so they don't fold when they spread out around the track."

When she didn't say anything more, Claire threw her hands up. "You use them for?"

"Basically a 360-degree screen for images. See those projectors up there?"

Claire looked where she was pointing and saw three projector lenses attached with brackets to the ceiling. "Cool. It's like a mini movie theater when you have the curtains closed."

"Yeah, it can be." Austin took a swig of water. She avoided looking at Claire as her face heated up.

"You don't use it for movies, do you?" Claire asked.

"Not really, no. Sounds like a great idea. I can't believe it never occurred to me." Austin answered, stepping past Claire toward the work table.

Claire followed her but kept glancing back at the set-up. "Are you going to tell me?"

"Tell you what. Let's get this out of the way. If there's time after, I'll show you. It's totally geeky though. Consider yourself warned." Austin pushed up the sleeves of her shirt, handed Claire the flashlight and picked up the GoPro. "Now, let's find out if I'm any good at measurements."

To her relief and ego gratification, Austin's measurements were fine and the camera fit in the casing without any noticeable gaps. Austin grinned. She was pretty good. This was what she loved most. Math and applicable engineering coming together. "Sweet!"

"Snug as a bug in a rug," Claire said. "Now, let's see this baby roll."

They tested the rover first on Austin's hardwood floor, then on the sidewalk outside her apartment. As a final test run,

Austin drove it over the gravel parking lot next to her building.

At first, Claire stayed glued to its side, peering at the open casing. Finally, she shrugged and walked back to Austin. "Not even a jiggle. You're a genius. I'm satisfied. Now show me what you use the darkroom for."

"You're a curious creature." Austin guided the rover back to where they stood and looked at Claire. "You like mysteries?"

"Is that a bad thing?"

"Of course not." Austin decided then to tell Claire everything she had learned. She had a mystery, and Claire was right time, right place. "You were right about the birth certificates."

Claire raised her eyebrows. "Really? Which part?"

"All of it. One was an amended version of the other. Turns out I am adopted and somehow my parents have managed to never mention it. I can only assume Brian doesn't know." Austin told Claire about meeting with Jeremy and what he told her.

"Oh, Austin." Claire squeezed her shoulder lightly. "I'm so sorry."

Austin looked at the ground. A cricket hopped over her foot. "Let's head back. I think I felt a raindrop."

"I was thinking later that night, after you left, how I just threw it out there. About it being amended, about adoption. It was pretty thoughtless."

Austin shook her head. "I didn't think there was a chance in hell that could be the case. I didn't give it another thought. Not your fault you were right."

They carried the rover up the front steps and got into the foyer right before the rain came down so hard, Austin couldn't see the buildings across the street.

Claire paused outside her front door. "What's this?" she

asked, running her fingers over the ornate rectangular capsule on the doorframe.

Austin pushed open the front door and guided the rover to the table before returning to the front door. "It's a mezuzah."

Claire shook her head. "I don't know what that is, but this is gorgeous workmanship."

"A mezuzah is something Jewish people put on their front door as a reminder of our commitment to our faith and our home as a holy place. It has a tiny scroll inside, with two biblical scriptures from Deuteronomy." Austin looked at the mezuzah, affixed to the right section of the doorframe, tilted slightly inwards. It was a beautiful wooden casing, with elaborate minuscule decorative carvings on the curved body. The top and bottom, where the screws attached the casing to the wooden frame, were carved into curlicues. Rivka had brought it back from Israel for her.

Claire glanced at Austin. "I didn't know you were Jewish."

Austin shook her head. "Most people don't unless I say something. I don't look Jewish."

"Isn't that a stereotype, thinking all Jewish people look Jewish?" Claire followed Austin into the apartment, shutting the door behind her.

Austin shrugged. "Maybe. I think it came about because of the number of Ashkenazi Jews being from a similar region, like Eastern Europe, and being a somewhat enclosed community, which fosters a lot of the same genetic physical traits."

"But most people from similar regions, regardless of faith, look genetically similar, don't they? And there are Jews from all over the world, right? Not just Eastern Europe."

Austin smiled. "You sound like a lawyer."

Claire moved toward the table and put her camera away in the bag. "My dad's a lawyer. We have lots of discussions."

"Discussions or arguments?"

"Both." Claire laughed. "Anyway, I'm certain not all Jews look like Woody Allen. Your dad doesn't look like Woody Allen, does he?"

"No. Basically the opposite." Austin laughed with her. "I guess I've always thought of my parents and brother as being Jewish looking, and I look so different." She scrolled through her cellphone photos. "Here, see?"

She handed Claire her phone, showing a picture of her family taken last Thanksgiving. That picture, like their other family portraits, had bothered her every time she looked at them. There was something odd about her standing with her parents and brother, the three of them looking like they were cut from the same mold—same dark curly hair with dark penetrating eyes—while she, though tucked in the middle of them, appeared like an other. Her wispy light brown hair hanging down, her pale skin, high cheekbones. All of her looked so conspicuous next to them. She often thought the pictures would be much improved were she not in them.

"There's a similar look, but they don't necessarily look Jewish to me." Claire held the phone up, looking between the picture and Austin.

"Maybe it's just more that they look like a group," Austin clarified. "Like they belong to each other. It's like that game, which one of these things isn't like the others." She chuckled. "It seems so obvious now that I was adopted. I'd feel stupid for missing all the clues, but genetics are a funny thing. Lots of people don't look like their parents, but they're a dead-ringer for a great-grandmother or someone. Maybe I just think they look Jewish because I know they are. And I don't know if I am, now."

Claire handed her phone back. "Great picture of you, by the way."

"Thanks." Austin stared at the picture a moment before placing her phone on the table.

A minute, then two, passed before Claire spoke again. "As far as looking Jewish goes, people who convert to Judaism may not look Jewish, but they still are, aren't they?"

"Sure, in the eyes of the religious community. Definitely."

"But not in your eyes?"

Austin caught her breath in surprise. That wasn't what she had meant. Was it? She hadn't ever considered it. Did she think converted Jews were less Jewish because they weren't born a Jew? "I don't know," she admitted. "I don't even think I know anyone who's converted. I've never really given it any thought."

"And now you have to, because you might not be Jewish by birth."

Damn, Claire could be blunt. Austin leaned against the square table, folding her arms across her chest. She hadn't considered any of this when she stopped by the synagogue last night to make a date to talk with Rivka. She had only thought of asking her about whether Rivka had known about it and decided that could wait. It hadn't occurred to her that being adopted might change the way her synagogue viewed her Jewish identity. Suddenly, she was grateful that she had until Tuesday to meet with Rivka. She needed the time to look into this.

"I'm sorry. I didn't mean to upset you." Claire stood awkwardly in the center of the room, hands tucked in back pockets.

Austin waved off her apology. "Not your fault."

If she had been converted as a baby, would she regard that as being more Jewish than an adult who converted? And why was she thinking in terms or being more or less Jewish, anyway? Jewish was Jewish, wasn't it, no matter how you came to be? "I was thinking I should ask Rivka, my rabbi, about this. Well, she's my rabbi, but also a really old family friend. She used to babysit me all the time, even when she was way too old to babysit."

"Sounds exactly like what you need."

Austin rubbed her right temple. "She's like a sister. So much better than Brian."

"I'll be sure to let him know. Do you think Rivka knew? About the adoption, I mean?"

The question caught her off-guard. The possibility that Rivka might have known this family secret all these years caused her knees to buckle. "God, I hope not." Austin walked across the room to look out the French doors leading to her porch, before turning back to Claire. "I'm the only one in my family who even goes to synagogue, who's at all faithful. I guess I'd call them more secular. Wouldn't it be just icing if I turned out not to even be Jewish?"

Claire, after hesitating, moved to Austin's side. She slid an arm around Austin's shoulders and squeezed lightly before stepping back. "It must be upsetting to have something so close to your heart be so uncertain now."

Austin took a step back. "Were you raised in a particular faith?"

Claire shrugged. "Not really. My parents are Methodists, but we only ever went to service on Christmas Eve."

"Oh. And now?"

"Mark me down as agnostic, I guess."

"Not a quiz, but okay."

"So, being a person of strong faith, agnostics and atheists don't bother you?"

"Of course not. It's really personal, isn't it? Who am I to judge what other people believe? As long as they don't try to tell me how to live. Any external expression of my faith will only be in the form of mitzvah, a good deed for others." Austin headed toward the living room and tugged at the black curtains. "Enough of the serious. How about I show you my geeky side now?"

"Because your insane crawling robot isn't geeky enough?"
"Not even close."

***

Austin gestured for Claire to sit on the couch. "Turn the lamp on, please. It's gonna get dark in a sec."

She drew the blackout curtains around the track, then unrolled the black canvas top to completely enclose their section of the living room.

Claire moved to the edge of the couch as Austin knelt on a center cushion, pulled a wire connector from behind the couch and connected it to her tablet. "All right, ready. Turn the lamp off?"

Claire did and they were enveloped in midnight black, mitigated only by the dim light of her computer screen. Claire's voice floated toward her in the darkness. "You really went all out. Ceiling frames, rollers. I'm jealous."

"You have unlimited use of the darkrooms at work, don't you? I'm sure Brian must let you…"

"Yeah, yeah. But how great would it be if I had one like this in my apartment?"

"Really great? You should set one up. I'll help." Austin could see Claire's silhouette, still seated on the edge of the couch. "Sit next to me. You won't see it right if you're next to the curtain."

Claire inched closer to Austin. "This is so exciting."

"You must not get out much. You might be overhyping the event."

"Oh, it's an event!"

"Yeah, an event. I'll collect your ticket in a minute." Austin stood up on the couch, wobbling on the cushions.

Claire grabbed her legs to keep her from toppling over.

"Thanks. Now I have to make it all like a big thing. Thanks a lot. Close your eyes. " Austin flipped the switch on the projector, glancing at the curtain facing them. Everything was working. She extricated herself from Claire's grip and flopped down on the couch. "Okay. Now you can look."

The image of a full moon, projected onto the taut black drapery, reflected just enough light for Austin to make out Claire's face. Claire looked surprised, but Austin couldn't tell if it was in a good way. She tapped the settings on her iPad to enlarge the moon so it filled the screen before them, a pale disc hovering above the edges of the curtain brushing the floor. Austin kept her eyes on the moon, but her ears were attuned to Claire. She heard nothing; no rustling, not even Claire's breathing. Why'd Claire have to build this up into a big deal? Now, she was probably disappointed. A weight sank into Austin's chest. It'd be nice to have at least one person in her life that enjoyed this type of thing.

Then, she heard Claire whisper, "Oh," as a crescent of black encroached on the moon's surface, edging its way across the brightness, replacing light with delineated darkness, sliver by sliver. "An eclipse! How are you getting this?"

"It was recorded last month." Austin leaned back, folding her arms across her stomach. "I subscribe to this online astronomy site. They do live-streaming. I did see this live. It's an eclipse as seen from the Canary Islands." Austin pointed to the projector box attached to the ceiling, "I set all this up so I could feel like I was really watching it in person. A city geek's next best thing to star-gazing."

"You set all that up just to watch this eclipse?"

"Oh, no, I stream from the site all the time. You can rent telescope space in ten-minute increments to actively look for things or just join in when they're streaming an event like this or meteor showers, events like that. Also, you can download events or loops if you're a member, which I do all the time as well."

"Of course you do. It's like a playlist for stars, instead of music."

"Yeah. A geek playlist."

"Very geeky," Claire agreed, leaning back against the couch. "And totally cool."

"Sometimes I loop a random night sky clip and just let it run." Austin patted the arm of the couch. "This is actually a sofa-bed."

"Explaining why it's so damn uncomfortable," Claire interrupted, tucking her feet up beside her, shoes left on the floor.

"Yeah. I just pull it out and lie on my back, staring up at the night sky over the Canary Islands."

"Just chilling, looking at the stars?"

Austin could feel rather than see Claire's smile, could detect the gently mocking tone that didn't sting. "Yeah. I really love looking out there. I love the idea of it."

"Idea of what?"

"Looking back through time."

***

Rivka called at noon on Sunday to confirm their Thursday night plans, and to tell her that her mother had called Rivka once again to check up on Austin. "Whatever is going on, Austin, can you at least call her to let her know you're okay?" She'd asked.

"She knows I'm fine. I texted her this morning, as a matter of fact."

Rivka had sounded like she wanted to say something more, but simply said she looked forward to seeing Austin on Thursday.

Every time Austin managed to push the adoption thing to the back of her mind so she could focus on studying, her cellphone would vibrate, constantly flashing 'Mom' as if the phone itself was glaring at her. Finally, when it rang for the fourth time within two hours, Austin tossed her notebook down and answered the phone.

"Well. Thank you for finally deigning to take my call, Austin."

Austin imagined her mom standing in the den, back straight, hair perfectly straightened then curled so it bounced lightly on top of her shoulders, hand loosely holding the phone next to her ear, painted fingernails matching the dark pink Otterbox-encased phone. "Mom."

"It's good to know you're still alive," her mother continued.

Austin was in no mood for the guilt trip. As if her mom had any right. She resisted the urge to hit the 'end' button. "I sent you a text telling you I was fine."

"Anyone can send a text, Austin."

"I've had a lot going on with school."

"Being busy doesn't mean you shirk your social obligations."

Austin opened the fridge, not sure what she was searching for and therefore not finding it. She shut the door. "I didn't realize I was under a social obligation to you. Are there other obligations you want to fill me in on?"

"Austin! What has gotten into you? Why do you sound so angry?"

Didn't she really know? Was she playing dumb, hoping Austin hadn't figured out the truth?

"Austin, answer me, please." Her mother's voice sounded tinny, thin, almost childish.

Anger warred with guilt and guilt won the first round. She could hear the sound of her mother shifting the phone from one ear to the other and Austin knew she had sat down on her ottoman. Her free hand was likely rubbing her right temple, maybe moving to the bridge of her nose briefly before returning to her stress spot, as she called it. "I am angry, Mom. I wasn't answering your calls because I'm angry, and

I'm not ready to talk about it."

She left the kitchen and strode into the living room, waiting through her mom's silence.

Finally, her mom spoke reluctant words. "What in the world are you talking about, Austin?"

"Do you really not know? Isn't it what you were so concerned about when you kept calling about whether I got the right birth certificate? I did get the right birth certificate, Mom. My original birth certificate. You know, the one that wasn't amended."

"Austin, I—They aren't allowed to do that." Her mom's voice rose in pitch. "It's against the law for them to give that to you."

It wasn't the response Austin had expected. No denial, no sudden rush of explanation, just indignant self-righteousness. "It was a clerical error, an honest mistake." Austin didn't flinch at lying, feeling more loyalty toward Jeremy in the moment then her dedication to truth telling. "But, seriously Mom, you guys were never going to tell me, were you? If this hadn't happened."

Her mom wasn't listening to her, going on about needing the name and address of the exact office that had made this horrific mistake. Austin refused to provide the necessary information. "That's not the point, Mom. I'm more interested in getting a confirmation."

"Confirmation?"

"Amended birth certificates usually mean adoption, Mom. Am I right?"

"Darling, it's not- "

Never before had her mother's use of that endearment grated against her like it did now, stinging like skin scraped along concrete. "Yes or no, Mom."

Her mom hesitated for several seconds that stretched for so long, Austin felt an eternity had passed before her mom finally, softly, answered, "Yes. But—"

"Not now. I don't want to hear it right now." Austin tugged the darkroom curtains around the ceiling track until she was fully enveloped in the darkened space. "I'll talk to you later."

She hung up without waiting for a response. Thankfully, her mom didn't call back. She sank onto the couch and closed her eyes.

After the call, she'd tried to recenter herself, staring up at the stars for what seemed like hours though, when she checked, only thirty minutes had passed. She tried working on classwork, but nothing made sense. Now that she knew, absolutely, she felt incapable of doing anything other than trying to learn more. She went in search of the Post-it with Jeremy's number.

~

7

She spotted Jeremy waiting for her in a booth near the front door. She had suggested the Village this time. Its familiar tan walls, covered in student art pieces, all for sale, comforted her. She didn't think of Jeremy as creepy or threatening, now that she understood his behavior. He had been sympathetic to a fault, apologizing again for springing this on her.

She slid into the booth across from him. "Thanks for meeting me."

"Anytime. I'll help however I can. I feel terrible about this."

"You can stop apologizing." Austin ordered a Coke when the waitress popped by. "I don't know if I think what you did was right, but it's done, and I think I'm glad to know. But I have so many questions about what to do now. I feel kinda lost. I've done a little research. Enough to realize the original birth certificate is the holy grail for adoptees, right?"

Jeremy nodded. "Adoptees who are searching often request a copy of their birth certificate a couple of times a year, hoping a clerical error might send their original birth certificate to them instead of the amended one. It's the only surefire proof you can get of knowing who your birthmother is. Unless you get your records unsealed and that's close to impossible in most states."

Birthmother. The word sounded alien. There were a few terms Austin had learned about, but they all sounded just as foreign. Biological mother. Natural mother. What did they prefer to be called, these mothers without their children?

"That's why they amend the birth certificate, isn't it? To erase any trace of who you were and where you came from so you can start all shiny and new with a new family." Austin shook her head. Such an elaborate deception aided and abetted by the government. Who made these choices? The parents or birthmother? Both? It seemed outrageous to her. She glanced sharply at her companion. "What you did, sending the original birth certificate to me, I'm guessing that's against the rules?"

"If you reported me, I would be fired." Jeremy met her eyes. "You were the first chance I found. It's awful you found out from me, but I don't regret doing it. People have a right to know where they come from, who they come from. It's our birthright. I don't believe anyone has the right to seal it away from us."

"Us. You're adopted?"

He nodded. "I spent twenty years searching for my biological family."

He spent several years, he told Austin, first trying to find a way to unseal his adoption record without success, having no dire medical reason for needing its content and lacking the funds to take it up in the courts. It's impossible, he explained, to get those records opened without sufficient cause, which usually means you have to be dying or your life is imperiled, and you require blood relatives for bone marrow or organ donation to save your life. Being in fine health meant he had no legal standing to approach the courts to open his file. Then, he discovered that he was adopted through an agency.

"My parents told me I was adopted when I was very

young, four or five I think, but we never discussed it. I found out about the adoption agency when I went snooping in their safe. I didn't even tell them when I started searching. I figured I'd tell them if something ever came of the search."

"Why?"

"Fear of hurting their feelings, of them being angry at me." Jeremy stirred his coffee slowly, tapping the wooden stirrer twice on the lip of the mug before placing it carefully on the table napkin. He propped his elbows on the table, folding his fingers together. "Fear of being considered ungrateful. Fear of their rejection."

"So, fear." Austin mulled the word over in her head. She didn't know enough right now to feel any fear. If this was true, what Jeremy was saying, then her parents had lied to her for years. People who lie are usually afraid of being exposed. How afraid were her parents, she wondered.

Jeremy told her how he obtained non-identifying information from the adoption agency, most of which turned out to be untrue. He said it was common for unwed pregnant women to often obscure the truth, to save face or be spared judgment from the health professionals. He was born in the seventies, when closed adoptions were common and unwed mothers were still looked down upon, especially pregnant teenagers.

"In any event, the information didn't help me at all. I was stuck on square one for years."

"And where are you now?" Austin pushed her empty coffee cup toward the waitress passing by with a pot of coffee. She stopped and filled the mug. Jeremy shook his head when she offered him a refill.

"A few years ago, I was checking the registry boards. I hadn't looked at them in a year, maybe more. You'll find that, after you've been checking them for a while, it gets depressing. I did my usual search and this time, something popped up. A birth sibling was searching for the son his mother gave up for adoption several years before he was born. His information was pretty detailed, matched mine closely, so I reached out. Turns out his mother had died, and he'd found paperwork from this adoption in her safe when he was going through her things, including the original birth certificate."

Austin sipped her coffee, eyes glued to Jeremy's face. "And it was a match to your amended one? Did you compare the file numbers like mine?"

Jeremy nodded. "Long story short, he of course absolutely embraced me. After all, he had posted the information I used to find him. I have two half-siblings, Jeffrey and a lovely woman named Allison, but my mother, well, I was too late."

"If you had had the information earlier…"

"I would've been able to meet her, or at least communicated with her."

"So that's why you helped me."

"It's not right that these secrets are kept. Maybe it won't be too late for you if you decide to find your birthmother."

Austin couldn't think about that yet. She was still reeling from the realization that all this was true and her parents had not only adopted her, but kept it secret from her. "Are you still in touch with your siblings?"

"Oh, yeah. They're terrific. Very open, very sharing. It's been a blessing." But Jeremy was only half-smiling and didn't look up from the table as he spoke.

Austin didn't know how to read that. "What about your birthfather?"

"I never have discovered who he is. His name wasn't on the original birth certificate either, and he was not the man my mother ended up marrying and having children with so, basically a dead end."

Austin would've liked to ask more questions, but Jeremy

looked at his watch with a sigh. "I'm out of time. I have to get going. Wife puts dinner on the table at seven. If I'm not there, I don't eat. Same rules as the kids." He grinned.

"How many do you have?"

"Two. Ben's twelve and Melissa's sixteen."

"You have your hands full." Austin smiled. Looking at Jeremy now, with his bald head, round face and gentle smile, she felt vaguely embarrassed that she had ever found him creepy. Even her anger had faded. Why kill the messenger? "Thanks for talking with me. Again."

Jeremy fished in his jacket pocket and pulled out a pen to write on a napkin. "You can learn more visiting these websites, maybe find some support in the forums. Once you've had a chance to think about this, you're gonna have a lot of questions."

"I still have a hard time believing this, just so you know," Austin said. "My mom even confessed, and still, I keep thinking maybe it isn't true. I'm so stupid about it."

"I understand. I've never met an adoptee whose parents didn't tell them. I can only imagine what that must be like." He jotted something else on the napkin. "My email address. You can write or call me anytime, if you have questions or just need some help with this. You will find, if you talk to people about this, that it's very difficult for non-adoptees to understand what it's like for adoptees and others in the triad."

"Triad is the three parties to adoption, right? I was reading a little about it. Adoptees, birthparents, and adoptive parents."

"Yep. And bear in mind all have different ideas about what adoption is, what it means to be adopted, whether people have the right to search for the birthparents, and all the rest of it. There's a lot of conflicting opinions and people get pretty heated over discussing them, especially online." He handed over the napkin.

"Thanks." Austin folded the napkin and tucked it the front pocket of her jeans. "I guess it gives me somewhere to start."

***

Austin had managed to do some reading between classes in the few days since her talk with Jeremy. She'd gathered a decent amount of material on open versus closed adoptions, search legalities, and other bits and pieces from websites. She bookmarked sites and printed pages, highlighted insights and underlined facts before slipping them into her binder as though this was just one more class project. She would read them more thoroughly when she had some better idea of what she wanted to do about all this. Gather information first, then plan.

The hunt for information also kept her mind occupied and confusion at bay. There were numerous articles and blogs written by adoptees or for them, talking about pain, loss, grief, abandonment issues, intimacy issues. None of it resonated with her. She couldn't find many pieces about adult adoptees who hadn't known they were adopted. The few she did find, she devoured. Most of these adoptees found out after their parents passed away. They found adoption papers in boxes or safes while going through their parents' belongings. Their depth of anger at the betrayal, the proven deception and the inability to confront their deceased parents were pervasive throughout their writings. Immersed in their emotions, Austin found herself poking around at the knot of her own tangled feelings. Though she couldn't unravel it, not yet, it was comforting to know she wasn't alone.

It was on a sub-forum of one of the adoption boards that she found reference to what she and Claire had talked about yesterday (only yesterday?), the process of Jewish conversion for adopted infants. A potential adoptive mother, Jewish, had posted, asking what the correct protocol was for adopting an infant from a non-Jewish mother. What needed to happen was that they would bring their newly adoptive infant to the synagogue for a naming ceremony. There were other varying answers, some involving some kind of water bath-type ritual. Austin couldn't quite find a straightforward explanation. Requirements seemed to vary from one synagogue to another, one branch to another. Austin scribbled some notes down for her talk with Rivka.

Three hours later, Austin was exhausted. She was vaguely surprised her mother hadn't called back. Then again, what could her mom possibly have to say? Austin glanced out the window at the gray world. A gust of wind whistled through the frames as a light rain sprayed the glass. A walk was out of the question. When had the rain started? She glanced around her living room, feeling restless and trapped. She almost dialed Claire, then remembered she was out of town. When had Claire become her go-to friend?

Her phone buzzed with an incoming text. She glanced at it with dread but saw with delight it was from Claire. Uncanny. Austin smiled as she glanced at the text, which was actually a photo of two golden retrievers covering a sitting Claire, who was grinning while holding up arms to fend off the canine invasion. She sent a smiley back to Claire.

It occurred to her, while looking at the photo, that she could perhaps find a picture of her birthmother online. She had her maiden and married name on the certificate. She was ahead of the game. She had a place to start. Something she could trace back to the—to her—beginning. It was more than most people seemed to have. Those who posted on the adoption forums and registries, searching and sounding angry or hopeless or hopeful. She had a name. Such a simple thing held hostage, locked in file cabinets under the watchful eye of some bureaucrat determined to follow policy. Except for Jeremy. Thanks to him, she had a name.

It should be a simple thing, taking a name and tracking it down to a state (should she start with country, she wondered), then a city or town, drilling it down to a street, a house or apartment, until the name is distilled into exactly this person, this woman who gave birth to her. Of course, her name could be different now. It was unlikely she would be found currently under her maiden name. The married name was useful, if she hadn't remarried. Although that brought up another question for Austin. If her mother was married when pregnant, what drove her to seek out adoption as an option? Divorced before giving birth? Austin picked up a pen, pondering whether she should start a list of questions for her birthmother. No. She wasn't ready to tackle that yet. She didn't want to meet her right now. Just find her so she had the option.

Austin pulled her computer onto her lap and opened a search page, typing in her mother's name in quotes. She was rewarded with 263 results, including a row of images at the top. She glanced over pictures. A blonde with a bob cut, too young. A right-aged African-American woman in a business suit, possible but not likely. As she looked at the images, Austin thought about whether she would recognize her birthmother if she saw her in a photo. What about face-to-face on a street? You'd know the woman who carried you for nine months, who gave birth to you. Wouldn't you? There had to be some kind of psychological quantum entanglement at play. The kind of thing when one got hurt, the other ached in pain. Surely, she and her birthmother existed in some type of quantum state.

She scrolled through a second page of results, then realized she could narrow it down. Her birthmother's age was listed on the birth certificate. Add Austin's age to that and she got forty-four. First, she typed "Elise Brouchard" + "44", but all that came up were results from some genealogy site, referencing an Elise Brouchard born in 1888. No good. Next, she tried Elise's actual birthdate, typing in variations of the whole date separated by backslashes, dashes and then periods, but nothing relatable appeared. She got hopeful with one result from a school reunion site, but quickly discovered she couldn't get identifying information. The woman seemed to be from Colorado and probably too young. Again, possible, but not likely. The story of her search, so far.

She tried similar searches, switching to the married name on the original birth certificate. It led to even fewer results, none of which appeared helpful. Frustrated, Austin snapped shut her laptop. She was going to need more help. The websites she looked at had lots of search tips, but maybe she wasn't applying them right. If having the name was the easy version of this search, how did anyone without a name ever succeed? DNA? She jotted down a reminder to research the cost of the top DNA testing sites.

She opened up her laptop again to write an email to Jeremy, asking if he had further search ideas as she was feeling stuck. Crazy how this complete stranger had become one of her go-to persons as well. In the space of one week, she was struggling just to recognize her own life.

~

8

Jeremy had responded to her cry for help with a detailed email on what free websites she could use to track down information about people, and how to use them effectively. He had also alerted her to a local adoption support group meeting, which is why Austin found herself, on Tuesday evening, standing in front of the Cathedral of the Sacred Church.

When Austin found the front doors of the church locked, she almost returned to her car. It was a sign, perhaps, that she didn't need to be here; that this was a waste of her time. As she turned away, she caught sight of a sign reading, 'Adoption Support Group' with an arrow directing her to the side of the building.

She turned down the narrow path, lit by small solar-powered lights staked along the path every four feet until she came to a nondescript gray door. She opened it and stepped into a cavernous empty room with white-painted windowless walls connected by a white-speckled tiled floor. A door on the far side was open, but darkened beyond. She backed out of the doorway and glanced down the side of the church, but there were no other doors.

"Come in." The sing-song voice floated out from the

hallway. She re-entered the room as an older woman, in her late 40s, struggled through the internal doorway with two folding chairs. "Adoption group?"

Austin nodded and walked toward the woman, who was setting up the chairs. "Can I help?"

The woman introduced herself as Jacqui and she quickly took Austin up on her offer to help with the setup. She brought two chairs at a time from the closet down the hallway and Jacqui set them up in a circle, laying a flyer on each chair. At twelve chairs, Jacqui brushed her hands and nodded at Austin. "That should do it, I think."

Two people bustled into the room, ladened with several gallons of iced tea, platters of cookies and veggies, and a couple of shopping bags with cups and utensils. Austin stepped over to help them set up on the long table pushed against the back wall.

Austin turned to newcomers. "I didn't realize we were supposed to bring something."

The young woman, probably about Austin's age, said. "It was our night."

Jacqui spoke from the entryway, where she was propping the door open. "We have a volunteer list. It'll get passed around the group later."

The woman stretched out her hand. "I'm Arielle."

The man standing next to her extended his hand as well. "Matt."

"Austin," she replied, as she shook both their hands. The man was older, maybe in his early thirties, clean-shaven and in a well-tailored business suit. She looked at him. "Coming from work?"

He nodded and brought a hand up to loosen his tie.

Austin felt a measured wave of relief when she saw Jeremy come through the door. How quickly he'd shifted from stranger to mentor and friend. She gave a quick eager wave when he spotted her. He came right over, grinning.

"You made it!" He started to put an arm around her shoulder then altered course, merely patting her arm.

Austin removed a flyer off a chair and took a seat. "Sit with me, will you?"

"Nervous?"

Austin nodded.

"Don't worry. Participation's totally voluntary." He sat to her right, looking at the flyer. "No meeting next month."

She glanced down at the paper. There was a note about May's meeting being canceled, as well as who was next on the list for drinks and snacks for June. She read the words in flowery font along the top and bottom of the flyer. "Out of love, she gave you a better life."

She pursed her lips. "What's that supposed to mean?"

He shrugged. "It's like an affirmation, reminding adoptees not to feel abandoned, you know, like it was a sacrifice to give us up so we could have a better life."

"Nice thought, not necessarily true," Austin said. "I've been reading and there are all sorts of reasons birthmothers relinquish their kids for adoption. Sometimes, it wasn't even their choice. This makes it sound like some kind of idealized sacrifice."

Several attendees glanced at her. She lowered her voice. "It sounds like a line. Disingenuous."

Jeremy shifted in his seat, running a hand over his bald head. "This group is sponsored by Catholic Charities, so they are going to offer a positive spin on adoption."

"What's Catholic Charities?"

"They've been an adoption agency since like 1900. They handled a lot of private adoptions back in the sixties and seventies, mostly, maybe early eighties. You know, unwed pregnant teens needing help. I think they do both now, private and open."

"Oh, so the kind of group that probably coerced those same girls I was reading about into giving up their babies. If you love your baby, you'll give it to a nice married couple."

"Something like that." Jeremy shrugged. "But come on. It's not that bad to remind yourself that most birthmothers gave up their children so they could have a better life."

"I guess. But not all of them were some type of snarky, snappy Juno."

"Who?"

"That movie. Juno. Gee, Jeremy, that's more your age than mine, and you never saw it?"

Jeremy shook his head.

"High school kid has kid, wants to kick it old school with closed adoption. Never a word about what's best for the kid's kid, though. And again, it's not about the why of adoption. It's about creating a wall between you and the person who gave birth to you." It rankled Austin. This all-for-the-best approach felt like a cover-up, like something being told to a group of children to obscure the reality of what adoption actually did, which was separate mothers from babies, regardless of reason. Adoption could be, often was, a good thing. But the sealed files and bureaucratic gatekeepers created a whole legal system designed to keep people from knowing themselves; to allow these barriers to exist ignored the damage done to a person's sense of self, even when intentions were good.

Her discontent only grew as individuals in the group started talking. There seemed to be some kind of pervasive need to first state how lucky, how grateful they were in their current life. Only then would they go on to talk about the issues or dilemmas they were facing with being adopted.

Suddenly it was Austin's turn to speak. She considered opting out, but finally decided to say what she had been thinking since the conversation began.

She introduced herself, then said, "I noticed a lot of you talk about being lucky and grateful for being adopted. I don't really understand. Why grateful?" She glanced around the room. People looked puzzled. Jacqui actually seemed horrified, staring at her, mouth agape. She tried to clarify what she meant. "Do you actually feel grateful for being adopted? Or are you grateful for having a great family? I'm definitely grateful for that. Or is it maybe other people are saying you should feel grateful?"

"Well, I'm sure grateful I was adopted instead of aborted." An older man spoke out from the opposite side of the circle. There were a few murmurs of agreement.

"I'm sure I have a better life now than I would've if I hadn't been given up." This was quietly spoken by the girl who had come in with the refreshments. She looked at Austin, arms folded across her chest, as if daring Austin to argue with her.

Austin wouldn't dare. She held up her hands against the ripples of hostility emanating from many of the attendees. Even Jeremy was looking down at the floor. She tried again. "I'm not arguing with you. I'm curious. As I said, I feel grateful that I have parents who paid attention to me growing up, made me do my homework, and tried to give me a good start. I'm thinking, though, shouldn't anybody with parents like that feel grateful? It's not just limited to adoptees, is it? Same goes for being aborted, really. Every woman who chooses to have a baby, whether she keeps it or not, is choosing against abortion, right? One's a choice between having a baby and the other's a choice about whether to keep the baby. It's two different things."

"What's your point?" Another young guy stood up, squaring off to her.

"That adoption isn't the flip side of abortion?" Austin was sorry she had opened her mouth at all in this group. Clearly there was a proper etiquette here she wasn't up to speed on.

"I don't mean to ruffle feathers. Truth is, I just found out I'm adopted. My parents lied to me about it, so I guess I'm still working on what it all means to me. Equating being adopted with being grateful just doesn't feel...accurate. At least not to me."

She sat back down with a sigh, looking at her feet. Suddenly, she felt like she was twelve years old again, getting dressed down by a teacher in front of the class.

"Well, it certainly makes sense that you would be angry about that right now." Jacqui spoke up as she looked around the group. "It can be very difficult to process all the emotions that you must be going through."

Austin felt the tension in the room start to dissipate as people started shrugging off her comments. New to the knowledge of being adopted or not, she thought it ridiculous that all these people couldn't even begin talking about the issues they faced without at least trying to preface it with flowery baloney about how it had all been for the best. Like if only they could deal with the residual effects, everything would be just peachy. It was as if they were trying to assuage the guilt they felt for even talking about having issues with being adopted by first saying that being adopted was great. How could they be honest about their issues if they were constantly battling back guilt they felt about having those problems in the first place? Like any of it was their fault.

Austin kept silent for the rest of the meeting. It was all she could do not leave after her epic fail to be a part of the dialogue. She didn't, however, stick around for refreshments afterward. She was at her car, key in the door, when Jeremy caught up with her, slightly out of breath.

"So, that was fun, right?" He asked. "Same time, next month?"

"No meeting next month, remember?" Austin opened the door. "And no, it's safe to say I won't be returning. I don't see what support's being offered. It's just one giant guilt-fest. I don't know what I was expecting, but this wasn't it."

"I thought it might be of help, but I guess it's pretty hard for people, even adoptees, to understand what it must be like to suddenly find out you're adopted as an adult. It brings a whole mess of other issues into the mix."

"Yeah, maybe." Austin held up the flyer. On the sheet of paper, there was a code for a discount from a DNA testing group. "Not a complete loss, though. I might do this DNA testing. Have you ever done one?"

Jeremy shook his head. "It was too expensive when I was looking and then, I didn't really see the point, after learning who my folks were."

People were drifting out of the church. Austin really didn't want to interact with anyone so she quickly said good night to Jeremy.

She drove home, feeling unsettled and a little guilty. She had been a bit snarky with the group. More than the situation called for. It wasn't her place to judge them. Jeremy was probably right about giving them another chance. She needed more time to come to terms with her situation, stop feeling like a pinball. The DNA test excited her and troubled her for reasons she hadn't wanted to get into with Jeremy. She knew that being Jewish wasn't defined by blood. That there was terrible danger in defining faith through genetics. But she also knew that, if her DNA test came back with evidence of a biological Jewish heritage, she'd feel a whole lot better. Her desire lacked logic. Only Ashkenazi Jews could be identified from DNA, as far as she knew. Even then, it wasn't foolproof, but she didn't care. If she could prove she was genetically Jewish, then she wouldn't have to worry about conversion, or any of the rest of it. She pushed away the kernel of disgust that swelled up as she thought about it, this notion of a blood tie to her faith. If it worked, it'd be worth it.

***

All day Thursday, Austin could barely contain her impatience to meet with Rivka. She paid no attention to lecturing professors, checking and rechecking her notes on the questions she had for Rivka.

Austin navigated the route to Rivka's house that night, thinking about her parents. Given the secrecy that surrounded her arrival into her family, Austin couldn't imagine them telling the rabbi at their synagogue, much less doing a naming ceremony. If they had gone to services regularly, people may have noticed her mom wasn't pregnant. She seemed to recall they only went on high holidays when they were together. After the divorce, her mother stopped going at all, only dropping Austin off if she asked. The forum post made her wonder. If she did nothing, told no one at Beth Israel, then no one would know. If she didn't tell Rivka, she could continue being the daughter of Ben Nobel and Rachel Blankenship, no questions asked. She would be as she had always been. Jewish. An active community participant. Nothing would change. Except inside her. She would know, would worry, if somehow it came to light, would her community no longer welcome her as one of their own? Being Jewish was central to her being, a core part of how she moved through the world. Once she told Rivka, this key facet of herself could be redefined without recourse, if not now, then perhaps later in life. The thought was unfathomable.

If she kept it secret, would she be satisfied not knowing the truth? Down the road, if she did have children and they needed to verify their heritage for some reason, what would happen if it came out then? Would she want to pass along an unknown, uncertain legacy? Either way seemed to threaten more loss than she could bear.

She parked at the curb in front of Rivka's house. Rivka had

a way of pulling things out of her, so she was going to have to make a decision before going in and stick to it.

Rivka opened the door as Austin was raising her hand to knock. "I didn't know you were psychic, Rivka."

"I am a woman of many talents. That, and I saw your car pull up five minutes ago." She latched the door and followed Austin into the kitchen. "David's upstairs with the baby, who just fell asleep, so shhh with the voice. What were you doing in the car?"

"Just thinking a minute." Austin peered into the open fridge and snagged two water bottles. "I'm parched."

Rivka took the second bottle from Austin. "Let's go in my study. It's private."

"Like David doesn't know everything about me. Why have they made these caps so small now?" Austin struggled to get the bottle cap off. Rivka exchanged her own opened bottle for it. "Thanks. Actually, I guess I do have secrets now."

"That sounds intriguing." Rivka opened the glass-paned door to her study, pausing while Austin studied the geometric shapes of the glass. "It's new."

"It's beautiful." She glanced through the room at the back doorway leading out to the patio. "Does the evening sun reach it?"

"In the winter. December and January, I think it should." Rivka strolled through the room, removing the decorative pillows from the sofa and piling them on a nearby chair.

"This is so strange, Rivka. I feel like I've stepped into the twilight zone. I keep moving forward, following the right steps, and with each new step, I keep thinking I'll discover the right missing bits and it will all make sense. Nothing will be what it looks like, and I can just go back to living my life. But that's not what keeps happening."

"This must have something to do with why you're avoiding your mother. You're going to have to fill me in, though, because I have no idea what you're talking about."

Rivka steered Austin to the sofa. She retrieved the afghan off her desk, spreading it over both of them as she sat down. "Start from the beginning."

Austin told her about the birth certificate, what she learned from Jeremy and the terse conversation she had with her mother on Sunday, essentially confirming what she couldn't seem to believe—that she was adopted. At the end of her story, she turned slightly to look directly at her friend and rabbi. "Rivka, I need to know. Did you know?"

"Did I know you were adopted?"

Austin nodded.

"I had no idea. Your parents never mentioned it. I certainly never suspected it. I hope you believe me."

"I do." Her shoulders dropped as she relaxed and sank into the couch a little more.

"I've been doing some reading, Rivka, about adoption and being Jewish and I came across some information. It was upsetting." Understatement of the year, Austin thought.

"Tell me." Rivka leaned sideways, resting her arm on the back of the couch.

"What if I'm not Jewish?"

Rivka frowned. "What do you mean?"

"Exactly that. I'm adopted. I don't know all the facts yet, but that part's definitely true. That means it's possible my birthmother isn't Jewish. Likely, even."

"But your parents are. Legally, there's no distinction—"

"I'm not talking legally. I'm talking religiously, in the eyes of the Jewish community. Our Reform community, our synagogue. That's what I'm asking about."

"You want to know, if your birthmother isn't Jewish, are you still Jewish? Is that your question?"

"Yes."

Rivka leaned back into the sofa, grimaced, and rubbed the

back of her right shoulder. "First of all, your faith is defined by your beliefs. Your faith, not the faith of your ancestors. You grew up in the Jewish community. You're an active member of our synagogue and our community here. Faith is not defined by blood, Austin."

Austin shook her head and stood to pace in front of the couch, turning away from Rivka. "That's true but not true, plus you're not answering my question. You know that being Jewish, identifying as Jewish, is more than just following a set of religious beliefs. It's a culture, a heritage, a community. A history. As you know, my parents are pretty damn secular, haven't stepped foot in a synagogue since oh about 2003, I guess, is the last time I went with them. But they're totally Jewish. They might disagree, but it's so primary to who they are, in their own way."

"And primary to who you are. You are a part of the Jewish culture and community. I don't see how that changes." Rivka stood as well, walking over to the desk to perch on the front edge. "Maybe I'm not understanding your question correctly."

"I read online that if a Jewish couple adopts a baby, at least in the Reform community, as long as they have a naming ceremony for the baby at the synagogue, that baby is considered Jewish."

"A naming ceremony, usually during a tevilah," Rivka agreed.

"I don't remember my parents ever having a ceremony, Rivka."

"It would be remarkable if you did, given it's done when one's an infant."

Austin frowned at her and ignored the wink she got in return. "What's a tevilah?"

"A tevilah, or mikveh, is a ritual immersion in water, a ritual cleansing."

"Oh, the baptism-like thing I read about it. I'm certain my parents didn't do that. It would go against this big secret they were hiding from everybody."

Austin walked over to the oversized glass door leading out to the backyard. Two solar-paneled pathway lamps illuminated the small patio just outside the doors. A small wrought-iron picnic table and four chairs took up most of the bricked area. It looked exactly like the backyard patio at Rivka's parents' house, where she had spent considerable time when she was young. She wondered if the furniture was a gift from her parents, or whether Rivka had simply gone for comfort of the familiar when decorating. She turned to see what Rivka was doing and saw her jot something down on a notepad.

Rivka said, "I'm not certain how adoptees, as infants, are brought into the Reform community, what type of conversion or affirmation is required. I'm equally uncertain about what the religious implications are for adopted adults who did not go through that ceremony. What I do know," and she waited until Austin looked at her again, "is that although you didn't complete your full Jewish education or have a Bat Mitzvah, you do, by what I can see, daily affirm your commitment to the Jewish faith."

"I was reading that even if a person believes in the Jewish tenets and lives their life as a Jew, even as an Orthodox Jew, if they aren't born to a Jewish mother, converted as a baby or undergo full conversion as an adult, they aren't considered Jewish, by any branch. So, where does that leave me? As a non-Jew practicing the Jewish faith? How does that work? That's not okay with me." Austin turned away again, toward the back door. She wanted to kick out the glass, rattle the frames, throw the broken painted wood pieces against the wall until she was exhausted and couldn't think about this anymore.

"You know, you're assuming some things here. Why don't we roll it back and tackle one question at a time."

Austin slowly turned around, with a wry grin. "Right. Let's start the deconstruction of my false identity one step at a time. That was my plan, too."

"Honey, I know this must be distressing, but we will figure it out." Rivka came toward her, wrapping an arm around Austin's shoulder and pulling her into her body, like she did when Austin was ten years old, sobbing as she watched her parents pull out of Rivka's driveway on their two-week vacation to France. Even as a young college student, Rivka had enough empathy to intuit that young Austin had doubts about this odd vacation taken in the middle of fall, and she had—without exactly telling her what was going on—comforted Austin, promising that they would get through those two weeks, and whatever came afterward, together.

Her parents hadn't really gone to France, Austin realized later. They had dropped her off at Rivka's apartment, then driven back to their home to pack up all of her father's belongings and ship them off to Arizona and, Austin assumed, to deal with the lawyers and paperwork. By the time they returned to pick her up, her home had been reorganized to cover up all the gaps of her father's missing items—a favorite recliner in the living room, a small secretarial desk in the den, the communal closet holding winter clothes and her father's cross-country skis—as if she wouldn't notice the changes, the lack of her father after they had calmly and politely, because that's how they did everything, told her they were getting a divorce. She had cried then, too, and Rivka had been there for her, just as she was today.

But Austin wasn't crying now. She was too confused, too in-the-dark to know what it was she might lose with this discovery. The thought almost made her laugh. Discoveries were supposed to bring you something new, not take everything away. For a brief moment, she hated Jeremy directly and with a razor-sharp focus, but this wasn't his fault. He was right. She did want to know the truth, now that she knew there was a truth to be known. Of course, it followed that to find the truth, she'd have to discover and unravel the whole yarnball of lies she had been told or simply been led to believe over the years.

Nonetheless, she was comforted, being in Rivka's arms, as always. She was a big sister without any of the baggage of growing up together. Maternal without the awkward years of slammed doors and veiled insults. She had never kept secrets from Rivka, trusting her with the knowledge of the first (and only) time she skipped a day in high school, of her first kiss with a girl (which took place the same day she skipped school). Now, she leaned into her, smelling Rivka's familiar perfume, the etrog citron scent blended with delicate mint and ambergris, among other fragrances. Austin had given her the bottle, a custom fragrance designed by a prominent Jewish perfumer living in Canada and meant to encapsulate the scents of Israel.

"I'll tell you what I can do. I'll look into this, call Rabbi Adler, find out exactly what is supposed to occur at the time of adoption. Then, I'll find out what can be done if those steps weren't taken. Okay?"

"Can you look into it first without talking to Rabbi Adler? I'd rather not…"

"I won't mention names, if that's what's worrying you. This is absolutely between us."

"Okay." Rivka's arm tightened around her shoulders once more and Austin rested against her, blowing her nose with the tissue Rivka had just handed her. "I'm so confused by all this, Rivka, and I'm so angry at Mom and Dad. I just don't understand how—"

Rivka waited to see if she would finish her thought. When Austin remained silent, she spoke. "We'll get through this, Austin. I promise."

~

9

"I ordered a DNA kit," Austin confessed to Claire as they were running Inquiry down the river path Gil had marked off for them. She had already told Claire about the meeting debacle and her big mouth during the drive over. Carpooling had been Claire's idea, and Austin offered to drive today. If Claire thought she'd been an ass at the meeting, she didn't say so. Austin maneuvered the rover across a protruding root. "Is the speed okay? I can't go much faster."

Claire trailed slightly behind Austin, left hand on Austin's shoulder for guidance as she viewed the live feed on her phone. "It's fine. We can always speed it up in edits if Gil wants. What's the DNA test for?"

"Crap." Austin set the controller down and hurried over to the crawler, which had attempted to clear a clump of weeds and was now precariously tilted, the right two wheels spinning in the air. Long weed stems had wrapped around the wheel bearings, preventing them from turning. Carefully, she cut through them with a pocket knife. "I thought it might be helpful to know what my biological heritage is, you know? Who knows, maybe I'm Irish, or French. I mean her name is Brouchard. That's French, isn't it?"

"Sounds like it."

"I figured it couldn't hurt. The more knowledge, the better, right?" She tested the rover, removed a few straggling stems, and resumed course. She couldn't bring herself to admit her interest in finding Ashkena

"That lets you find DNA relatives, right?"

Austin nodded. "Yeah, but it doesn't give exact relationship matches, just ranges. Like a fifty percent match is for parents and full siblings, and twenty-five percent is for grandparents, but it gets tricky because twenty-five percent can also be half-siblings or aunts, uncles, nieces, you get the drift."

"That's cool." As they reached the end of the path, Claire stopped walking and reviewed the footage. "You could talk to them and maybe learn more, if you match up with someone close enough."

Austin made a face. "I don't know if I want to communicate with anyone yet. What would I say?"

"That you're interested in finding out how you're related to them."

"I'll have to think about it."

"You know, if you do a test, they can find you too. They might reach out first."

Austin hadn't considered that. If she did the test, the results would be out there, and everything would be out of her control. Crap. Austin waited for Claire to look up from her review. "Do we need to do another pass?" They had already gone down the path twice, taking two slightly different approaches. She was relieved when Claire shook her head. The wind had picked up over the last hour due to another cold front on its way. Mercurial April weather.

As they loaded up Austin's car, Claire asked, "Have you thought about reaching out to your birthmom, since you have her name? Seems like she'd be the easy find."

"I tried to see if I could find out about her online. There are registry boards, where you can post your info so birthfamily members can try to find each other, but I'm not ready for that. I didn't have much luck in my info search. Jeremy sent me some tips and tricks, so I thought that's what I'd do this afternoon." Austin slid into the driver's seat as Claire made her way around the car.

"Do it at my place. I have to work on my gallery stuff, so I won't get in your way. Much."

Austin readily agreed. It felt good that Claire sought out her company, seemingly enjoying her presence. She liked that someone wanted to be around her. They dropped off the rover at her apartment, then headed to Claire's.

An hour later, her stomach painfully full with empanadas, Austin stretched out on Claire's bed, pillow cushioning her back against the wall, her adoption research binder splayed open on her lap.

"Twenty-three is kind of old, don't you think?" Austin looked over at Claire, who sat at her desk working on her computer.

"Old for what?"

"To give a kid up for adoption. You'd think she'd be a teen mom or something. It'd make more sense, giving up a kid for adoption at that age."

"Yeah, but there are probably a lot of reasons women do it."

"I know. I know. It's just the more I try to find information on her and can't, the more curious I am about her and her life and how we ended up like this."

"You won't know for certain unless you talk to her." Claire turned around in her chair, wrapping her arms around the back and resting her chin on the top.

"I'd have to find her first. This was supposed to be a walk in the park, according to Jeremy." Austin tossed her iPad onto the coffee table and stretched out her legs and arms. "I can't find anyone who matches that name on Google or social media or anything. I know it can't be that hard, but I really suck at this searching thing."

"Okay. You said you've tried her maiden name and the married name on the certificate and you haven't found anything definitive, right?

"Yeah." Austin rubbed her forehead, then the bridge of her nose. She leaned down and grabbed her water bottle off the floor.

"She probably remarried."

"Yeah, but how do I find that name? I tried searching for marriage licenses, but all these websites charge for information and I don't want to pay when I don't even know if I'm selecting the right person."

Claire stood, stretched her arms in front of her, then walked to the bathroom doorway, leaning against the wooden frame. "I have an Ancestry account. Maybe you can search on there."

"Isn't that for dead people?" Austin regretted the words as soon as she spoke them.

"You can't get census reports past 1940, and you usually can't see living people in people's trees, but they have current marriage licenses if the state allows digital access. I don't know what criteria they use for making them public, but it might be worth a shot."

"But I don't know what state she's in, or was in."

"Just try her maiden name and birth date and see what comes up." Claire glanced at her watch. "We got thirty minutes. I'll show you how it works and give you my login info so you use it whenever you have time."

"Thanks." Austin watched Claire pull some clothes out of a dresser drawer then go into the bathroom. Claire had mentioned when they arrived at her apartment, almost apologetically, that she'd had plans tonight at seven she'd forgotten about. She didn't give details. Austin now wondered if it was a date. She'd almost asked earlier, then reasoned if Claire had wanted her to know what she was doing, she would have told her.

When Claire reappeared in worn jeans and a faded gray long-sleeved shirt, Austin thought a date unlikely, but she still didn't ask. She stood behind Claire's chair as Claire showed her the basics of searching on the Ancestry website.

"Thanks again." She took the scrap of paper upon which Claire had written her account information. "Why did you get an Ancestry account?"

"I thought I might be able to learn something about my mother's family, but I haven't had much time to spend on it yet." Claire stood and switched the computer off. "Let me know what you find?"

"Definitely." Austin quickly gathered her bag and jacket and headed out of the room, toward the front door. "Um, have fun tonight."

"Thanks. I'm sure it'll be a blast." Claire paused, hand on the door knob, as if waiting for Austin to say something more. When Austin didn't, she pulled the door open and smiled. "I'll see you soon, I'm sure."

"Yeah. Night." As Austin walked down the sidewalk to her car, she glanced behind her and was caught in the act by Claire, who was locking her front door, jacket draped over her left arm. Austin waved with assumed intention, hurrying away after Claire waved back.

***

It was past ten on Sunday morning when Austin finally woke up. Though she often spent Saturday nights at home, she had been restless after leaving Claire's. She had driven through downtown Richmond to the other side of town to a little pub she'd discovered last year. It had four tables and a five-stool length bar, definitely not a place for hip college students, which suited Austin fine. She preferred the low-key atmosphere and keep-to-themselves customers. The bar was only half-full when she arrived and steadily decreased in occupancy as the night wore on, country rock playing softly in the background as a muted TV showed some soccer match playing somewhere. She'd eaten fried pickles and a beer, which she nursed for most of the evening while browsing forums on her tablet.

It had been close to midnight when she arrived home, with little more to show for it than an acquired sense of melancholy and a few more helpful search tips from an online adoption group she joined a few days earlier. But, as she was lying in bed, she remembered Mitzvah day was coming up. Her last thought before drifting off to sleep was wondering whether Claire might like to volunteer with her this year. Too drowsy to reach for her phone to make a note, she hoped she would remember to ask.

She did remember, while in the shower, and called Claire as soon as she was sure her voice didn't sound froggy. To her disappointment, Claire didn't answer. She left a message. "It's not super important, just something I thought you'd be interested in. Give me a call when you can. I'll tell you all about it."

Although eager to hit the genealogy site and get started on her research, Austin forced herself to work on schoolwork. She had taken the hardest remaining required classes last semester so this one could be fun and engaging, like the robotics engineering class for which she built Inquiry. Fun or not, there were still readings and quizzes and exams to pass so she settled onto the couch with her textbook and notebook and a cup of coffee.

A knock on her front door pulled her from the not-so-wild world of feedback control systems. She looked through the peephole and swung open the door.

"What're you doing here?"

Brian grinned, pushing up his sunglasses over his short hair. "You ready for brunch?"

"It's after noon. It's just lunch."

"It's Sunday and it's called brunch. Ready?"

"Did we have plans that somehow slipped my mind?" Austin left the door open and ambled to the nearby table, where she grabbed her jacket and slipped it on.

"I know you're not gonna turn down brunch with your brother, who's paying, right? Plus, I'm hoping you know why Mom and Dad are flying into town Friday night."

"Oh, hell," Austin muttered. She locked her door and followed him out of the building.

***

Brian took her to Willie's Diner, a tiny red-brick building with several wrought-iron garden tables and chairs in front, sheltered by a tan multi-tiered awning. Of the three booths inside, the middle one was just being cleared as they entered. Austin slid onto the bench as her brother gestured toward the restroom sign.

They didn't talk much until the waitress had come and gone with their order, returning to bring water for both and coffee for Austin. Her brother eschewed coffee, for some strange reason Austin would never understand. She measured precisely a teaspoon of sugar and stirred it into her mug as her brother watched, shaking his head.

"My coffee, my way."

Normally, he'd tease her, but not this morning. That her parents, both of them, together, were making such an abrupt trip, was obviously bothering him.

Her creamed chipped beef over toast arrived first, then Brian's twice-as-big omelet platter. He was halfway through his plate when Austin finally decided to ask him. "When did you talk to Mom? Or was it Dad?"

His fork paused midway between plate and mouth as he glanced at her, then the table, then his forkful of egg. "Mom. This morning."

Austin took another bite of her food. "Did she tell you anything about why they were coming into town?"

"No. It's so weird. I mean, if they were coming in to surprise us, Mom wouldn't have mentioned it at all, right? And, if it was just Mom driving in, that's not surprising because you two are always spending time together." He paused to shovel in some food. "But then she said Dad is coming too. Something about him flying into Norfolk, then driving up here with Mom. Nothing about why they're doing it. I don't know. Something's going on. Mom totally had that 'divorce talk' tone happening, you know? You think one of them's sick? Jesus. You think Mom has breast cancer? Why would they come here together?"

"Calm down, Brian. I'm sure no one's sick."

"Mom said they want to spend Saturday with you, and then a family dinner Saturday night with both of us."

Austin dropped her fork. "Really? That's not gonna happen."

"You know what's going on." Brian wiped his mouth. "You wanna fill me in?" He slid his empty plate to the side.

"Did you even taste any of that?"

"Don't avoid."

"I found out I'm adopted."

Brian narrowed his eyes. "That's a stupid joke and I'm being serious. I'm worried."

"That is why." Austin pushed her half-empty plate next to his. A wave of nausea at the idea of lunch with her parents squashed her appetite. "I found out when I got the wrong birth certificate. Well, it wasn't wrong. It just wasn't what I expected."

She gave him the abbreviated version of her discovery,

leaving out her conversation with Jeremy. She didn't need that getting back to her mother. Brian didn't say anything as he listened, just observing her with a somber expression. On Brian, it was disconcerting. She wrapped up by saying, "I'm guessing they want to come in and talk to me in person about it."

"You're really not kidding." Brian stared at the table. "They never told you?"

Austin shook her head.

He looked at her. "They never told me, either, so you know."

"It doesn't change anything between us." Austin winced slightly at the lifted tilt of her statement, making it sound more like a question.

"Why would it?" Brian leaned back from the table. "Have you talked more about it with Mom? Has she told you anything about the circumstances or anything like that?"

Austin shook her head. "I haven't wanted to speak with her, honestly. Too angry."

"Because they didn't tell you?"

"Yeah."

"I can see that. I'm sure they had their reasons, though." Brian drummed his fingers on the table, making the silverware rattle against the wood.

Austin scoffed. "It's a pretty big lie, Brian, no matter what reasoning they had. There are a lot of components to a lie like that."

"I think you owe them a chance to explain where they're coming from."

"Would you be saying that if it were you they lied to on this?" Austin folded her arms and leaned forward. "Don't bother answering that. You can't know. You can't understand."

Brian held his hands up. "All I'm saying is that Mom and

Dad love you. More than anything. I get that you feel betrayed, angry. Give them the benefit of the doubt, okay? Talk to them. Can you do that?"

Austin sighed. "I'll try, Brian. No promises."

***

Austin let herself into the apartment, waving to Brian as he sped off. She wondered why her parents hadn't told Brian the purpose of their visit. Was it because they thought she should be the one to do it? Or were they embarrassed to admit they had kept it a secret? Maybe they were even hoping she might not tell him either, though that seemed unlikely. They could hardly expect Austin to keep it from her brother.

She perched on the edge of the couch and checked her email on her phone. Sure enough, there was a note from Mom, subject line: *Keep Saturday free. We're coming to visit.*

It was just like her not to ask, to make the plans and expect Austin to accommodate it. She didn't blame her mom for not calling, though. Austin didn't want to see her, didn't want to see either of her parents yet, or talk to them and now it was out of her hands. It wasn't fair not to give her some breathing room on this.

She opened her laptop and debated how to word her response. Maturity would go over better than a rant, so she chose her words carefully, telling her parents that she didn't think the visit was a good idea. She was still upset by what she discovered and thought it wouldn't be a particularly fruitful discussion. However, if they still insisted on coming into town, she would appreciate if they would bring all paperwork pertinent to her adoption with them and leave them with her.

She knew the dispassionate tone of the note would rankle her mother, but it was the only way she could communicate with her right now. She would have to do the same when they talked in person. Otherwise, there would be only tears and mumbles and her points would be lost. She quickly reviewed the text and hit 'send'.

Her phone rang. She braced herself for seeing her mother's name, but it was Claire returning her call, apologizing for the delay though not providing a reason. Austin didn't inquire. "I'm doing this volunteer thing with my synagogue. It's ongoing this month, actually, but Sunday, April 19th is the day where we put it all together. It's called Mitzvah Day. Would you like to come help?" When Claire didn't answer right away, Austin added, "You don't have to be Jewish."

"I'm glad to hear it." Claire laughed. "Sure, I'd love to, but what exactly are you putting together?"

"Family food boxes. We did a Hunger Drive this year, among other things."

"That's great." There were rustling sounds in the background and it sounded like Claire was holding the phone away from her ear a moment, before saying, "That's really awesome for you to do."

"It's not like I do it on my own."

"No, of course not, but still. It's cool." Again, more rustling, Claire shooing someone away from the phone. "I have to go but I'm sure I'll see you before then. Call me when you have the details for Sunday."

"Yeah, of course." Austin hung up and wondered why Claire was hiding the fact that she had company over. The thought bothered her. She pushed it out of her mind.

It was after three. She still had homework for class the next day, but didn't feel like working on it. Her thoughts were too scattered, anxiety too high, and science was not enough distraction, for once. She wandered from kitchen to living room to bedroom and back to living room, unsure what to do. It was a gorgeous day outside, sunny and in the mid-seventies, a fantastic spring afternoon. They should've eaten outside, she thought as she dropped back down on the couch.

She heard a paper crinkling in her jeans and pulled out the scrap paper Claire had given her last night. She smoothed it out and propped her laptop on her legs once more and decided she could distract herself from one set of parents by trying to find out more about her second set.

The first few search attempts on Ancestry were as fruitless as her web searches, with even fewer results and none that were relevant. However, as Austin got the hang of the search parameters, she tried a combination of names and dates, using her birthmother's birth date from her birth certificate. No family tree or document data appeared, but she did find an obituary that made her catch her breath. She clicked on the link, which led to an index card notation and another link to an outside source. She held her breath all through the navigation. It hadn't occurred to her that her birthmother might be dead.

The link led to an archived Falls Church News-Press webpage that showed the obituary in its entirety. With relief, Austin noted it was for a woman named Elaine Brouchard (neé Marchand), born 1940 and life-long resident of Falls Church, Virginia, died November, 17, 2009. She skimmed the rest of the article until finding Elise's name in bold, listed as a surviving daughter. No last name for Elise was given, and no indication of her age either. Still, it could be her.

Austin reached for her binder and flipped it open to the birth certificate. Elise's hometown was listed as Falls Church. What were the odds? She returned to the laptop and printed the obituary. She almost hit 'save to shoe box', then remembered this wasn't her account. Would Claire mind? Then, she realized that, in the toolbar at the top, Claire had started her own family tree. She hovered the icon over Claire's tree for a few seconds, but decided not to look. She wasn't going to take advantage of Claire's generosity by invading her privacy. It was hardly an action that would inspire trust. Better to remove the temptation entirely.

She clicked on membership options. She could afford the monthly fee if she only used it for a month or two. She logged out of Claire's account and signed up for her own, digging out a debit card from her wallet. If she was interested in knowing more about Claire, she should damn well ask her, not poke around in her files.

Feeling better, Austin returned to the obituary index page, saved it, then retrieved the printed copy from her printer in the bedroom. As she read it through more carefully, she underlined the names and dates referenced, including her likely grandfather's name as well. There wasn't a photo accompanying the article. There might be in the genealogy database, though.

Austin started a fresh page in her binder and recorded her potential grandmother's name and life dates, along with locations mentioned in the article. Using that information, she searched under her grandmother's name, hoping to find more information. She wasn't disappointed. Several family trees popped up. The first she dismissed, as Brouchard was listed as the maiden name. The second proved more fruitful, with 'Elaine Marchand' listed as marrying 'Leonard Brouchard,' the same name mentioned in the obituary. She found the right track. Her pulse ratcheted up a notch as she clicked on the first available family tree.

Elaine and Leo had a daughter, but the name was listed living so her name, details of birth, or any locations, were all hidden as private. Still, now she had two names and the mention of a daughter, all matching up with the obituary she found. If the obituary was correct and connected to her Elise, she was looking at her own family tree. With that thought, a shimmer of guilt passed through her as she considered that she did have a family tree, with faces and names familiar to her, nothing withheld as private. Fully known.

She clicked on the tool bar at the top and created a new family tree, labeling Nobel Family Tree. She added herself, and then her parents and Brian. Satisfying the niggle of guilt for the time being, she returned to the Brouchard tree.

This tree had an associated gallery of pictures. Austin clicked on the link and squinted at the tiny thumbnail pictures and descriptions. Most were of people with names she hadn't heard of, black and white portraits, cracked and faded. Then she saw it. A color photograph of a young woman with some kind of shag haircut and a tight light blue knit jersey. Were those yellow corduroy bellbottoms? Oh, good God. Austin peered at the caption, which read "Elaine Marchand, '71."

Excitedly, Austin clicked on the image, but the picture remained frustratingly small on her laptop. She didn't need a larger picture, though, to see she had the right family. Her own hazel eyes, same round expression accentuated by the same thin eyebrows, were staring back at her from the screen. Somewhere deep inside, Austin felt the visceral sensation of a puzzle piece sliding into place.

~

10

After class Tuesday afternoon, Austin swung by the three UPS stores to pick up the boxes to drop off at the synagogue. As this week had worn on, she felt the knots beneath her shoulder blades tighten and the muscles in her neck stiffen. Lengthy hot showers failed to manage the aches borne of her anxiety over her parent's impending visit.

Strangely, looking at the picture of her newly-discovered grandmother calmed her. Last evening, she had downloaded the photograph to her iPad and propped it up like a portrait in a frame, so she could glance up and look at it at any time.

She worried, though, that she was not just projecting a connection to the woman in the photograph, but also her own desire to see herself reflected in the image of this woman. She needed confirmation from an outside source. Much to Austin's chagrin, Claire had been tied up most of Monday and Tuesday and it wasn't until last night that they were finally able to connect, making plans for coffee tomorrow. She couldn't resist telling Claire about the photograph over the phone, though, promising to show it to her. Claire asked her how it felt to see a picture of someone she was biologically related to, that she actually resembled, for the first time.

Pretty damn amazing, Austin had responded. It feels pretty

damn amazing.

It still felt amazing, three days after her discovery. She caught herself looking at the picture on her phone while sitting in class, getting in her car, any random downtime. She resisted the urge to glance at it again after parking in Beth Israel's parking lot.

The synagogue doors were unlocked and Rivka's Prius was parked in the lot. Austin didn't find her in the office so she carried the flattened boxes, one bundle of twenty-five at a time, into one of the two classrooms in the back of the building. She was slicing the straps off when Rivka appeared in the doorway.

"Hey," she said, coming into the room and taking a seat. "Saw your car out front."

"I picked these up. Figured I'd drop them off since I had the time." Austin leaned against the wall.

Rivka surveyed the stacks on the various desks. "You got a lot of boxes."

"Five hundred. Hope it's enough." Austin grinned. "Have you seen the food donations?"

Rivka nodded. "I have. I can't believe it. More than last year, even, and that was a record."

"The beauty of social media."

"I guess so. Good job."

"Don't tell me, tell Alexa," Austin said. "She's a social media wiz. I don't think I even have accounts on all the channels she used."

"Still, you've done an amazing job organizing this, Austin."

"Thanks." Austin gathered up the white straps. Though Rivka often doled out compliments like candy, she sounded earnest. And pensive. Austin felt the euphoria of finding her grandmother's picture fading away. She wrapped the white straps around her hand. "Do you think I should leave them flat and have a couple of volunteers unfold them as we go?"

"I looked into that question we talked about the other night." Rivka folded her hands on her lap and looked at Austin. "And I talked to Rabbi Adler. No names, of course."

"Oh. Good." Austin pursed her lips, still staring at the boxes. "Why don't I unfold a few. Give them a head start. Do you know where the packaging tape is? I'll have to tape the bottoms."

"In the supply closet. I'll get it."

Austin watched her leave the room, then rested her hands on the table, taking a deep breath. Whatever Rivka had found, it wasn't great or she would've just launched into it. She had four boxes folded and ready for taping by the time Rivka returned with the packaging tape dispenser.

"Thanks." She grabbed the tape and started sealing the bases of the boxes. "What did you find out?"

Rivka must've realized Austin wasn't in the mood to sit so she talked while Austin worked. "First, I took a look at "Conversion for Adopted Children" in the Reform Responses for the 21st Century volume. It's in our library if you want to take a look. It has a section on adoption in Jewish families. Some of it was more or less what I thought."

"Which is?"

"From a legal standpoint, you're your mother's daughter, who is Jewish. Thus, in the eyes of American law and Israeli law, you're considered Jewish. That means, if you ever wanted to relocate your citizenship to Israel under the Law of Return, you could do so."

Austin could feel Rivka watching her, waiting for a reaction. She looked up. "Good to know. I hear they have excellent opportunities for women engineers."

Rivka offered her own deadpan response. "It's a silver lining."

Austin moved the finished boxes and stacked them on the floor in a column against the brick wall. "But…"

"That's from a legal standpoint only. I know you were interested in understanding this from other viewpoints, namely religious. The truth is, it varies. Not only between branches like Reform and Conservative, but also among Reform rabbis themselves."

Austin leaned against a table. "So, what does that mean?"

"Generally, if an adopted child received a Jewish name at infancy—"

"Which I didn't."

"—receives a Jewish education up to celebrating a Bar or Bat Mitzvah through confirmation in high school—"

"Which I also didn't do."

"—then he or she is considered Jewish within the Reform community."

"So, I'm not considered Jewish is what that means."

Rivka frowned. "I know this is upsetting, but if you're going to interrupt me every other word, this conversation is going to take a long time."

Austin flushed and looked at her fingernails. "Sorry."

"There are other options. The manual goes on to say that adults who were adopted, but who didn't receive these conversion rituals—the naming ceremony or tevilah—are encouraged to consider formal conversion."

Austin leaned back in her chair, rubbing her face with one hand. She wanted to interject with how ridiculous this was, how wrong it was to act as if she was some kind of intruder, some uneducated Jewish wannabe. Was this what being excommunicated felt like, a total rejection of self? You're just not Jewish enough, kid. Sorry.

Rivka said, "It's made very clear that this advice has nothing to do with doubts concerning the quality of the adult's Jewish commitment. It's simply a method by which your Jewish status would be accepted in the broader Jewish community, well, except for the Orthodox community, which has a specific Orthodox conversion process."

"So, that's my only option. Formal conversion." Austin could feel her eyes stinging. She looked up at the pockmarked, tiled ceiling, then the rough-pebbled tan paint on the walls until she felt she could look at Rivka again without threat of tears.

Rivka shrugged. "If only Beth Israel's acceptance of your Jewish status matters to you, we would do an affirmation ritual, which would include a tevilah and some additional one-on-one study with Rabbi Adler or myself, but nothing like what formal conversion would require. We would do that here because we know of your Jewish education—you did teach Hebrew school here last summer after all—know of your commitment and so forth. But, if you were to move and join another Reform synagogue, they may have a different view of it."

Austin sighed, shoulders slumped. She was exhausted. Too exhausted to feel the fury and sense of abandonment lurking just below her skin. "I don't believe this."

"Of course, even if you were to move, join another synagogue, unless you talk about this, or request some odd ceremony or something that would require an official validation of your Jewish status, no one would ever know, or ever question your status. It's entirely in your hands."

Austin glanced sharply at her, shocked. "I'm surprised you'd say that, Rivka. That sounds so—"

"Dishonest, is what you're thinking, right?" Rivka nodded. "I understand. What I'm really trying to say is that it only matters what you feel, what you need to do for yourself so that you feel right about this."

Rivka moved her chair across from Austin. "Austin. I can't imagine what this must feel like to you, but it's not insurmountable."

Austin shook her head slowly. "I don't know, Rivka. I can't

believe I'm in this position. My parents—"

"It would've been impossible for them to think of all the far-reaching ramifications of what they were doing at the time, Austin. Think about it from their perspective."

Austin pulled her hand away and tried to stand. Instead, she rather ungracefully spilled out of the beanbag and onto the floor. She stood, straightening her t-shirt to muster up some dignity. "Why are you defending them? I get it, okay? It's not like I think they were purposefully trying to screw me over. They probably didn't consider, maybe couldn't consider, all sides of it, all implications, ramifications, whatever. I got it." Austin took a deep breath. Then another one. "How about my side of it, my perspective? How much did they really consider things from how it might be for me? Or were they just banking on my never finding out?"

"Have you talked to them about this? Not just gotten confirmation, but really talked with them to find out why they did what they did?"

Austin shook her head. "I haven't trusted myself." She raised her eyebrows at Rivka. "Do I strike you as being calm enough to discuss this with them right now?"

She went back to the table, opened another box, taped the bottom. "They're coming into town this weekend. Mom emailed me, but Brian told me before I saw it. She and Dad are driving up Friday night. They want to talk with me Saturday. The both of them. Can you say ambush?"

"It's good they're coming up. I'm sure their intent is not an ambush, Austin." Rivka stood and started moving the finished boxes to the wall. "Would you like a mediator? It might be helpful. Rabbi Adler won't be able to as he's still in Louisiana, but I could if you want."

Austin shook her head. "No." She tucked her hair behind her ears and finally looked directly at Rivka. "Thanks anyway. What I need, Rivka, even if it's just for this short period of time, is for you to be biased. I need you to pick a side to support. My side, if you can. That's what I need."

Rivka came around the table to take Austin's hand. "You know I'm always here for you."

***

She saw Lauren's Instagram post the next morning as she killed time by flipping through her social media accounts while waiting for her robotics engineering class to start.

Lauren had posted it three days earlier. It took her breath away to see Lauren's impeccably made-up face beaming at the camera. Her dark hair was down, brushing the top of her shoulders. The picture had been taken outside and Lauren seemed to glow in the sun.

Lauren was perched on the knee of a young man who looked vaguely familiar to Austin, though she couldn't place him. It was the caption that captured her attention. For a moment, she wasn't sure she had read it correctly. It took several more attempts to understand that it did indeed read: 'We're engaged!'

Her chest contracted. The air squeezed from her lungs. Full of surprises, that girl was.

Then, the professor walked into the classroom. Austin slid her phone into her back pocket, only to take it out three seconds later and toss it in the flap pocket of her bag. She wanted to kick her bag, shove it further away from her feet, but it held the controller for the rover and she couldn't risk damaging it. She stared at her rover sitting at the front of the classroom, focusing on its metallic shiny surface. She was third on the list of presenters in this precursor to the final. She needed to calm herself, focus on what was important. She glanced through her presentation notes. Public speaking didn't terrify her, but it wasn't something she'd do if she had a choice. Confidence in her work usually overcame anxiety and it did so again today.

When it was over, she took her seat, relieved to have it finished. The only thing remaining would be to turn in her "instruction manual", which amounted to a final paper explaining what she did, and the footage of its capabilities. She tried to listen to the other presenters, but her thoughts kept returning to Lauren's post. It bothered her, which was stupid. She hadn't loved Lauren, wasn't even sure how much she liked her before Lauren turned tail and trekked across the country. Why would she give a damn if she got engaged, got married, did anything at all?

It wasn't really about Lauren at all, she realized. It was about being left behind, deserted without a word, without explanation. It was about not understanding why she was left standing, watching someone disappear from her life. Before, it felt like a one-off. Now that she knew about her adoption, it felt more like a nascent pattern.

She struggled to understand her emotions. Everything recently was just loss, wasn't it? All of herself, in bits and pieces, were floating on a river and one by one they were sinking to the bottom, getting ground into the mud and muck. The once-easygoing trust she shared with her mother, the back-and-forth bickering camaraderie with Brian, the unalterable irrevocable sense of belonging she felt with her faith, all of it floating away from her and she was left behind, as who? What was left?

During her drive home, Austin realized why the man in the photo looked familiar. He had been there the day Austin had met Lauren on the photoshoot. He was part of the magazine's crew, working on the set design, maybe? She vaguely remembered them talking between shots, when Lauren hadn't been talking with her. She hadn't given it much thought. She hadn't given Lauren much thought either until after the shoot, when Lauren had changed back into street clothes as Austin gathered up wires, looping them together in color-coded bundles.

This part she did remember with perfect clarity, so surprised was she that Lauren had pulled her by the arm into the supply room turned makeshift dressing room. She had, with little warning, grabbed the belt loops on the side of her jeans and pulled her close so that Austin could smell the lemon lotion on the skin of her neck, and taste the cherry lifesaver on her lips as she kissed her. Austin hadn't kissed her back. Instead, in her surprise, she'd turned around and walked out of the room, back to her wires and heat lamp cases and surge protectors.

Lauren had followed her, had knelt down and whispered, not an apology, as Austin expected, but an invitation to dinner. What else was there to say but yes? The first dinner was followed by others, most often at Lauren's apartment, rarely out in public, which was fine with her. She figured Lauren appreciated privacy. They did go out, too, particularly on those Fridays, but to movies and plays. Darkened rooms. Now she wondered whether Lauren had stayed in simply because she wasn't comfortable being out with her. Was she dating her in secret and this guy in public? Not that Lauren was a public figure. Her modeling career was just taking off and she had just landed a series of commercials for a local car dealership, but none had aired yet.

Austin preferred dates at home simply because it was quiet and she could focus on her company rather than the clatter and bustle of surrounding activity. If, as she suspected, Lauren wanted to keep their dates private because she had a public image she was trying to cultivate, Austin's preferences played right into her hands. She didn't begrudge Lauren for it, didn't even care if Lauren had wanted to date other people. They certainly had never laid claim to monogamy in the short time they'd been seeing each other. But Lauren had never mentioned it. It was, as seemed to be the growing theme in her life these days, these omissions and deceptions.

It then occurred to her that Claire might have known. She had been present at all of Lauren's photoshoots. If there had been something going on between them, Claire certainly could have known. Was that why she had seemed so uncomfortable when they talked about Lauren? Not, as Austin had thought, because she wanted to spare Austin the humiliation of discussing being ditched so unceremoniously but because Austin was so oblivious to Lauren's real life?

She parked her car and began the laborious process of moving Inquiry into her apartment. Was anybody in her life interested in telling her the truth? She was meeting Claire for lunch in an hour. No better time to ask.

***

"I can't wait to see the picture!" Claire exclaimed, sliding into the booth across from Austin. Claire was on her lunch break, so they had met at The Village, which was walking distance from the studio.

"What?"

"Your grandmother's picture? The one you haven't stopped talking about for the last three days?"

Austin couldn't believe the picture had slipped her mind. She took out her iPad, brought up the photo and slid it over to Claire. She nibbled on her fingernail as Claire studied the picture, looked at her then back at the screen. At long last, Claire handed the tablet back, grinning. "The resemblance is uncanny," she said, "not only in features, but in expression, too. That must feel so incredible."

"It does," Austin responded, looking at the picture once more before sliding the tablet back into her bag. "I can't even explain what it's like to see someone who looks like me. Or, rather, who I look like."

"I'd have thought you'd be a bit more psyched, given how you've talked about it. Is anything wrong?"

"No. Yes. Sorry." Austin paused as the waitress came by for their orders. "It's just, shit's about to hit the fan, I think."

Austin then filled her in on her parent's impending visit and conversation with Brian. Then, there was a lull in the conversation. Briefly, she considered mentioning her conversation with Rivka, but it was depressing, and she didn't feel like getting into it. Claire, Austin reminded herself, didn't exist solely for Austin to dump all her woes. Austin chewed her nails again, wondering how to broach the topic of Lauren's engagement. Finally, she decided just to say it. "I saw a post from Lauren yesterday. She's engaged."

Claire's eyebrows shot up. "Really? That's crazy. To who? She hasn't even been out there a month."

Austin nodded, trying to determine if Claire really was surprised. If she wasn't, she was very good at acting. "I don't know the guy."

As Austin pulled up the post on her phone and handed it over to Claire, she watched for a reaction. Claire frowned at the picture. "That's what's his name, from the February photoshoot. He was with the magazine, though I don't recall him doing anything other than just standing around."

Claire handed the phone back. Austin remarked, "I wonder how long she'd been seeing him."

Claire shrugged in response.

"Obviously, while we were dating." Austin tried again, "Did you, by chance, know that they were…"

"I had no idea!" Claire sipped her iced coffee. "I would have told you."

"But we didn't really know each other until recently."

"I would have told you if I'd known," Claire stated. "I knew you guys were dating. If I had noticed her dating someone else, I would've found a way to mention it. If you had known, no harm done. If you hadn't, well, being cheated on sucks."

"Personal experience?"

Claire nodded. "Once is all it takes."

Austin agreed though she hadn't ever knowingly experienced it. She closed the app on her phone and slid it in her back pocket. She believed Claire about not knowing and she really didn't care about Lauren's issues, so what did it matter? The melancholy that had so gripped her earlier in the day faded as she sat in this cafe, dishes and drinks clattering around her, while she and Claire drank coffee. She wondered, as she finished her drink and caught eyes with the waitress for more, why someone would ever cheat on Claire.

~

11

Saturday came far too quickly. Austin felt as ill-prepared now as she had when Brian first alerted her to their trip. She paced the length of the walkway in front of the elevator bank on the third floor of the public parking lot across the street from her parents' hotel. She glanced at her phone. Ten minutes left to change her mind. She was hard-pressed to come up with any reason for backing out. She could call them and tell them the truth. What a novel thought! She didn't want to talk with them, wasn't up for this conversation, or this whole situation, for that matter. There was too much drama, too much confusion, too much emotion, and too many fucking lies.

Or, instead of calling, she could show up and spew that bit of honesty all over the cloth-covered table and their turkey and tuna sandwiches. Her maturity would be called into question. Instead of conversation, there would be her parents' pointing fingers and shiny eyes telling her this, this was why they didn't tell her. Look what the truth had done to their lovely, once well-behaved daughter.

The best course of action, she decided as she punched the elevator button, was to simply keep her mouth shut. Let them talk. Let them explain their reasons, excuses, whatever they wanted to call them, and sort it all out later, when she was alone, calm, capable of reasonable thought. Austin stepped into the elevator, avoiding the wad of gum stuck to half of the street-level button as she pressed it. It was a good plan. The question was, could she do it?

Apparently, Austin wasn't the only one with a plan of silence as a method of communication. After a brief, awkward greeting that involved half-armed hugs and avoided gazes, the three of them sat at the table in the hotel restaurant and substituted rustling napkins and clinking water glasses for conversation. But after the orders were placed and the saving grace of the waiter's presence disappeared through the kitchen door, it was clear someone would have to start talking.

Her father ran a hand through his dark hair, now highlighted with silver, Austin noted. He opened his mouth to speak. Then closed it. He glanced over to her mother, eyebrows raised. Austin followed his gaze and gesture, waiting.

Her mother shrugged helplessly. "We don't know what you want us to say, Austin."

There was a truth to that. What did Austin expect them to say? "Maybe you could start with why you guys felt it was the right decision to lie to me about being adopted."

Her father looked down at the pristine white plate in front of him. Her mother flinched but met Austin's eyes as she spoke. "We did not lie. We didn't decide to deceive you. You were just a few days old when you came home with us."

"So, because I wouldn't be able to remember it, you thought it best to omit the fact that I was born to another woman?"

"We're not insensitive, Austin. We did it for your well-being. Your father and I knew several adults who had been adopted. They told us how they felt abandoned by their birthparents. How badly it hurt their self-esteem, and their difficulties with close relationships. We didn't want that for you. We didn't want you to ever feel abandoned. You were so wanted, so loved. Isn't that what's important?"

Austin watched her mother tug a cotton tissue out of her purse and dab her eyes. It sounded so convincing. So true. And it probably was. But that couldn't be all of it. She looked over at her father.

He was nodding. "We also had very little information about your birthfamily or the situation that led to your being available for adoption—"

"No information, actually," her mother interjected.

"Right," he continued. "We had nothing to tell you, no answers to give you. We just thought it would cause you grief, without opportunity for relief."

She had wondered, had thought perhaps they didn't tell her because her situation had been tragic, a hideous history so disturbing that they wanted to protect her. She could have at least tried to understand that. "But I knew I was different. I knew. What about my difficulties coping with that? Didn't it occur to you that adoptees might have an innate sense about it?"

"There's no way you could remember it, Austin," her mother said.

"I'm not talking about remembering it. I'm talking about knowing it." She leaned back in her chair, glancing from one parent to the other, suddenly overcome by the notion that they had morphed into intimate strangers. Her mother's thin lips, her brown eyes and rippled dark hair now highlighted with gray. Austin stared at these familiar now alien features. "When I was twelve, I asked you if I was adopted. You said no."

"I don't remember that." Her mother took a sip of orange juice, then stared down into the glass.

"We were on vacation in Arizona. Touring the Grand

Canyon." Austin could remember the blistering heat of midday, the glaring brightness of the sun reflecting off the cragged cliffs surrounding them on all sides as they blindly followed a guide down a switchback path.

"The tour guide had asked me if I was a friend of the family invited along. When we went to dinner afterward, I asked you."

Her mother shook her head, but Austin remembered it now clearly. Her mother had not actually said 'no'. She had said, 'Don't be silly.' Austin had been too young to realize she had been given the slip.

"I knew, even without knowing. How could that not have been a sign that maybe you should have told me?"

Neither of them attempted to answer as the waiter returned with the lunch tray. Turkey sandwich for her mother, tuna for her father. She knew them so well. Yet, she could not crawl inside their heads to understand this. She thought back to what Jeremy was saying about his fears. The waiter retreated to other tables. "I think," she said slowly, "that maybe you didn't want to tell me because you were afraid."

Both parents only looked at her. Her mother opened her mouth as if to protest, then pressed her lips firmly together. Austin waited. Finally, her mother broke. "We weren't afraid for ourselves. If anything, we were afraid for you, what knowing might do to your self-esteem."

Austin felt the blood flushing her face, resisted the urge to throw her napkin down on the table and jump up. "Stop saying that everything you did was for my own good. I don't think you really thought about what was for my own good, only what was easier for you."

"Austin."

"No. You need to listen. If you had really thought about what was good for me, healthy for me, you know damn well that lying to me about how I was born, to whom I was born, and where I came from in general, would be exactly the opposite of caring for my well-being." Austin realized she was half-out of her chair, body rising in sync with her voice.

"That's enough, Austin." Her father pulled up out of his seat, so he was half-standing, hunched toward her. "Sit down and behave."

Austin laughed. "What am I, a five-year old? I have a right to be angry at you. Don't you dare deny me that."

"Austin, keep your voice down, please." Her mom leaned forward, lowering her own voice, perhaps hoping Austin would follow suit.

Austin sat down. "I asked you not to come this weekend. I told you I was not ready to hash this out with you."

Maybe, Austin thought, her parents had mentioned lunch at a restaurant in the belief that the public venue would keep the conversation civil. Too bad for them.

"We know it's important for us to talk about this with you, but you need to give us a chance to explain. You need to be an adult about this." Her mother dabbed at the corner of her eye with the tissue again. A tiny black smear of mascara marred the cotton.

"An adult. And just how would an adult handle this?" Austin's lower back twanged. She wished she could get up, walk around. She felt her anger building from the base of her spine, like building blocks stacking up, stiffening her posture.

Her father spoke up. "Please, just listen to us. We know this is difficult. We know you feel angry, hurt, but—"

"Don't forget betrayed."

He leveled his brown eyes at her. "I think that's overstating it, don't you? Everything we did, we did out of the belief it was the right thing to do. We did it for your peace of mind. We wanted you to have a normal childhood."

We. Austin hadn't heard her parents use the term 'we' so

much since they gave her the 'divorce talk' when she was fourteen. "Do you really think knowing I was adopted would've prevented me from being a normal kid? I mean, really? Because I'm thinking plenty of adopted kids have grown up just fine, knowing the truth. This wasn't all about me. I think this was about you, what made you comfortable. You were threatened by the fact that I had biological parents out there. Maybe you were scared they'd want to find me. Maybe you were scared I'd want to find them, know them. And I do plan on talking to them. Not that it should have any impact on you or my relationship with you. It has nothing to do with you. In any case, whatever the reason, it's a poor excuse to deceive and, yeah Dad, betray me by not telling me the truth."

So much for the keeping silent plan. Her parents looked shocked. Austin felt shocked at her own surprising declaration that she was going to speak with her birthparents. If she could find them.

Finally, her mother spoke. "I think that's a very poorly thought-out idea, Austin. That woman chose a private adoption, chose to remain anonymous, likely for good reason. Don't you think she has an expectation of privacy that you would be violating by hunting her down and accosting her?"

Austin was taken aback. "Jesus, Mom. I'm not committing some kind of violent act. There are sensitive ways to do this. And it's not that woman. It's my birthmother, you know, the one who carried me in her womb for nine months?"

"Austin, private adoptions exist for a reason. To protect the birthmother's privacy. If she wanted an open adoption, she would have chosen it."

"Would you?"

"Excuse me?"

"You chose a private adoption, too, didn't you? If you didn't want the adoption to be a secret, you would have chosen an open adoption for me, right? But you had decided from the beginning, before you even adopted me, that you weren't going to tell me. You know, even in cases of private adoption, the parents usually have the decency to tell their child she's adopted, even if they don't know who the birthparents were. So, the privacy wasn't just for her. It was for you too."

"And you," Austin's father broke in. "It was for your protection."

What a bunch of baloney, Austin thought. "Protection from what?"

"The stigma," her mother answered. "We didn't want you to feel different or be treated differently because you were adopted."

Seriously? Like Austin didn't have a million reasons to feel different, anyway? She just shook her head at the thought. "Who would know, if I didn't tell them? That makes no sense."

Her mother sighed. "Austin, we're telling you why we didn't tell you. It may not make sense to you, but I assure you we gave it a great deal of thought and had your best interests at heart. Getting back to your plan, I strongly recommend that you reconsider reaching out to your birthfamily. The pain and disruption you could cause by doing so, have you even thought about that?"

Austin hadn't, of course, but didn't say so. "I think that, when a woman gives birth to a baby, that woman does not have a right to privacy from that baby. That's what I think. She has right for the rest of the world, her family, her whoever, to not know, but not from the baby she gave birth to."

Her parents didn't have a response to that. The conversation continued but did not improve, with her parents alternating between being angry at her anger and attempting to smooth things over with declarations of love. Finally, Austin was exhausted and said so. She wiped her mouth with her napkin, folded it neatly next to her plate and stood up. "I need to go."

Her mother stood as well. Austin saw her gripping her napkin. Her hands were trembling. Austin closed her eyes against the weight of ache pressing against her chest. Her mother reached out for her hand and said, "No matter what you think, Austin. We love you."

Austin squeezed her mother's hand. "I love you, too." She saw her mother's eyes brighten. She withdrew her hand and looked at her father. "But it's not enough right now. It's not enough to help me with this."

She left soon after. Her parents implored her to have dinner with them that evening and she declined. She told them to have dinner with Brian, though, as he was expecting them. They might find a more sympathetic ear with him. She was too tired to hear anything else they might say.

***

Although Austin had told her parents she was going to communicate with her biological mother, now, sitting at home, alone, faced with going through with it, she hesitated, thinking back on what her parents had said, about the expectation of privacy, not just for them, but for her as well.

Would a woman who gave birth really expect or want to be hidden from her own child? The reading she had done after her coffee date with Jeremy suggested that many women were strongly encouraged to walk away afterward, try to resume a normal life, as if it never happened. Was that possible? Some women, she supposed, could do that, but she couldn't fathom that most of them did. In any case, those stories were mainly from unmarried women who had children in earlier decades, when they were shipped off to unwed mothers' homes or distant rural relatives. Her birthmother was married, in any case.

Options were different in the 1990s, too, with the advent of open adoptions. But her birthmother hadn't chosen that option. Why? Was it because she did want to remain a secret, like her mom said? At twenty-three, she was certainly old enough to resist her parents' influence. Was it related to the man who got her pregnant? That would be her birthfather. She certainly hadn't given him much thought. What if he was the reason? Was her father not her mother's husband? An affair, perhaps? Crap. She didn't have room in her head for considering the both of them, so she focused back on Elise. What if, for whatever reason, Elise Brouchard didn't want to be found? It was possible. Anything was possible. That was the problem. How was she supposed to put herself in her birthmother's shoes, try to understand where she was coming from, when Austin didn't know anything about her, about the circumstances around her birth. It wasn't right to assume she didn't want to be found, just as the opposite was true.

Well, she could start with the registry boards, if she could muster up the courage. If she could find herself there, then the question would be answered. She pulled her laptop from her bag. While doing so, she had an idea and texted Jeremy to see if he was free for coffee later. It was a Saturday, and he was married, so she didn't have much hope. Much to her surprise, however, he texted back with an invitation to meet at seven. His kids were at sleepovers and he and his wife, Angela, were itching to get out of the house, apparently. He'd asked if she minded Angela being there. Austin didn't and told him so. In fact, she probably owed the woman an apology for monopolizing her husband's time.

There were three huge search and reunion registries that Jeremy had provided her earlier. She hadn't tackled them yet because reunion wasn't on her mind. Until now. She started with the largest one. Using the quick search function, she typed in her birth date and state. When the drop-down box asked who she was searching for, she chose Birthmother. No matches came up. She revised her birth date to leave off the actual date, leaving just the month and year. Jeremy had said sometimes mothers were in such a foggy state, they couldn't remember the actual date of birth. It was an interesting loss, this negation of a date, how it blurred the identities of the people involved. A woman gave birth to a girl in April, some day at some time unknown. Like the erasure of the hospital name on her amended birth certificate. She was born on this date in April in this year, some place unknown. Little pieces of the puzzle scattered, never meant to be fitted back together. These reunion registries must have been revolutionary when they started. Austin wondered if there had been outrage when they started getting noticed, being used. And who were the outraged? People like her parents, terrified all their carefully constructed lies would be dismantled by the short block of code allowing a search function? Birthmothers? Terrified that their secret would be laid bare to the world?

She found nothing listed under her birth month and year and so just started scrolling through the listings. So many of the searchers were adoptees. Such a clear indication of a basic human need to know your point of origin, to those who would ask, why do you need to know? You don't need to know who you are, where you came from. Live in the moment, love and be grateful for the parents you have. You were lucky.

Lucky. She thought back to the one and only adoption support meeting she had gone to. She was lucky, she knew, for having two parents who loved her, who supported her dreams and goals. Who, even though money was never plentiful, had made sure there was enough. Enough for occasional family trips to Rehoboth Beach and summer camp and most of her college expenses. Like she had said at the meeting, wasn't any child who had parents like that lucky? It wasn't a factor of being adopted. She had read some horror stories too, of adoptees growing up with abusive, neglectful, lousy parents. She wasn't lucky to be adopted by the parents she had; she was just lucky they were the parents they were. So was her brother, Brian. One day, when she could look at them without wanting to burst into tears, without feeling the weight of their lies wrapped around her, containing her love for them within her locked, maybe she would be able to tell them this. Right now, it was too much to ask.

She thought back to how they looked at her over lunch. Her father's eyes searching her face, trying to see how much damage had been done. He knew, maybe more than her mother, or maybe she was just better at hiding things, like Austin used to be. He knew how fragile trust was, like a spider's silky web, so strong when attached from one point to another to another. So easily destroyed in sudden motion. And once destroyed, the filaments still clung to their respective end points, ends swaying in the breeze, unsalvageable. The three of them were coated in its stickiness. In her father's face, she saw the understanding of how the years would stretch before them, each of them starting at the beginning, spindling a thread toward one another without the surety of knowing they would once again connect to each other.

Her mother's face reflected an entirely different kind of fear, one that journeyed from anger–at how this happened, at who was to blame, at everything outside of herself, to disbelief– to an uncertainty that caused such anguish that she retreated back to anger. But Austin couldn't find room within her to accommodate her mother's fear, so great was her own upwelling of anger and disbelief and sense of loss. She wasn't ready to stand inside her parents, consider all the fears and hopes that drove their decision all these years. Perhaps, once she knew that truth, she could and would go back over what they had been telling her at lunch.

She searched the other two large registration sites but, again, found nothing. She didn't want to look at these lists any more, these thousands of faceless names all on the same journey, all crying out for the right to know who they are, where they came from. Many of them had nothing more than their own birth date and state to search by, while many of the birthmothers searching had old names and the impersonal names of doctors and lawyers their children would never know. She wondered if these searchers checked back frequently, daily even, to see if someone was looking for them. Did their desperation make them do what she was doing, removing her date of birth, even her month and town and state, just in case something, anything, had been remembered enough to make them found? She would not return to these sites, these testaments to the damage of tricking potential parents into believing that there's no harm in separating a child from their mother, even if it's for the greater good. There was harm and had it been acknowledged, perhaps more could have been done to heal the wounds in the aftermath. After all this, Austin didn't believe adoption was wrong, couldn't believe it when she thought of her life. The harm came from the lies, the deceit, the power struggles. Didn't it always?

She shut her computer down and placed it on the floor. She lay on her side on the couch, curled into a half-fetal position. Fitting, she thought. If her biological mom wasn't on these sites, did that mean she wasn't looking for her? If so, did it necessarily follow that she didn't want to be found? Or was she, like Austin and her parents, afraid too? Afraid of being found, or was that too simplistic? Austin knew, after her lunch with her parents, how full of fear they were about this once-secret, even though they refused to own up to it. She could work out some of what shivered through them, but what were all the fears her biological mother might carry in her, in the place of the child she once carried?

She must have dozed off. Much of the room was draped in shadows when she awoke to her phone buzzing in her back pocket.

"Hey. It's Claire."

"I know that. Hey."

Claire said something she couldn't understand. She sat up. "Sorry, I just woke up. What was that?"

"I was just checking how things went with your folks. I'm guessing exhausting."

"Among other things," Austin replied, stretching out her legs. "Thanks for asking."

"Are you okay?" When Austin didn't reply, Claire said, "I didn't mean to stump you."

Austin smiled. "Stumped, yes. I don't know. I must be okay, though, right?"

"Very convincing." And then, "Do you want some company tonight?"

Austin didn't answer right away. She imagined Claire at her apartment, her presence permeating the room, settling like a warm blanket over her nerves. And what would she offer in return? She couldn't keep taking advantage of Claire's need to take care of someone. Anyway, it would be rude to cancel on Jeremy after just making plans with him. "I have plans with Jeremy and his wife, to get their advice on this adoption stuff."

"Oh. Cool."

Austin couldn't tell if Claire was disappointed. She rather thought Claire would feel relieved. Austin wasn't great company these days and she couldn't quite understand why Claire didn't mind. Tomorrow would be better, though. Tomorrow, she would show Claire that she did have an external life, that she did give a damn about something other than herself and being pathetically mired in family drama.

Claire's voice sounded quieter when she next asked, "Are we still on for your Mitzvah day tomorrow?"

"Heck yeah, if you're still up for it." Austin held her breath.

"I'm excited to go."

She breathed a sigh of relief. "Me too."

***

Like she felt with Claire, Austin felt guilty for taking advantage of Jeremy's willingness to help her. Didn't mean she wasn't going to take advantage of it. After all, he was the one who set all this in motion.

"One of the reasons I'm reluctant to do it is because she's not looking for me on any of the reunion boards, at least not that I can find."

Jeremy shrugged and took a sip of his beer. "That's not unusual. The thing is, you need to try and think of this from her point of view, you know?"

Austin thought a moment. "Well, wouldn't you think it means she doesn't want to be found? All the tools are out there. When I was looking for reunion registries, there are a bazillion of them. Not that hard to find, so if she wanted to find me, she easily could. I've registered on all of them."

"Recently, though, right?"

Austin nodded.

Angela chimed in. "She may not have checked since you registered. People go in cycles. They look and look and look, get exhausted or depressed or whatever so they stop for a while before going back and looking again, sometimes even years later."

"True. But she didn't have to wait for me to register to find me. She could've registered. That's why I feel like she doesn't want to."

"She may not feel like she has a right to. After all, she signed the papers giving you up. She may not feel like she has any right to look for you at all."

"I hadn't thought of that."

Jeremy sighed. "There're a lot of things you need to be prepared for when you start searching, and none of its black and white."

"Like what?"

Jeremy leaned back, almost losing his balance, forgetting apparently, that he was on a bar stool. "Well, like you said, she might not want to be found. Maybe it was traumatic for her. Or she could be in a situation where it's not feasible for her to look."

"Like jail?"

"Sure. Or, and you have to consider all of this to be prepared, you know, she could be a drug user, or just in a bad situation. There are so many reasons. You just can't assume that she hasn't looked because she doesn't want to. If you search, you really need to consider what expectations you might have, so that you're able to handle the reality if it's disappointing."

"I don't have any expectations," Austin argued.

"Yeah you do, like just assuming she's alive."

"True." Austin had briefly considered it before when she saw the obituary, but now she realized she hadn't touched upon how she might feel if it turned out to be true. Jeremy's birthmother had died before he found her, but he was much older and by the time he searched, his birthmother would've been in her eighties. Austin's birthmother was only forty-four. But people don't just die of old age, she reminded herself. Anything could have happened to her in those twenty-one years.

She hadn't at all considered that her birthmother might be in jail, or a drug user, or any of those things. It was so far removed from her own life, her own experiences with her family and those around them. A typical staid middle-class existence bereft of drama. Or, was that atypical these days?

So, in doing this, in pursuing this woman, not only was Austin expected to consider every angle of how her birthmother might feel about being found, but she was also expected to try and emotionally prepare herself for every possible outcome, dead sick alive in jail a successful business woman or a strung-out junkie. She felt dizzy with possibilities and finally just laughed.

Jeremy and Angela stared at her.

Austin shook her head. "It's like the Schrödinger's cat thought experiment."

Both shook their heads.

"Schrödinger thought that some of the principles underlying quantum mechanics were totally nonsensical, right? To illustrate how ridiculous they were, he came up with this thought experiment where you put a cat in a box without windows. Inside the box is a lever. If the cat performs a certain function or series of functions, the lever releases a cyanide capsule and the cat dies."

"Depressing," remarked Angela.

"Thought experiment only," Austin reminded her. "Anyway, if the cat doesn't do any of those trigger things, the capsule isn't released and the cat lives. The point, Schrödinger was saying, is that the rules of quantum mechanics state that, until you actually open the box and directly observe whether the cat is alive or dead, the cat exists within the box as being both alive and dead, as well as all the infinite number of states in-between. He figured that would explain how fantastical the ideas were, and how unreasonable."

"What does that have to do with what we were talking about?" Angela asked, rubbing her chin and glancing over at Jeremy with raised eyebrows.

"I'm not nuts," Austin remarked wryly. "In fact, it's a perfect explanation for trying to understand how to approach this birthmother thing. She's the cat in the box, see? Without direct observation, she's alive and dead and well-off and a druggie and any other number of things. So her being is not just any number of things, but the whole infinite spectrum of things. And how she feels about meeting me also has every possible option. The entire spectrum of possibility is present. That's what I'm saying."

Jeremy was nodding as she spoke. "You're right. It's a great analogy, even though I don't know a damn thing about quantum whatever."

Austin waved that off. "But the real question is, if that's the case, if the concept of her encompasses all these possibilities, how in the hell can you reasonably expect to be emotionally prepared for what you actually find?"

Neither Angela nor Jeremy were able to offer an answer. Austin sipped her coffee and wondered if she was at all ready to embark on this search. Would it actually be worth it, at the end? Then she thought of something even more alarming. Would there even be an end?

~

12

Claire was sitting on the stoop outside her apartment building when Austin drove up ten minutes early on Sunday morning. She hopped into the car, holding up the camera hanging around her neck. "All right if I take some pictures?"

"Have at it," Austin replied, pulling away from the curb. "If you do, would you mind sending a couple to me? I bet Rivka would love to have some great pics for the website."

"Sure."

It took only six minutes on the quiet Sunday morning to reach the temple. A couple of times, Claire opened her mouth to say something, then apparently decided better of it and the drive was completed in amicable silence.

Around a dozen people were milling about between pews and in the aisles when they entered the sanctuary. Austin greeted people here and there, introducing Claire, who snapped away with her camera after asking permission until Austin guided them to a seat and some privacy.

"Wow. You know a lot of people here," Claire remarked, glancing around as the room started filling up further.

"I've been coming here since I was a freshman. Rivka came here a couple of years back as the junior rabbi. She was in Israel for the two years prior. I think I mentioned she used to babysit me when I was tiny?"

Claire gazed at her so long Austin started to squirm and said so. Claire laughed. "I was just trying to imagine a tiny Austin. It's tough. Did you hook, what did you call them, calipers to your belt-loops?"

Austin flushed. "Probably. I was even more serious than now. I remember I drove her crazy with questions."

"About what?"

"Everything, of course." Austin laughed along with Claire this time. "Yeah, I was the embodiment of the Science channel slogan." She grew serious. "Of course, I didn't expect that I would now be taking 'question everything' quite so literally."

Claire turned toward her, enveloping Austin with the scent of apple and cinnamon. Austin heard her stomach growl and hoped Claire didn't. "Tell me about your crazy lunch with your parents yesterday."

Austin closed her eyes and groaned. "I suppose I didn't handle it as well as I should have."

"I don't think there's a script for how this should be handled. It's a bit ground-shaking."

"To say the least," Austin agreed. "Still, I was rude." She shook her head. She had been rude, but not unforgivably so, given the circumstances. It ticked her off that her parents had tried to explain and defend their decision, rather than admit what they had done. Austin interpreted it to mean her parents didn't think they were wrong in keeping this from her. That, more than anything, set her blood boiling. How could they not see what they denied her?

Claire must have sensed her rawness on the subject. "Tell me more about Mitzvah Day."

With something akin to gratitude, Austin shifted her thoughts to the day and explained how the synagogue originally just participated in one event that took place on Mitzvah Day itself, a food drive or delivering meals on wheels or creating a city garden. It was celebrated internationally, too, but usually in November in other countries. 'Mitzvah', she said, was a Hebrew word that meant 'command', which could also be interpreted as 'obligation.' Austin always took it as an obligation to give back to the community. Gradually, it expanded into being a month of charitable drives and social actions that culminated on Mitzvah Day.

She stopped talking when Claire suddenly scooted herself back on the bench and whipped up her camera, taking several pictures before Austin even knew what she was doing. "Hey now!"

"Sorry." She didn't look sorry. "You just had such an interesting expression on your face, talking about something obviously so important to you. I just wanted to capture it."

Austin gestured for the camera and Claire handed it to her, with the picture on the preview screen. "I can delete it if you want," Claire said. "But I'd rather not."

Austin handed the camera back. "It's fine. I'm not going to censor an artist."

"Thanks."

There was a squawk from upfront as a rail-thin middle-aged man with thinning hair cleared his throat, shuffling some papers in front of him. "That's Dan," Austin whispered. "He's gonna give a talk on what the congregation has done over the past month and other stuff. If you can get a picture of him, that'd be great."

Claire nodded and snapped a few while the room quieted down.

In the community room half an hour later, Austin set Claire up at the first in a row of packing tables. Each table had a different food item and the person at each table would put in their food supplies, then slide the box down to the next table, where more would be added until it reached the last table, where the box would be folded up and placed on a dolly. She felt like she was apologizing to Claire every five minutes for not being there with her, but Claire shooed her off with a hand and a smile.

Austin spent the next hour running from one end of the room to the other, ferrying empty boxes to Claire's table and transporting full dollies to the back receiving doors, where volunteers with pick-up trucks were waiting to deliver the boxes to a local food donation center.

It was by these receiving doors that Rivka finally caught up with her. "Woo, girl, you've been a hot potato, hard to catch."

"It's been busier than I thought. Lots of donated food showed up in the last couple of days. I'm so glad I picked up extra boxes. The volunteers here today, it's been great." Austin swiped at her forehead with a handkerchief from her back pocket.

Rivka held out a bottle of water and gestured to the side of the room where several tan folding chairs were propped open. "Take a load off. It won't kill you to take a break."

Austin looked at the pick-up truck pulling away from the doors and then back toward the inner door. "I should go check in on Claire. I keep deserting her."

"She's fine. I've delivered water to everyone in there. Claire's chatting away, snapping pictures." Rivka guided Austin by the elbow to the chairs and sat her down, taking a seat next to her. "I gave her my email address so she could send me some pictures."

"Yeah, I asked her to do the same. She's a terrific photographer. I mean, really talented."

Rivka nodded but said nothing.

"What?"

"Nothing." Rivka leaned back, trying to look casual, arm wrapped around the back of Austin's chair. Austin kept looking at her until she broke. "Okay. I was just wondering if you were dating. She's seems like a great person and it seems to me, as an outsider, that she likes you a lot."

"Well, I like her a lot, but that doesn't mean we're dating." Austin was flustered. Rivka didn't usually bring up her dating life unless Austin mentioned it first. This was an odd turn of events.

"I see. I know you have a lot going on in your life these days."

"Did my mom call you? Because we had a pretty wretched lunch together yesterday."

"Nice change of subject." Rivka bought time with drinking some water, then answered slowly. "Yes, last night. I did tell her that I wasn't going to be a middleman between you. That this was obviously a private matter within your family."

"Bet she said you were family so what did it matter."

Rivka tried and failed to hide a grin. "More or less. It's true I'm an old friend of your family, that I love all of you very much. It's also true that I spend the most time with you and, in addition to being your friend, I'm also your rabbi, your confidante when you need one so I don't feel comfortable discussing things with your mom that you and I have discussed in that role. Right?"

Austin nodded. "The conversation didn't go very well yesterday."

"I gathered. When I refused to talk about you, your mother spilled all."

"They're furious that I want to track down my biological mother."

"They may have sounded furious, but I'm thinking maybe, inside, they're just afraid." Rivka looked up as a teenage boy entered the room, looking around until he caught her gaze.

"Hey," he said, shuffling over, hands deep in his pockets. "We need more empty boxes."

Rivka looked at Austin, who said, "They're stacked in the

kid's playroom. Sorry. Tell 'em I'll be back in a sec."

The boy shuffled off and Austin returned to the topic at hand. "It seemed like that to me, too. But afraid of what, exactly? It has nothing to do with them. Nothing to do with my relationship with them at all. My problem is not that I'm adopted. It's that they never told me. They lied about everything, Rivka, and for so long. How can they not understand that? How can they not understand I'm angry at them for lying, not for adopting me? What do they have to fear from a woman I've never met but want to learn more about? I'm an adult. It's not like I'm going to run away to her because I don't like my parents right now. How juvenile can they be?"

Rivka stood up. "All good questions and complicated ones. The answers all involve emotions. No matter how much you may want to, I don't think you're going to be able to reason your way through this. Listen, I know you want to get back out there and run the crew ragged some more but let me leave you with a couple of thoughts, okay?"

Austin rolled her eyes at Rivka, but smiled too. "If you must."

"I must. First, as hard as it might be, try to understand a little about where your parents are coming from, and the reasons they gave you for not telling you. You don't have to agree with them. You don't have to believe they are right in any way, shape or form, but try putting yourself in their shoes. It might help you find some patience to handle your current circumstances with them. It might help you manage your own emotions, too."

Austin clenched her jaw. It seemed unreasonable to ask it of her, but reluctantly she nodded. "Maybe if they call you again, you could tell them the same thing about me."

"I did. That's the only thing I said about it to your mom." Rivka glanced at the doorway. "The second thing is, and I'm totally meddling on this one, I know."

"Are you really going to talk to me about my love life? Do you want to talk about safe sex next?"

"Hell no." Rivka held up her hands. "Hear me out. This is coming from your friend, not your rabbi. It's pretty clear to me that she likes you, I wouldn't presume to know in what way, of course. It also seems that maybe you're not quite on the same page yet with each other. I think it wouldn't hurt to clear the air with her, sort out where you guys stand right now with your expectations, just to make sure no one's feelings are hurt."

"Oh my God." Austin covered her face with her hands. "Not everything has to be talked through, Rivka. Sometimes, it's best just to go with the flow." Austin stepped away a few paces, glanced at the doorway, then moved back in close to Rivka. She lowered her voice. "But did she say something to you?"

"No."

"I've known Claire for like five weeks. That's it. And, in fact, it's the same amount of time since I found myself suddenly single, which Claire also knows. I sure hope she doesn't think I'm the type to jump from one bed to another, so I'm fairly certain there aren't any expectations to worry about."

"I'm not saying you're wrong. I wanted to mention it, in case you hadn't thought about it."

Austin hadn't thought about it, had actively worked against thinking about it, just one more complication she didn't want to add to her growing pile. This conversation really needed to be over. Austin nodded at Rivka, mumbled a thanks, and darted out of the room. Thankfully, Rivka didn't follow.

When she got back to the packing room, she found most of the food supplies had been packed, and the last few boxes on their way down the line of tables.

"Hey!" Claire greeted her with a wave. "I was going to send out a search party."

"Sorry. Rivka waylaid me. She made me take a break."

"Oh, the horror." Claire grinned, wiped strands of hair back from her eyes, then grimaced at her blackened hands. "Wow, talk about dirty."

Austin pointed at a doorway on the far side of the room. "You can wash your hands in the kitchen through there, unless you need the restroom."

Claire did so Austin showed her the way, then hurried back to the room where the last three dollies were waiting. She pushed one out to the loading dock, with two volunteers pushing the other two behind her. She returned again to the room and found Claire taking group pictures. She stayed in the doorway. Claire had a way to make people smile, even these tired, grubby volunteers. Rivka's conversation fresh in her mind, Austin tried to see Claire objectively, but really, all she saw were long legs in a pair of fitted jeans and a long-sleeved jersey-knit shirt that clung to the curves of her body. A reminder why she had, in the past few weeks, so diligently not looked at Claire in this manner, not considered the possibility of attraction. She had done so well in leaving it unacknowledged, invisible. In this moment, thanks to Rivka and her own curiosity about how she actually physically felt toward Claire, she had to admit the attraction was there.

Whatever. Physical attraction wasn't everything and Austin had plenty of experience in resisting it. That wasn't the direction she wanted to go in right now with Claire. At least that wasn't a direction she could handle. But was Rivka right? Was Claire expecting something more? Wouldn't she have said something? Tried to make a move? Because she hadn't that Austin could recall. In fact, they rarely even stood within two feet of one another, no accidental-on purpose touching, no embarrassed caught gazes or half-started sentences fizzling into awkward sentences.

Just then, a volunteer in the group photo spotted her and enthusiastically waved her over. Claire turned and walked toward her, looping an arm around her shoulder to take her to the group.

As Austin stared toward the camera, looking over Claire's shoulder at the wall, she felt the warmth of Claire's arm still on her shoulders. Maybe they should spend less time together.

"One more, folks. No frowning this time, Austin."

Austin worked on her smile.

As she and Claire were heading out, Rivka trotted up and handed her a small, wrapped gift box. "I almost forgot. Happy Birthday!"

Austin looked at her blankly. Rivka frowned. "It is tomorrow, right? I know I've been frazzled but please tell me I've gotten this right."

Austin glanced at her phone to check the date. "No, you're right. It's tomorrow."

Claire turned to her. "Tomorrow's your birthday?

"It is." Austin was shocked she had forgotten it. Particularly considering the recent revelations of what actually happened on her actual birth date. Wow.

Claire bumped her shoulder. "Well, aren't you one for keeping secrets."

It was after three by the time Austin got Claire back to her apartment. Claire paused, one foot out the door, a hand upon the car latch. "Do you want to hang out?"

"What?"

"This afternoon. Hang out. Unless you've had enough of my company."

"I should probably study."

"Bring your stuff over."

Damn Rivka, Austin thought even as she replied. "Love to."

~

13

At Claire's apartment, over deli sandwiches, Austin filled Claire in on the details of her lunch with her parents, with some attempt to be honest about her own less-than-stellar behavior. Claire didn't say much until she finished the story, not sugar-coating her abrupt departure.

"So, you're actually going to do it? Contact your birthmom?"

Austin nodded. "I didn't know I wanted to until I said it to them. I think that's the only way to get answers to my questions. I can't keep guessing at why I was given up for adoption."

"And it's important for you to know why."

Again, Austin nodded. Claire had as neutral an expression she had ever seen, and Austin couldn't tell what she thought of the idea. She was afraid to ask. So much of the support in her life of late had come from Claire. If she disapproved of this step, it would be a blow to Austin's courage. She shouldn't feel so dependent on Claire's presence or support, she knew. It would just be a burden to the both of them. Still, she wished she knew what Claire was thinking.

"What're you thinking?" Claire asked. Having finished the chips that came with her own sandwich, she was not-sosubtly snagging the remaining chips on Austin's wrapper.

"I hardly know anymore." Austin pushed the wrapper toward her. "Help yourself. I'm stuffed."

"Well, if there's anything I can do to help, let me know."

Why, Austin wanted to ask, but didn't. Why was Claire so willing to help her? Was it as Rivka said, because Claire was interested in her? If so, why hadn't she brought it up? There'd been no shortage of opportunities. It begged the question of why Austin hadn't brought it up. Austin was certainly interested in Claire, though in what ways, she adamantly refused to consider, even when alone. It was enough, wasn't it, to enjoy her company right now? Something simple. Understandable.

Surprisingly, Claire really meant that hanging out didn't mean having to entertain one another. They spent the afternoon in the same space, separated by different work projects. For the next few hours, they barely spoke, as Claire worked on her computer while Austin sprawled out on the sofa, iPad on her lap. Claire appeared in the hallway entrance, leaning against the doorframe. Austin stifled a yawn as she rubbed at her eyes. "This is exhausting."

"No luck?"

Austin shook her head. "No. Without her current married name, assuming she is married since I can't find her listed under her maiden name or previous married name anywhere, I'm just not making any headway finding her."

"What're you going to do?"

"This lady, Sue, on one of the adoption message boards I've been posting on, said she'd look for me, see what she can find. She's what they call a 'search angel.' I've just sent her a scanned copy of my birth certificate and the other info I've gathered. So, fingers crossed."

"I hope she's able to help." Claire sat next to her on the couch. "I think a break is in order. I know I could use one."

"What are you working on, your show?"

"I need to make my final selections. I took some pictures of the space I've been given, so I just want to see what will display well there, with the light."

"That's coming up soon, right?

"A week from this Saturday."

"You excited?"

"Yes. And nervous." Claire stood up and walked to the kitchen doorway. "I'm gonna make some popcorn and then we're going to watch a show."

"We are?"

"Yes. We need to chill. Seriously. So, popcorn okay?"

"Popcorn's fine. I'm still a little full." Austin sat up, uncertain whether she should offer to help do...something.

"Liquid?"

"Water's good. I can get it." Austin stood. Claire motioned her to sit.

"It's not a hardship." She slipped into the kitchen, rustled around in the overhead cabinets and popped a bag into the microwave. Leaning against the counter, Claire asked, "Do you want to come?"

"To your show?"

Claire nodded. "Not with me, of course. I have to get there way earlier. You'd be super bored, but later, when it starts."

"Yeah, I'd like to. I'm sure you'll have tons of support. Brian's going, isn't he?"

"He said he would," Claire plucked the popcorn from the microwave and wrinkled her nose. "They're a little burnt. Let me know if too burnt and I'll try again."

Austin took the bag Claire handed her and opened it to let the steam escape. She chanced a glance inside. "They don't look too bad. I think it smells more burnt than it really is."

"I wish microwave popcorn would smell like movie theater popcorn instead of like burnt hair."

"If it did, we'd never stop eating it."

Claire sat down next to her, setting down two glasses of ice water and picking up the remote. Her leg brushed Austin and she scooted a little further way as she flipped on the TV. Abruptly, she stood up and retrieved her laptop.

"What are we watching?"

"You'll see."

"Yeah, because surprises have done me so well of late."

Claire gave her a wry grin and tapped on her computer, bringing up a blurred image on the television screen. "You'll like this one."

Austin felt a dull pain blossom in her stomach and grimaced.

Claire frowned. "Are you okay?"

"Fine." Austin sipped at her water. "Just a cramp. I've had them on and off for a few days."

"Period?" Austin shook her head. Claire set the laptop on the coffee table in front of them. "Shouldn't you get that checked out?"

Austin shrugged. "I'm sure it's just stress. It's been a stressful week, you know." Actually, she thought it likely to be gas, but who would admit that out loud?

"Yeah, but still." Claire frowned, but Austin rolled her eyes.

The surprise Claire had in store for them was a bootleg copy of Wicked the Musical, which Austin had never seen. The image was blurred and grainy at times, but she found herself equally enthralled with both the storyline and the set design. Claire paused it at the intermission, when the screen went black while whoever was filming had shut off the camera to go relax for ten minutes. She imagined it must have been painful holding out the camera for so long.

"Do you like it?"

"Yeah. I bet it's great in person."

"It really is. I went to New York last year and saw it on Broadway. So amazing."

"I bet. The set is awesome. Forget aerospace robotics. I should do Broadway."

Claire laughed. "But then you won't be able to save the world. That's small potatoes, though. I mean, we are talking Broadway."

Austin laughed.

It was late by the time they finished watching the show, especially after Austin kept asking Claire to pause it so she could look at the set equipment. Claire didn't seem to mind, except for mumbling, toward the end of the show, something about how next time they would watch a show without any electronics in it at all. Austin apologized and tried very hard after that to keep her mouth shut. Claire paused it anyway, seeing Austin sit up straight and peer closer to the screen.

But the show did finally end and when Austin declared herself exhausted, Claire offered to have her spend the night. Austin thought she should decline, thinking of what Rivka had mentioned to her earlier, but she couldn't muster up the energy to do so.

***

Lying on her back in the semi-darkness, Austin watched occasional headlights illuminating the ceiling corner. Claire was on her right, pressed against the fake wood-paneled wall, giving Austin plenty of space. She could feel Claire's gaze boring into her from the side, the weight of questions Claire wouldn't voice and Austin couldn't answer. Not now, not yet. This is what Rivka thought it might be best to avoid, this traveling through the land of murky 'what-ifs'. She couldn't get up. Couldn't go home now. That would force the awkwardness into light. Austin didn't want to make any decisions yet. Despite the anxiety (or was it anticipation?), she wanted to linger in this moment of possibilities.

She knew without a doubt she could turn her head, slide her hand along Claire's arm, curl her fingers into Claire's thick tangles of hair and kiss her, pressing the length of their bodies together, and more. Austin was no expert, was actually adept at missing signals and misunderstanding cues, but in this shadowed silence, she thought Claire might be willing, even as Austin's body—well ahead of her mind—was already willing, heat and dampness spreading as she considered it, a tangible ache blossoming through her belly and chest, squeezing her lungs and forcing her to catch her breath as sensations traveled up through her throat, drying her mouth, flushing her cheeks, dimming her eyesight, blood rushing through her ears so that for a second, she was almost deaf and blind to everything but the desire expanding within her.

She heard Claire exhale a long slow steady breath and whisper, "What are you thinking?"

Willfully, Austin slowed her breathing, relaxed back into her skin, sinking into the mattress. She slid onto her left side, back to Claire, resting her head on her elbow, before whispering. "Nothing."

It was minutes or hours later, Austin wasn't sure, when she awoke and gasped as a sharp pain seared through her right side, below her ribcage. Gingerly, she rolled from her stomach to her left side onto her back, but the new position did nothing to ease the pain. She struggled to a sitting position, trying not to disrupt the still-sleeping Claire. As she reached down for her phone on the floor, a wave of nausea rippled up her throat. Her gaze darted around the room illuminated only by the glow of a surge protector power strip. Beneath the small writing desk on the far side of the room, she could barely make out the cylindrical shape of a trash can. As she pushed the sheet off her, she felt a cool dry hand on her knee.

"Hey." Claire lifted her head. "Everything okay?"

"Uh, not entirely sure." Austin winced as she touched her lower abdomen. "Really sharp pain here."

Claire sat up, brushing hair from her eyes. "I can't really see well." She crawled to the end of the bed and switched on the overhead light.

Austin covered her eyes against the brightness. "Ugh."

"Sorry." Claire moved closer to see where Austin was holding her side. "Lower stomach?"

"Yeah, below my ribcage. Really sharp." Austin held her breath as pain stabbed at her again.

"Do you feel sick?"

"I've been eyeing your trashcan."

Claire slipped around Austin and retrieved the can, setting it between her feet. "Be right back." She left the room, returning a minute later with a small trash bag to line the can. "Have at it if you need it."

"You're so efficient with this."

"I had a lot of experience with my mom. The chemo made her pretty sick at night."

"Oh. Right." Nothing like being here tonight, reminding Claire of her sick mom.

Claire sat down next to her, placing the back of her hand against Austin's forehead. It felt cool, dry and wonderful. "You're running a fever, I think. Is this the same kind of stomach pain you had earlier?"

"Nothing like this. The pain earlier today was higher up, not as sharp." Austin blushed. "I thought it was just, you know."

"Gas. Everybody passes gas." Claire winked. "That's a children's book, you know."

"I didn't know." Austin chuckled and immediately was sorry for doing so. Austin watched as Claire rummaged through her dresser, pulling out sweatpants. She tossed them to Austin. "They're big, but it'll be easier than having to pull on and off your jeans."

"Are we going somewhere?" Austin lifted the sweatpants, felt a tug within her side and doubled over, breathing hard. She briefly debated whether she should take off the shorts Claire had given her earlier to sleep in.

"Hospital. It might be your appendix. Have you had appendicitis before?" Claire pulled on jeans beneath the oversized t-shirt she had been sleeping in.

Austin shook her head.

"I did, four years ago. It sucked." She grabbed a bra and shirt from another drawer, then slipped into the bathroom, leaving the door slightly open. "Anyway, I'm betting I looked a lot like you at the time. So, we better go."

Austin slid out of her shorts and pulled the sweatpants on before Claire emerged from the other room. She might be in pain, but she was still conscious of being in Claire's bed, of the sensations she felt before falling asleep. If, at any point in the future, Claire was going to see her naked, it wasn't going to be under these circumstances. She glanced around the floor, finally finding her sneakers pushed against the wall. She let the wall hold her up as she wiggled her feet into her shoes. "I know you have to work in—" she checked her phone, "—like two hours. I'm sure I can drive myself."

Claire came out of the bathroom, pulling her hair into a ponytail. "Good idea. I can see the news report for a multi-car pileup already." She scooped her car keys off her desk. "Let's go. Can you walk, or do you need help?"

Austin felt her scalp prickle as sweat beaded along the edges of her hairline. "You better drive with the windows down. A ride doesn't sound so good suddenly."

Claire scooped up the trash bin and guided her out of the room.

An hour and half later, Austin shifted uncomfortably on the hospital gurney, a sedative drip attached to the back of her left hand. The beep of the cardio monitoring machine irritated her ears. She turned her head as the curtain moved and Claire slipped into the room. "I've called Brian, both to let him know you're here and to let him know I'm running late."

Austin could see circles beneath Claire's eyes and felt guilty. "Don't stay. I'm fine. Gonna be in any case."

Claire rolled her eyes. "I know. I'm staying until your brother gets here, then I'll go hold down the fort."

Austin fumbled for Claire's hand, finding it and giving it a squeeze. "Thanks, Claire. Appendicitis, who knew? I owe you one."

"Sure do." Claire squeezed back, then stepped back from the bed as a nurse entered the room and spoke. "The anesthesiologist is ready for us, so if you're ready?"

Austin nodded and lifted her eyebrows at Claire. "Ready as I'm gonna be, I guess." As the nurse started to wheel her through the curtains, Austin saw Claire give her a little wave. She returned a thumbs up and then the curtain closed behind her, cutting off her view of Claire.

***

"There she is."

As Austin struggled against the weight of her eyelids, she was surprised to hear her father's voice. She finally pried open her eyes. Not her father. Brian sat in a chair next to her bed. The curtains were closed around her little recovery space. Beyond the curtain, she could hear the soft murmur of conversation, see the white shoes of nurses tapping up and down the hallway. "You sound just like Dad. I thought he was here."

"Just me. With breakfast." Brian lifted a small cup of jello, waving a taster spoon. "Happy Birthday! I brought you goodies."

Austin groaned. Was Mitzvah Day really only yesterday? It

felt like an eternity had passed. "I feel like a train wreck."

"Well—"

"Oh, don't. It's too easy. It's beneath you."

He nodded. "True that."

Austin looked around. No windows and no clocks. "What time is it?"

He checked his watch. Brian was one of the few people she knew who still wore a watch. "Just after ten."

"A.m.?"

"Yeah. Geez, it wasn't brain surgery."

She wanted to respond but a wave of exhaustion overcame her. She knew she had dozed when she opened her eyes again and Brian was standing in the corner of the room, talking on his phone. When he hung up, she said, "Don't stay, Brian, unless they're planning on releasing me soon."

"Not likely. Can you even sit up?" He walked back over and stood over her, his hand lightly resting on her forearm.

She made a tentative experimental move to prop herself up but found herself too weak. "I'm practically prone here. With a little help, I'm sure—"

"Lie back down. The nurse said they won't release you before five and it's only eleven so kick back. Relax."

"Ugh." What a waste of time to be stuck here. She glanced back up at her brother. "You should go, then. Not like I'm going anywhere."

He headed around the bed, then stopped at the curtain entrance. "I'll be back before five."

"Go. I'm fine." She caught sight of the jello cup on her bedside table, now empty. "Hey! Did you eat my jello?"

"I'll have them bring you another," he called as the curtain flapped behind him.

***

Brian wasn't there at five o'clock when Austin was ready for discharge. Claire met her outside the recovery room, telling her she had volunteered since Brian was caught up in some big client negotiation. Austin didn't mind. She was not particularly cognizant of the car she was in, or even of Claire, as she wavered in and out of wakefulness on the drive.

She came out of her daze a little when they pulled into the densely packed parking lot of a pharmacy to fill her prescriptions. She had struggled to sit up enough to open the car door. Claire had laughed, grasped her shoulder and told her to stay still. Brian had already paid for it. Austin wanted to protest, to argue that she was capable of helping herself, but couldn't even find the energy do it. She settled back into the seat as Claire disappeared into the bright lights of the store.

She became aware of her surroundings again as Claire double-parked the car in front of her apartment building, leaving the hazards on as she guided Austin up the stairs and propped her against the door with a 'be right back.'

By the time Claire had parked the car, Austin had managed to unlock the front door and stagger toward her bedroom, discarding her zip-up hoodie on the floor. "Thanks," she mumbled as Claire entered the room, and helped ease her into a sitting position on the bed with an arm slung loosely beneath her left arm.

"You know..." Austin paused, then shut her mouth.

"What?"

"It's too bad I had to meet you now. When I'm so scattered." She picked at the hem of her t-shirt. "I used to be so well-put together. And now, you can see. Not so much."

"I can see you're still put together nicely."

Austin kept talking, pulling words from her muddled, doped-wrapped thoughts like tugging cotton off a Q-tip. "I'm mostly just broken bits, it feels like. What use are broken bits? Can only use them for scrap work, for extra weight."

"Wow, those pain meds work fast, huh? I'll take your

word for it. Stop swinging your legs." Claire knelt to pull off her sneakers.

"Don't. Please." Austin tried to pull her foot from Claire's hand. "You don't have to. I can. It's so embarrassing."

"I'm sparing you the embarrassment of dressing you in pj's. Isn't that enough?" Claire retrieved both feet and removed one sneaker, then the other. Setting the shoes aside, she folded the bedsheets further back, lifted Austin's legs onto the mattress, then covered her with the sheets, pulling the blanket up to Austin's shoulders.

"Too hot," Austin mumbled, folding the sheets down to her waist, grimacing as her forearm brushed her bandaged side. "You gotta be exhausted. It's late."

"It's seven-thirty."

"Really? It feels so late." Austin patted the bed. "You should lie down a minute."

Instead, Claire crossed the room toward the window, closing the Venetian blinds and lowering the shade over them. Through the light-headed drowsiness induced by the hydrocodone, Austin felt something rising up around Claire, a barrier of sorts, a distance. And why shouldn't it? What reason did Austin give her to stick around? In fact, Austin was sure she had done the opposite. Maybe Rivka had been right. Maybe she should've addressed this with Claire earlier, but what if she had been wrong? What if Claire had never been interested in her? She just figured Claire would say something, do something if she was. Now, as she swam in Claire's silence, she wondered, did Claire think the same thing about her? "Claire?"

"It's not a good idea," Claire finally answered, leaning back against the wall, hands tucked in her front pockets.

"I know," Austin admitted. So, that was that, it seemed. "I told you. I'm broken."

Claire stared at her for so long, Austin squirmed while

struggling not to look away from Claire's face. A fresh sharp searing pain sliced along her side. She gasped, squeezing her watering eyes shut against the pain. When she opened them, Claire was sitting, tentatively, on the edge of the bed, near her feet. "See, that's why it's not a good idea. You need all the space you can get."

Austin watched, through half-closed eyes, as Claire moved a few inches closer. She closed her eyes and sensed, rather than felt, the light pressure of Claire's hip against her left arm, a warmth soon replaced by sliding cool skin on her forehead. She opened her eyes as Claire withdrew her hand and abruptly stood up. "I think you're clear of fever, but don't ignore it if you start feeling hot. Oh, that reminds me."

Claire stepped out of the bedroom, reappearing a moment later with a cold water bottle that she placed on the floor near the bed, along with the pharmacy bag containing the antibiotics and pain killers. "I got you a small bottle of ibuprofen, too."

Claire leaned down and quickly kissed Austin on the cheek. "Happy Birthday."

"Thanks." Austin wondered if she really looked as helpless as Claire was treating her. "For everything." Even her voice sounded tiny and fragile, like it had traveled light years before leaving her mouth.

"You're welcome." Claire turned to leave, then paused, leaning against the doorframe. Most of the hair around her ears had escaped her ponytail, curling around her jaw and cheekbones, little coils springing about as she moved. "You're an engineer, right?"

"Almost."

"You're an engineer. For my money, there's no better bet than an engineer when it comes to fixing broken things, don't you think?"

Before Austin could respond, Claire disappeared through

the doorway. A minute later, she heard the front door close softly and two minutes after that, she was sound asleep.

~

14

Late the next morning and settled on the couch, Austin used her iPad to check the university's Blackboard website. She had emailed her professors first thing when she woke up, letting them know about her emergency surgery and faxing a copy of the hospital admission sheet as proof. They didn't require it, but better safe than sorry. She had a quiz due tomorrow. The professor said he would upload the quiz for her to take before end of day. Robotic engineering was the furthest thing from her brain but once she started studying, it was a relief to get lost in the solidity of mechanical equations and hypothetical applications. She had just finished her coffee and two chapters of reading when her phone buzzed. She groped for it beneath a sheaf of papers and checked the caller id. Lauren. "Yeah?"

"It's me."

"I know."

"I wanted to check in on you."

"Why?" Had someone told Lauren about her surgery? Who would know, other than Claire? Austin shifted on the couch, her lower back aching, her abdomen throbbing.

"I figured maybe you saw my post about being engaged and maybe you wanted an explanation."

Obviously she didn't know about the surgery. Somehow, that was a relief. "I don't want an explanation, Lauren. I'm good."

Silence on the other end of the line. Then Lauren sniffled. Austin waited. She knew Lauren wanted her to say something about it, ask if she was crying, offer some sort of balm for whatever was paining her, but Austin didn't care enough to do it. Finally, she said softly, "I don't give a damn that you got engaged, Lauren. Get married, enjoy your life. But stop calling me."

"But I—"

"No, Lauren. There's no reason for you to keep calling. You've moved on. I've moved on. Just be happy." Austin did want that for her, wasn't invested enough in her own minor hurt over Lauren's departure to not want it for her. She didn't think Lauren was going to find happiness running down this particular path, but it wasn't any of her business and she didn't want it to be.

"What do you mean, you moved on? Are you dating someone?"

"That's not—"

"It's Claire, isn't it? You know she's had a crush on you forever, right?" Lauren's voice got animated, heated. "I saw her looking at you, that night we hooked up, at that photoshoot. I bet she moved in on you as soon as I left. Right?"

Austin was too confused to speak. That Claire had a crush on her for that long, it didn't make sense. Lauren must've been imagining it. It didn't even matter. Whatever was going on with Claire and her was different now that they knew each other. Crushes were for strangers and they definitely weren't that now. Although, if it had been true, Austin felt a surprising, quick pang of regret that she had been suckered in by Lauren instead of looking over Claire's way. She certainly preferred their ambiguously defined relationship to whatever fleeting attachment she and Lauren had shared.

Lauren apparently took Austin's extended silence as confirmation. "That girl does not waste time."

Austin decided not to correct Lauren's perception. She repeated what she said earlier. "Lauren. Get married. Be happy. You made a choice. I'm not bothered by it, so you don't need to call me."

"God, you are so cold, Austin. You —"

Austin hit the 'end' button on her phone and tossed it by her feet on the couch. She shouldn't have answered it in the first place. She would not answer if Lauren called again. Irritated, she gathered up the strewn school papers and tucked them into her notebook. Her phone rang again. She ignored it. Setting her laptop on the floor, she stood, stretched and wandered out on the porch, where she sat in her wicker chair to think. After a moment, she went inside to retrieve the large envelope her mother had given her at the end of their disastrous lunch.

After some hesitation, she had just opened the envelope when her phone buzzed. A text from Claire, checking in with her. She smiled. Claire was really thoughtful. Nothing at all like Lauren, Austin realized. No wonder Lauren was jealous. But she was jealous of the wrong woman. She sent a quick text back and, on a whim, decided to send a small Incredible Edible basket to Claire at her work to thank her for the hospital business. She couldn't remember if she saw fruit or similar stuff in Claire's apartment, but figured no one could go wrong with chocolate strawberries.

She picked up a stapled set of papers. Her mother had attached a typed note to it with a paper clip:

Austin,
    This is the family medical history as supplied by

the birthmother to the hospital at the time of your birth. This is the same information I used, of course, when we went to visit your pediatrician, Dr. Sandler, when you were young. It is also the same information I provided in the family information packet I sent you when you left for school, in case you were worried about that. As you should know, we would never compromise your health and safety.

Love, Mom

The 'Love, Mom' had been signed with a pen.

Ignoring the pang in her chest, Austin flipped through the sheets, recognizing the various details as items she had noted on forms over the years. She set the papers down and leaned back, closing her eyes. She felt like a swordfight was taking place within her gut. On one hand, she was so relieved that her parents had not carried the deceit on to such a degree that they would sacrifice her health; on the other hand, that meant every time they filled out a doctor's form or school application, they were reminded that she was other than them, a different history, a different biology. They were reminded of the decision they made to keep it from her. It could never have been far from their minds, this tremendous thing they were hiding. Was it stressful for them? Did they regret making that decision? Telling her the truth would have only gotten more difficult as she got older. Did they feel trapped in their lies?

She set the papers aside in the 'to be read' pile and picked up the next packet, which was light powder blue and folded in half, stapled at the tops, not in the middle like a book. She flipped open the cover. It was a county circuit court document, stamped with a seal at the back, with dates and signatures of a circuit court in Fairfax county. She turned to the next page, which looked like it had been typed on an old-fashioned typewriter, the way the letters were shaped and the occasional offset of the letter 'n', slightly higher than the others. She felt like she was reading old documents in the reference section of the library.

She ran a finger under the type, reading slowly through the legalese, though it wasn't difficult to understand this was the legal document that transferred ownership of her from her birthmother to her parents. Not ownership. You couldn't 'own' a baby. Transfered legal guardianship then. Well, how was the document wording it? She retraced what she had read.

It didn't contain anybody's name other than her adoptive parents. That was another thing. Was she really going to have to keep distinguishing between parents by using these stupid qualifiers of adoptive or birth or biological? Oh, and here was a new one she hadn't heard—natural mother. That didn't seem right. Furthermore, even though she did have a name on her original certificate, the document only referred to her as female infant. The whole thing was so clinical, so dehumanizing. She tossed the document on the read pile.

She picked through the rest of the dwindling paper stack, flipping through only briefly the other legal documents, which were mostly correspondence between the lawyers. Well, her parents' lawyers and her birthmother's legal aide, it looked like, not even a lawyer. Yeah, that seemed like a fair set-up. So, doctors made money on births, but they make money on births no matter what so you can't really count that. Unless, of course, they were the ones hooking up the parents with the babies and wasn't that the way a lot of private adoptions worked? Hers was a private adoption. There wasn't an agency involved so, yeah, some doctor made some money as a broker no doubt. And then, of course, the lawyers made money by making sure the whole thing was legal. Her birthmother probably couldn't afford a lawyer and so went to some low-cost legal counsel clinic for help. The aide was just some randomly assigned *misken* probably paid some basic low-woman on the totem pole-type of salary just to ensure out and out theft wasn't taking place. Of course, her parents spent money; they were the cogs the whole business worked around. They were the jackpot for these lawyers and doctors separating mothers from babies and they were taking them to the cleaners. She had read enough on the high demand, low supply of healthy white kids so yeah, she had been a big prize, a majorly valuable commodity. So, no, babies weren't directly sold in this adoption business, at least not in the above-board adoption business. But they were definitely a money-making operation.

She shoved the papers back into the envelope. They wouldn't help her in her search and reading them made her feel nauseated. She was about to start on her homework when someone knocked on her door.

She glanced through the peephole and opened the door. Her brother swept past her and headed into the kitchen, leaving Austin to slowly follow.

"I thought you were going to pick me up last night. How come you sent Claire?"

Brian set the Chinese takeout bag on the laminate kitchen counter and pulled out two plastic soup containers. Austin plucked the lid of the one closest to her and immediately wrinkled her nose at the pungent smell.

"That one's mine." Brian pulled the container to his side. "It has shrimp."

"Explains the stench."

"Shrimp don't smell, you know. It must be psychological with you. It's so weird that you don't like seafood." He handed her the other container. "Here's your wonton boring tasteless chicken soup."

"Maybe it's genetic." She lifted the lid and sniffed. Perfect.

Brian glanced at her, but said nothing. He leaned against the counter, eating his soup.

"So, why didn't you pick me up?"

"Claire volunteered. I didn't want to deny a chance for the new lovebirds to share what is bound to be a story of epic proportions by the time you get around telling it to the second generation, yours or mine."

"We're not dating." Immediately, Austin felt guilty. She stirred around the wontons in her cup, trying to cut one in half with her plastic spoon. "Did Claire tell you we were dating?"

Brian looked surprised and shook his head. "No. I just assumed. I mean, she did drive you to the hospital in the middle of the night."

"I guess we're not not dating. It hasn't been discussed. It's not really the best time for me to get involved with someone right now."

"Maybe you should clarify that with her."

Really? First Rivka, now Brian? Brian rarely involved himself in Austin's personal life and Austin wondered if his interest with this was protective because Claire was an employee or something more personal. Either way, this was not a conversation she wanted to have with him. But she couldn't help asking, "Did she say something to you? Do you know something I don't?"

He held up a hand. "No, she's said nothing, I swear. It's just you've been spending time together lately. She's seemed happier lately. Two and two, you know."

Austin thought about the other weekend, when Claire had plans. And then, the other night, when she clearly had someone over, but didn't say anything. She shook her head. "Yeah, we've spent a lot of time together but, you know, she has a life. I think she's seeing someone, anyway. Which means if anyone needs to clarify anything, maybe it's her.

There's been no shortage of opportunities."

"Okay, yup, I'm out of it, promise." He lifted the soup container and drank the remaining broth. "It's just—"

Why were they still talking about this? "What? Spit it out."

Brian shrugged. "You can be intimidating to talk to, I think, maybe, for girls."

Austin set her soup container down on the counter harder than she meant to, splashing soup droplets all over her chin, nose, and cheeks. After feeling irritated for a second, she burst out laughing. Pain in her side made her clutch at the countertop and her stomach. Brian offered her a paper towel. "So intimidating," she muttered, wiping her face.

Brian smiled but refrained from laughing, probably sensing he was on delicate ground. "I won't say any more about it. As long as the two of you know what's going on, right? It's none of my business."

"Thank you for acknowledging that 'cause, you know, it's really not."

"I had dinner with Mom and Dad Saturday night."

"Jesus, Brian, can you find one topic I might actually want to talk about when you visit?" She left the kitchen and sat down on her couch, careful not to spill what remained of her soup. "Did you have fun? Cuz lunch was a blast. I'm sure you heard all about it."

Brian stayed in the kitchen to rinse out the container in the sink. "Mom was completely hysterical. Something about you saying you were going to try and find your—" He waved his hand, either because he didn't know what word to use or didn't want to say it.

"My birthmother."

He stepped into the doorway, leaning against the frame. "You really think that's a good idea?"

"Yeah, I do. I want to know who she is."

"Why does it matter? Is it worth hurting Mom and Dad

over? I mean, Mom was really out of sorts."

"It has nothing to do with them. Why can't they understand that? Why can't you?" Austin capped her soup container. All semblance of her appetite was gone as soon as Brian started talking about their parents.

He was staring at her, slack-jawed. "How can you say it has nothing to do with them? They're our parents. They raised us, loved us. Now, you're throwing them over for someone who abandoned you? How could they not be hurt?"

Austin opened her mouth to speak several times before the actual words came to her. "What are you talking about? I'm not replacing them, for God's sake. That's so ridiculous, and completely melodramatic. It's a simple fact, Brian. Mom, no matter much she loves me, did not give birth to me. I would like to know the woman who carried me for nine months and did give birth to me. I would like to know the circumstances surrounding my birth. These are common and simple questions."

Brian didn't look at her. "The answers won't be."

"Probably not."

"And what if she doesn't want to know you?"

"That would be painful," Austin replied truthfully. "But I believe I have the right to know the woman who gave birth to me. I don't have a right to a relationship with her, but I have a right to know who she is."

"She might not see it that way. You coming in after twenty-two years, invading her life."

"She might not." Austin clenched her jaw. That her brother was so far from her own perspective on this surprised her. If she had thought about it, which she hadn't, she would've believed he would play a mediator role, trying to see both sides of it, but he wasn't trying to see her side of it at all. It was as if he thought she was attacking their family, like somehow she was the one breaking it all apart.

Brian stood up straight, looking at her finally, arms folded across his chest. "I get that you're angry at them for not telling you. I'd be angry too. But this birthmother, she deserted you when you were a baby. Why in the hell would you want to go find her when it's clear she wanted nothing to do with you?"

Austin stared at him, then briskly hobbled over to the front door. She opened it and gestured for Brian to leave. When he started to object, she shook her head. "You better go before we start saying things that really are hard to come back from."

"Austin, I'm sorry. That sounded," Brian sighed as he walked slowly to the door, "really awful as I heard it coming out of my mouth."

"Yeah. It was bad." Austin pulled back as he reached out to hug her, motioning at her stitches. "Thanks for lunch. I need you to leave now, please."

Austin waited until she heard Brian's car engine roar to life from the street before locking the front door. Brian loved his Mustangs. Just like Dad. Nature or nurture, these similarities? Was there even an answer to that? Did it matter? That was the hardest part of all of this, Austin realized. Suddenly having all of these questions and not knowing which ones mattered.

She thought of Brian's last words, how she came from a loving home with two parents who loved her, which was true. But that's not where she came from; it was where she'd arrived.

She grabbed the soup and put it into the fridge and returned to the couch. No matter how great it was, and it was a good solid family despite a few rough patches, it wasn't her origins. She didn't sprout as a full-grown baby onto her mother's lap or in her father's arms. Someone, a real person, a woman named Elise, carried her around for nine months or thereabouts, went through the agony of childbirth, and made a decision that irrevocably changed both of their lives forever. Whose own good was that for? Austin's (or should she say Kaitlin, like the name on her birth certificate?) And some unknown, unnamed man contributed to her as well, half of her DNA, in fact, but when she tried to wrap her mind around who this was, how she happened, she felt overwhelmed, without solid footing.

Not lost, though.

If you're lost, that still implied that you were in some concrete place, had come from some place and to become unlost, you could theoretically retrace your steps back to where you began. But she had no beginning; thus, the path of her past led to nothing, an empty space. If she tried to follow, she would only find herself *tomber dans le vide*—falling into the void—a phrase that, oddly, she had learned in Astronomy 101.

Wasn't it a basic human need to ask, 'where did I come from?' Austin swept the lunch trash off the counter into the trashcan. That was the logical individualized form of humanity's question, 'where did we come from?' It drove the curious to search the skies, discover the solar system, the universe, the big bang, all of it. How could that be trivialized so intentionally, so intently, by lawyers and baby brokers and secret-keeping government policy-enforcers?

To have spent twenty-one years knowing the answer to where she came from, only to find out nothing she knew was true, losing everything she thought comprised her past, her history. Although, thinking about it now, perhaps that wasn't the way to look at it. Her brother had a point about being influenced and shaped by her parents. And then there's what she had said to Rivka about the cultural history and personality of Judaism. So no, it wasn't so much losing everything, not when she had still gained so much. It was more like suddenly feeling like an imposter in her own life.

She dug out the copy of her birth certificate from her messenger bag. Tracing a finger along the black border of the paper, she looked at her mother's name, not her real mother any more or less than her other real mother but still, one of her mothers. Elise. She was part of her beginning. Even then, it wasn't the whole story, her whole story. Would Elise, if she found her, even be willing to tell her?

She checked her email, hoping Sue may have written, but there was nothing from her. On a whim, she fired off a quick email to Jeremy, asking him if he could offer some recommendations on how she might write an email to Elise, provided she actually managed to find her. She slid the birth certificate back into her bag. As much as she wanted to continue her hunt, she needed to take care of schoolwork first. She'd be damned if she let her search for her past compromise her future.

After watching two video lectures, Austin couldn't keep her eyes open. She awoke an hour and a half later, not much refreshed. When she checked her email, her heart double-timed it when she saw an email from Sue. She skimmed through the note, then read through it more slowly. Sue had succeeded where Austin failed, finding a marriage certificate for an Elise Hargrave and Elliott Parham from 1995. Hargrave was the married name listed on her birth certificate. From her first husband, and her likely birthfather. She opened her notebook to where she had recorded Elise's maiden name—Brouchard, first married name—Hargrave, and added this married name—Parham. If she had divorced and remarried since 1995, this could be a another dead-end but it was a new lead, and that really quickened her pulse. Sue had included a link to the online archive of the Virginia marriage certificate as well as an attached pdf of the document. If Sue had been in the room with her, Austin would have kissed her in her gratitude. She wrote back an enthusiastic if overly effusive thank you note.

So, her likely birthmother's name was now Elise Parham, if she was still married or kept her married name if she wasn't. No point dwelling on the 'ifs.' Austin opened up her laptop and typed in the name in the Google search bar. Several portraits came up at the top, then a number of listings for Facebook, LinkedIn and a plethora of other search results. She glanced at the photographs. The first was a contender, a middle-aged woman, long brown hair—straight and darker than her own, though that didn't mean anything, right?—brown eyes, pale skin, slight smile. It looked like a business profile portrait. Hard to tell, definitely possible. The others didn't seem to match what she was looking for, too young or too old, though, Austin considered, it's not like she knew what year these pictures were from. No need to complicate things right off the bat. Pursue the obvious, then go back for the ones that required digging.

She opted to click on the Facebook results, scanning down the options. There were only four exact name matches. She clicked on the one that was listed as being in Virginia first, which turned out to be the woman in the picture she had been looking at. To her disappointment, as she skimmed through the woman's friends and found a brother and father with the last name Parham, it was obvious that was her maiden name as well. She typed the name in the search box and looked at the results again. This time she picked a name of someone in North Carolina and again was disappointed when the profile came up of a college student.

In the end, it was the last name she tried, the one who lived the furthest away, in Ann Arbor, Michigan. There wasn't a profile picture on the page, just a generic photo of a snow-covered hilly landscape with a red-roofed barn in the distance. Austin clicked the 'About' link, which was, Austin saw gratefully, partially filled out. Austin felt a ripple of relief and a lump in her throat as she saw that Elise had listed her hometown as Fall's Church, Virginia. That matched the info on her birth certificate. She was on the right track.

Austin jotted down Elise's current location on a blank sheet in her binder, then went back to the home page to look through the posts. There weren't that many, and none that were just notes or messages from Elise. Most were shared posts from other people, primarily animal rescue groups, memes of adorable kittens and puppies imploring people to adopt not shop, neuter your pet and other various slogans Austin couldn't find fault with, not that she was looking. Unfortunately, other than being an obvious animal lover, there was nothing of value in terms of identification that Austin could glean from the posts. According to her Friends section, Elise had seventeen friends on Facebook. Clearly, spending time on here wasn't a priority. Probably just shared things from her phone when she had time. Elise wasn't that old, not like her mom, who had been forty when she had, *when she adopted*, Austin. She rarely used computers beyond the basic word files, simple spreadsheets and email. Then again, maybe her mom was just stodgy because Austin knew plenty of older people who were better with computers than she was, well, maybe not exactly, but close.

This other mom of hers would be forty-four now, not so old that computer skills would've been difficult to pick up if she had chosen to. Looking at her paltry Facebook spread, Elise either didn't care much for social media or was too smart to put a bunch of information about herself on the web. The thing about the internet, though, is that all those little bits out there added up, each little morsel of information became a foothold into other sites, more information hidden beneath the initial Google searches. Though Austin carefully skimmed all the posts and tidbits, she couldn't find anything other than Elise's possible current location in Michigan. She'd saved the list of friends for last, thinking they'd be her best bet for another toehold into Elise's life.

First, she scanned the list for any with the last name of Hargrave. Maybe she had another kid by the man before cutting ties. No such luck, though, nor were there any people with her maiden name or her current married name. Either she never had any other children—and Austin felt a strange pang of sadness at the thought—or they weren't connected on here. Not surprising. Austin hardly ever updated her own Facebook page, occasionally posting brief updates on her life, like the internship, for a few old high school friends and some random cousins living in New Zealand, of all places.

It was curious that three of Elise's friends listed themselves as working at the same place in Ann Arbor, some company called Full Moon Productions. She jotted down the name and opened a new tab in her browser. Though she was tempted to send a note to Elise through her Facebook page, the note would go to that obscure message folder because they weren't connected as friends. No point in that. She resisted her impatience and brought up the company website she found. It appeared to be some type of full-service marketing agency. Finding a team page, she hastily scrolled down the page, then looked again more slowly. Elise wasn't listed. Damn.

Austin set the laptop on the floor and stood to stretch. Sharp pain shot through her side as she raised her arms and she quickly lowered them, grimacing. Still, she could sense the pain was lessening. Another few days, she'd be good to go.

After pouring a glass of iced tea, Austin picked up her laptop again. Her stomach growled, but her patience could only carry her so far. It would not stretch through a dinner break. She was so close. She could try LinkedIn; that would actually contain some real information about work and career she might be able to use if Elise was on there.

Austin typed in Elise's full name and got several hits. Naturally, she was blocked from seeing the full profiles unless she created an account. She did so. She could always delete it later. It took her less than a minute to discover Elise worked as a Senior Graphic Designer at a company called Meyers & Franklin. In another minute, she had Elise's work email off the company website.

She hated using it. But at least it would be easier to take Jeremy's advice now. He had sent her an email earlier, responding to her request for help in composing an email. She had in mind some kind of a personal letter, letting Elise know who she was, how she was, and expressing hope that Elise was well also. She didn't really know what she had wanted to write, just that it should be personal. This was a personal thing, wasn't it? This connection they shared. Was there anything more personal?

Jeremy had advised exactly the opposite in his response email last night. He had provided a basic script she could use, something short and somewhat vague and containing nothing of the odd twist of emotions wrapping around her gut. She opened the word file he had sent and filled in the missing info, then read it over.

First, the harmless, if not quite honest subject line: Re: Genealogy, surname Brouchard.

Then, the even more obfuscating text of the email itself:

Dear Ms. Parham,

I have been doing some family genealogy this past year and have reason to believe we are related. My name is Austin Nobel, but I've recently discovered evidence supporting that my original surname was Brouchard. I was born April 19, 1998, in Falls Church, VA.

Based upon my research, I know there were some Brouchards in that town during that year, possibly related to Leo and Elaine Brouchard. If you know the family I am talking about, or think you can help me in this research, please answer this email, or call me at the contact info listed below my name. Thank you for your time and any help you may be able to provide.

Sincerely,

Austin Nobel

Then she listed her cell phone, email address, and mailing address.

She hated doing it this way, so vague, so against her instinct to be direct and to the point. Jeremy said that it would be better this way. It would protect Elise if someone else in her family read the email. It didn't give anything away. Didn't unveil a secret world, expose a lie. It was benign. Easily explained. Perfect, she hated to admit, now that she's sending it to Elise's work email.

Austin copied and pasted the text into her Yahoo account and read it through several times, checking for typos. She wanted to make a good first impression. Finally, she had no more reason to delay. She hovered over the 'enter' button. Her hand was shaking. Her whole body was shaking. Finally, she hit 'send', then immediately felt her throat sink into her chest.

~

15

Austin pushed her plate toward Claire, sighing as she gazed at the half-eaten empanada. "Sorry for the waste. I just can't."

Claire pulled the plate in front of her and nibbled on the empanada before saying, "I can't imagine. Waiting on a response like this. It reminds me of a children's book my dad read to me. It was about this baby bird that falls out of its nest while its mother's hunting for food. Then it walks around, asking each animal it comes across, "Are you my mother?""

"Oh. The poor baby bird." Austin mustered a wan grin that faded as she imagined a little bird hopping about, tapping farm animals on the shoulder with its little wing, looking up with huge imploring eyes. They always had huge adorable eyes, right? That's how she felt these days, spending endless hours staring at a perpetual stream of pictures and social sharings of maybe-moms. Her eyes started to sting and she shut them tight, bowing her head and rubbing her forehead in an effort to keep Claire from noticing.

She felt slightly set-up by Claire, though, as if she had mentioned this book as a means to elicit some sort of reaction from Austin. It was a ridiculous thought. Claire wasn't calculating like that, and what purpose would it serve? Still, the feeling lingered, along with a low-level resentment that Claire felt sorry for her. Like she was some kind of foundling. Austin's eyes misted then cleared. She looked over at Claire, who was slipping the plate into the dishwasher. Was that how Claire thought of her? A flash of irritation rippled through her and she quickly glanced down as Claire looked back at her. She couldn't trust what she was thinking right now. There was this rumbling, this static-like noise filling in her brain, making it hard to think.

"I didn't mean to upset you." Claire walked past her but stopped just beyond Austin's peripheral vision.

Austin felt the slight pressure and warmth of Claire's hand on her shoulder. She stiffened, though without intent, and Claire slid her hand off, backing up toward the hallway wall as Austin turned around on the stool to look at her. Claire, now leaning against the wall, looked back. Again, Austin looked down. She stared at the worn beige carpet, then at Claire's red canvas slip-ons before lifting her gaze to Claire's hands, which were tucked into the front pockets of her jeans.

She didn't remember moving, wasn't sure how her left hand had gotten hold of Claire's waistband, or how her right hand had tangled itself in Claire's hair at the nape of her neck, but there she was, pulling Claire to her, lifting her face to meet Claire's lips. She felt a vague sense of surprise that Claire was kissing her back, that Claire's hand was resting on the center of her chest, gathering her t-shirt into her fist. She was just as surprised when she felt Claire pull back, push her gently back toward the kitchen counter.

For a disconcerting moment, as her fingers found and gripped the counter edges, again, she wondered if any of it had happened, or if she was just experiencing some kind of reality break. But a glance at Claire's flushed face, the tingling she felt in her own lips and the heat in her own chest confirmed something had occurred.

This time, Claire was looking down. Austin looked at her,

waiting until she caught Claire's gaze. "I know I haven't misread this thing between us."

Claire slowly shook her head. "No, but," She stepped forward, hesitated then returned to leaning against the wall "this isn't—I don't want to be your distraction, you know?"

Austin frowned. "I don't."

"You were here the other night and something could have happened, but it didn't. Maybe you weren't ready."

"Maybe it was the appendicitis?"

"Before that. That's fine. Everything in its own time, right? But, then, why now? I mean, you're here tonight and you've got a lot going on in that head of yours, most of which you're not sharing, and that's okay. But since I'm pretty sure that what's in there doesn't have anything to do with me, then that makes me the distraction, right, from what's going on with your family?"

"What's wrong with a little distraction? Unless you're not interested, in which case just say so." Austin knew she sounded peevish and didn't care. The energy boost from their brief encounter buzzed through her, Suddenly, the air inside the apartment was stifling. She pushed away from the counter, toward the front door.

Claire didn't move away from the wall, but she did stand up straight and reach out an arm to stop Austin. "There's nothing wrong with having sex, or fooling around or whatever, to take your mind of things. I don't want to start off that way with you."

"I didn't know you wanted to start with me at all." Austin flicked the chain lock off its track. "As I recall, we were both there the other night. I don't recall any hints on your part."

"There didn't seem to be a non-awkward way to bring it up."

Austin glanced at her and shook her head.

Claire shrugged. "I was working up the courage. Why did

you kiss me now?"

Austin didn't answer. If she did, her answer wouldn't be fair. She wanted to lose herself, yes, distract herself in Claire, in the heat and rawness she knew a night together could be, instead of going home where the shadows of angst and anxiety would entangle her like vines. It didn't mean the attraction wasn't real, but...Claire was right. Bad timing. She held a hand against the door, allowing it to hold her up for a second before turning back to the counter to grab her cellphone. At that moment, it flashed an alert. New email.

Before she could stop herself, she swiped open the screen and checked the email address. Claire remained motionless against the wall, watching Austin sag onto the stool. "Is that her?"

"I think I'm going to throw up."

***

Austin read the email as soon as she got home from Claire's. She hadn't wanted to read the email with Claire watching, and now she was glad she hadn't. Embracing her with open arms wasn't exactly on Elise's to-do list, apparently. She needed advice but it was too late to call anyone.

She slept little and fitfully. As soon as the time became decent, she picked up the phone and dialed Jeremy.

"Read it to me," he said, after she explained the gist of the response.

Austin put Jeremy on speaker and set the phone next to her computer. "She wrote, 'Austin, I'm uncertain what led you to me, but I am not who you think I am. Please don't write me again, as I would not like my family to learn of this, however erroneous the correspondence might be. Respectfully, E. Brouchard.'"

"Well, that's certainly to the point."

"Yeah." Austin flipped her laptop closed. "Kinda sucks. I

think she's lying."

"How sure are you that you have the right woman?"

"Scale of one to ten? Nine point nine. I'm meticulous with research." Austin drummed her fingers along the arm of the sofa. "Plus, all my email said was I thought we might be related. I used your template. Why would she be so certain? Plenty of people have second cousins and distant relatives they never knew about it. Most wouldn't find it threatening. Rationally speaking. She knew exactly who I was because I put my birthdate in there."

"Right."

"So, what do I do?"

"Nothing."

"Really, Jeremy. That's what you got for me?" Her call-waiting beeped. She glanced at the screen. Her mom. She could leave a message.

"Sorry, kid. Unless you want to email her back with all your proof, but—"

"That would be a big FU that pretty much destroys any chance of a decent conversation down the road, huh?"

"Yeah. Listen, Angela's on a business trip and I gotta go pack the kids' lunches and stuff. I know it's hard but let her sleep on it a couple of days. Take a break from it yourself, if you can. You never know how things will play out. I know this is all new to you, but at least you've had a few weeks to know about this. She's only had a couple of hours to digest being found, and what that could mean. What she wrote you might be instinct, you know, self-protection. She probably needs to work herself through a few steps here. You see what I'm saying?"

"I suppose." Austin glanced down at her hand resting on the keyboard. She was still shaking.

"On the positive side, your mom's alive. Hang in there, Austin."

"I'll try." Hanging up the phone felt like disconnecting from her only lifeline. When she first read the email, her first instinct was to call Claire. She'd dialed the numbers and hit the call button. Then she remembered what happened with Claire earlier and promptly hung up. Claire was right. She couldn't use her for a distraction, even if she needed her as a friend.

Austin snacked on a banana before returning her mom's call. She didn't bother listening to the message. That her mom actually left one made it clear she wanted Austin to phone her back. They'd only spoken briefly yesterday morning, when her mom had called to ask how she was doing after surgery. Austin was still fuzzy on pain pills and the conversation was short and hardly memorable.

Her mother picked up on the first ring. "Hi, Austin."

Oddly, she felt disappointed her mom hadn't used her usual 'darling' in her greeting. "Hi, Mom. I was on another call."

A brief silence. Austin bet her mother was biting back the question of 'with whom.' She waited out the silence.

Her mom finally spoke. "I'm calling about graduation. It's three weeks from next Saturday, isn't it?"

Silly for her to make a question out of it. Her mom had that date circled on the calendar the moment she bought it. Austin supposed she was working sounding (or was that too cynical?) conciliatory. "Yeah, at ten. Why? Are you planning on coming down?"

"That's why I was calling you. To ask," she responded. It seemed so unlike her mom to make this a question, to sound so cautious. Not walking on eggshells extreme, more like dipping a toe in water. She'd never heard it in her mom's voice before. She didn't want to hear it there now. It turned her mom into a stranger.

It hadn't even occurred to Austin to ask her parents not to

attend her graduation. They, more than anybody, had supported her engineering dreams, sending her to geeky science summer camps and countless after school math club meeting and endless, no doubt boring-as-hell for them, state science fair projects. They'd always been so proud of her. They didn't understand a damn thing she was doing, but they were proud. Not the kind of proud where they took some type of credit for Austin's accomplishments, just proud of her. She owed them so much. But of course, her mother would just say 'that's what parents do.' But Austin knew she was lucky. And not because she was adopted, she reminded herself.

"Austin?"

"Of course, Mom. I'll email you the details today."

"Wonderful." And then the mom she knew emerged, launching into her usual instructional voice. "Make sure you do send it today, Austin, so I can plan appropriately. Also, I'll check with Brian to see if he can make it for your graduation and lunch afterward. I'm sure he'd love to."

Her mom just jumped right in there, making plans for all of them. Typical. The momentary comfort she'd felt at speaking with her mom dissipated and annoyance blossomed in its place. Austin gritted her teeth, tuning her mom out a bit, reminding herself it was better than the hesitating note the conversation started off on. She heard her mom say something about dinner. "Dinner? We just agreed on lunch."

"Weren't you listening? I'd like Brian to be there, so if he can't make lunch, you and I can grab something simple to eat, and then have a celebratory dinner. I think that's better, anyway."

"Not for me," Austin replied bluntly. "I have plans that night. It's graduation. There're people I'd like to see before they go off to...wherever." She didn't actually have plans, but her mom's assumptions and brisk reversion to behaving as though a recent earthquake had not recently shaken up the whole family ticked her off.

"Austin, don't you think you can squeeze in dinner with family before you run off?"

"I really need to check my calendar. I'll have to get back to you on it, but don't make plans before I do." Austin felt pretty good about not bending on this. It was so out of character for her. She usually just went along with whatever her mother wanted, whatever anybody wanted, really. Suddenly, something clicked with what her mom just said. "Wait. You said you and I would grab a bite for lunch. Dad's not coming?"

"Honestly, Austin. I just explained this. Your father has to travel to Texas for work. He wasn't able to delay it, unfortunately."

Her mother's tone suggested she thought her father probably hadn't tried very hard. Austin doubted that. Her dad would be there if he could. Her father worked for a computer security firm that had a lot of contracts with the military. It meant he traveled a lot, with little flexibility in the when and how of it. Anxiety swirled in her chest at the thought of spending the day with her mom without her dad as a buffer. "It's fine, Mom. I know he doesn't have much control of those things. I gotta go. I'll send you the details and stuff. Plan on lunch. I'll reach out to Brian and see if he can make it. You know he's the boss, right? I'm confident he can swing it. Having lunch will also ensure you'll make it most of the way home before it gets dark." Austin didn't want her having any illusions of spending the night or making a weekend of her trip.

"I'm not that old, Austin. I can drive in the dark."

Her forced playfulness made Austin cringe, transforming her irritation into an ineffable ache. Would things ever return to the easy camaraderie of before? "Sorry. I'll guess we'll talk later. "

"Talk to you soon. Love you."

"Love you too," Austin mumbled.

She texted Brian immediately to see if he could make her graduation and lunch afterward. He promptly replied in the affirmative. She emailed her mom, letting her know Brian was in for lunch. She could handle lunch with the two of them. She wasn't going to tell them about reaching out to Elise, though. She didn't need their silent satisfaction at her rejection. They wouldn't mean to hurt her, but it would hurt anyway if they said anything about it. She was better off keeping it to herself.

She wasn't naive about things, of course. Jeremy warned her denial was a possibility and this was definitely denial. Austin had double- then triple-checked her research to see if there was a mistake. There wasn't. That this woman was her mother was irrefutable. She had also read the posts cluttering the online adoption registry and reunion forums, from distressed adoptees whose found birth families wished they had remained unfound and unknown, but her imagination could take it so much further, when she was struggling to comprehend all the possible negative outcomes of hitting the send button on that email. It was true, what she told Jeremy that night they had drinks. It was impossible to imagine all possibilities in that Schrödinger's box. When she'd gotten home that night, she'd reasoned her way into thinking that if she just made herself really think through all the worst possibilities and try to prepare for those, then maybe it would be enough to help her handle the rest. She hadn't really thought through this possibility. It seemed rather minor compared to the others. However, now she was stuck, with nothing she could do.

***

The week dragged on. There were only three weeks before

finals, but Austin struggled to maintain focus on her schoolwork. She compulsively checked her email account every hour, disappointed each time. Claire had texted a few times, but Austin wasn't up for hanging out. There was a conversation waiting to happen there about where they stood with one another. Austin's brain was just too muddled for that one.

By Friday, cabin fever got to her. She was tired of studying the same three pages of notes over and over again. The weather outside was mercurial, alternating between sunny and quick, tropical downpours. At one point, she'd looked outside and it was doing both. Lovely. She could go to the Beth Israel. They had a good library. She could at least do some reading on what she'd need to do if she decided to participate in a formal conversion. The internet had a lot of information, much of it contradictory. There was a comfort and reassurance in a book splayed open on a table.

She had been in the library for over an hour when Rivka appeared in the doorway. She hadn't seen Rivka's car in the lot when she pulled in, but Kathy had let her in. Kathy was the secretary and often there on weekday afternoons.

Rivka wandered the small room, then over to the table where Austin sat. She glanced at the book covers. "Doing your research?"

"I have no idea what formal conversion entails. I thought I ought to see what I'd have to do."

"So, is that what you've decided to do?" Rivka perched on the edge of the table.

"I haven't decided yet." Austin stood and stretched. "Frankly, Rivka, I'm pissed that I have to even consider doing this."

"You don't get to choose what challenges God puts in your path. All you can control are the choices you make in handling them."

"Jesus, Rivka, can you not be a rabbi for one second? Sometimes, it's really infuriating." Was Austin yelling? She hadn't meant to.

Rivka returned to the arched doorway then turned to face Austin. "Austin, I couldn't love you more if you were my own sister. But I haven't got infinite patience, either as your friend or your rabbi, to deal with your emotions for you. This would go a lot better for you, I think, if you would just embrace being angry and work through it, instead of exploding at random points in a conversation."

"Oh, I'm embracing being angry all right."

"No, not really. You tend to keep things under wraps, but the result is that you think you have everything under control until you don't. And that's where you're at right now. So, if you want a therapist, I have a number. If you need a punching bag, not the human kind, I've got one set up in my basement."

That surprised Austin enough to draw her out of her scowl. "Really?"

"You think I'm this calm naturally? And, if you want to talk with me, I'm here, but you have to be willing to be honest with yourself. Feel everything you're feeling at the time you're feeling it and learn how to deal with it. Otherwise, it will keep coming out in these little explosions and you won't be able to listen to anybody, even yourself."

Austin opened her mouth to argue, wanted to argue even though she suspected Rivka was right, because she could feel that slow bubbling lump of lava anger rising within her chest, totally out of proportion to the conversation. She sat back down at the table and said nothing. She glanced over at Rivka, fingers tapping her lips as Rivka gave her a small smile and disappeared down the hallway.

Austin wanted her parents there in the room so she could yell at them, throw a temper tantrum, shake them until they understood just what damage they had done. If only she could understand the damage herself, but she didn't feel like she had been hit by a tornado, only that she was the tornado, twisted and hurtling across the landscape, formed and driven by forces far outside of her understanding. She rested her head on the table and stayed there, focusing on taking deep breaths, until she felt her heart slow down to its normal pulse.

As she put the books back on the shelf, her phone vibrated in her back pocket. She pulled it out and saw a text from Gil.

Did you hear about Lauren?

She dropped into a chair. To respond or not respond. Gil didn't wait.

A friend texted me and told me Lauren's fiancé (?!?) put on Instagram that she overdosed last night and was in the hospital. Thought you might want to know.

Austin stared at the text for a long time. Finally, she messaged back. *Thanks.*

~

16

Austin awoke in complete darkness. It took a moment for her to register that she had fallen asleep on the couch, that she was in her own apartment. She heard the hum of the refrigerator. The faint buzzing of the streetlamp outside her apartment. Her iPad had fallen on the floor. After Gil's text, she had DM'd Lauren's fiancé through Instagram, hoping to find out more information, hoping, maybe, she'd gotten the wrong information. She'd drifted off to sleep without hearing a response. She picked up the tablet, then set it back down. She didn't want to confront certainty right now.

She swung her feet to the floor and gingerly stood up. Her stomach rumbled. She padded into the kitchen, not bothering with the light. It was just after midnight, according to the microwave. She opened the refrigerator, looking for something quick and easy to quiet her stomach. She had bread, peanut butter, jelly, and eggs. When was the last time she had gone to the store? A week ago? Two? A peanut butter and jelly sandwich would have to do.

Austin took the sandwich on a paper plate back to the couch. She glanced at her phone. Nothing about Lauren, but she'd gotten a text message from Claire. *You still alive?*

Austin started to respond, then thought better of it. She

didn't want to wake Claire. It could wait until morning. She heard the chime of an email notification. She turned off the phone, then turned it on again. Sleep would be awhile coming. She glanced at her inbox. The new email was from Elise. She could see the subject line from the locked screen.

Subject: I'm sorry. Please read.

The email had attachments as well, but Austin hesitated before opening it. Her heart, sluggish since awakening, was now pounding staccato. She set the phone down to wipe her suddenly sweaty palms. She picked the phone up again, then turned it off. She retrieved her iPad. Her finger hovered over the email as she closed her eyes to calm her pulse. Eyes still closed, she clicked open the message. She took a deep breath, then read the note.

> Dear Austin,
>
> I owe you an apology. All week, I've been thinking of you and my response to your email. I know who you are. I knew the minute I saw your birthdate. I have no excuse for lying to you, or for waiting so long to send this email. This past week must have been so hard for you, and it's my fault. I just wasn't able to find the same courage you had when you wrote me.
>
> You're probably angry with me, but I'd really like to talk to you. Can I call you this weekend? If that's okay, let me know when. Also, I thought you might like a current picture, so one is attached. Send me one?
>
> - Elise Brouchard

Austin reread the note several times. Elise was right. She was angry at her for the week of self-doubt and depression she'd gone through. She quickly shoved it out of her mind. That'd be a crappy way to start with each other. Compartmentalize, right? It got her this far.

But could she handle a phone call? What would she say? She didn't know what was okay to ask. She didn't want to offend her, or anger her by asking the wrong things, or being insensitive. She wanted to be honest, though. Was there a right way to do this?

Austin warred with her impatience. She did want to talk with Elise. Tomorrow was just too soon. Sunday, then. Late afternoon. Hopefully, Elise would be free.

She hit reply on the email. After some thought, she simply wrote that she wanted to speak with Elise too, and what about Sunday afternoon at four. She signed it the same way Elise did, only her name. Short, but not rude, she hoped.

Austin downloaded the picture to her iPad. She examined Elise's shoulder-length brown hair—a bit lighter than her own—but with the similar thickness and volume. That's all she could really see though. The picture was still too small. She couldn't even tell what color Elise's eyes were, even with the zoom function. Austin glanced up at her ceiling projectors.

She had so often scrutinized her mother's face, trying in vain to find a likeness, some common feature that would bond them together beyond words and family dinners and hospital trips and shared tears and laughter. That was enough on so many levels, but the most basic, the most visceral. She had, she realized now, been searching for some tangible proof that this being was her point of origin, and she always walked away disappointed. Not with her mother, but with herself, as if she, somehow, was flawed in her creation.

There was no disappointment as she gazed at this photograph. Elise, almost life-size, stared back at her from the photo projected on the curtains. With a touch of surprise, Austin did not have trouble seeing the similarities, recognizing the long but slightly upturned nose, slightly square jaw and bold cheekbones, her half-smile and the rosy paleness of her skin. Saw a version of these things every day in the mirror. For so long, without knowing why, Austin had avoided mirrors whenever possible because of the discomforted, unsettled feeling that washed over her every time she saw her reflection, as if a stranger was staring back at her. Now, as she stared at the photo of her mother, she understood. Without the benefit of growing up and seeing herself reflected in a jawline here and eyebrow there, she had no frame of reference for recognizing her face, a strange form of self-prosopagnosia, and her reflection remained a perpetual familiar oddity.

She sat on the couch. Oddly, she didn't feel as satisfied with the picture as she had when she found her grandmother's picture. This portrait wasn't enough. She wanted to talk to Elise, meet her. Who was she? Were they alike? What happened when Austin was born? She couldn't ask all of that at once, though. Elise would run screaming. And the answers might be worse than the questions. She hoped, when Sunday came around, she'd be brave enough to answer the phone.

***

Claire hadn't responded to her text by the time Austin emerged from the shower. She was probably on the road to work already. She could swing by to say hi. Someone would let her in if she got there before they opened.

She didn't have to worry about it. Claire was just locking her car when Austin pulled into the back lot. She waved at Claire, who looked at her then down to drop her keys in her shoulder bag. She didn't wave back.

Austin's enthusiasm downshifted rapidly to cautious wariness as she got out of her car. "Hey."

"Hey."

Austin waited, but Claire didn't say anything else. "What'd I do?"

Claire took off her sunglasses and tucked them in her bag as well. "Why are you here, Austin?"

Austin felt the blood rush to her face, its warmth almost making her eyes water. She rolled the gravel beneath her left sneaker. Before texting Claire this morning, when was the last time she had responded to one of Claire's texts? A few days? Longer? It wasn't what she did. It was what she didn't do. Crap.

"I'm an asshole, Claire," she finally said, shoving her hands deep in her front pockets.

"You drove all the way here to tell me that?" Claire stepped around her and walked toward the studio's back door. "You could've just kept ignoring me. That's a pretty clear message."

Austin placed a hand on Claire's arm. "I didn't mean to."

Claire shrugged and stepped away. She unlocked the back door and pulled it open.

Austin caught it before it shut. "It's not like that, Claire. I just needed some time to understand what was going on. Not with you. With other stuff."

"Because what's being going on with us has been so clear."

"Hey! That's not all on me."

Claire didn't respond.

Austin watched Brian's car pull into the lot. She looked at Claire. "Can we talk a minute. Over there?" She pointed to a corner of the lot.

"I guess." Claire turned toward Brian, now getting out of his car. "Be inside in a sec, Brian."

He gave her a thumbs-up, waved at Austin, and disappeared through the door.

They walked to the corner in silence. Claire leaned back against a tree, hands in pockets, waiting.

"I'm sorry I didn't get back to you, Claire. I wasn't in a good place."

"You could've told me that. You could've just texted me to give you a few days, a week, whatever. Instead, I get the silent treatment. Do you have any idea how that makes me feel?" When Austin didn't answer, Claire continued, "Like you were indifferent to me. Like you didn't give a damn."

Austin met Claire's eyes. "That's not true. At all."

"How would I know?"

"I care about you a lot, Claire. And I know you care about me. But look, I know how screwed up I've been lately, how much that—" Austin paused, eyes on the ground, searching for the right words, "—can foster pity."

"I don't pity you, Austin," Claire responded sharply.

Austin didn't believe her, but shrugged. "Sympathy, then. But what I'm saying is that close feelings, an attraction, can evolve from that."

"Wait, let me see if I understand you correctly. You think I'm attracted to you because you're super-pathetic?"

"I didn't say super-pathetic, gee." No smile from Claire. "I have no idea if you're attracted to me."

"You're a terrible liar."

"It's just, I mean, you're very—"

"What?"

"Caring. Empathetic. It's amazing." Austin looked at Claire intently. "You like to, maybe need to, take care of people. You're a caretaker. It's a good thing! All I'm saying is it can create feelings of intimacy that maybe aren't what they appear."

"Jesus, Austin. So, you've spent all this time analyzing how I must feel, and my motivations for feeling them. But what about your feelings? I know you must have them, but damned if I know what they are."

"I don't know." Austin immediately looked away from

Claire. "I'm not sure."

"I don't believe you."

"I didn't want to think about it. I thought maybe we were building something, but then, you started seeing someone and I figured I misunderstood things. But, then you invited me to spend the night." Austin's face felt like it was on fire. "I got confused."

Claire stepped away from the tree. "You thought I was seeing someone? Where in the world would you get that idea?"

"That Saturday afternoon I came over, not the one where I spent the night. You had plans but didn't mention where or with who. Obviously, you wanted to keep it private. And then a few days later, I called you and you kept shooing someone away from the phone. What was I supposed to think?"

"Damn, Austin, how many assumptions are you going to make?"

Austin jabbed her finger at the air between them. "You were being mysterious about it."

Claire opened her mouth to argue, then shut it as the back door opened and a laughing couple exited the studio, arms around each other's waists, stumbling down the stairs because they refused to extricate from one another. Austin hadn't even seen them arrive. How long had they been out here?

Once the couple were in their car, Claire turned back to her. "There was nothing to tell. I wasn't seeing anyone."

"Wasn't? Are you now?"

Much to Austin's surprise, Claire started laughing. "Honest to God, Austin. I don't know whether to laugh or cry with you. Answer me this. Why are you so passive? If you were confused, why not ask?"

Austin scoffed. "What?"

Claire uncrossed her arms and took a step toward her. "Do you just expect things to continue happening, or not happening, until you get pushed so far that you're forced to do something?"

Austin stared at her. Clueless.

Claire rolled on. "I mean, you didn't decide to look for your birthmother until your parents pissed you off. You wait until I'm pissed at you before telling me how you feel. Which you haven't even done yet. Why do you wait until you're on the edge of a cliff before you actually admit to feeling anything, before you actually do anything?"

"Why should I? Why should I make investments, be proactive, when everybody just keeps walking out the goddamn door?" Austin heard the petulance in her voice. Couldn't restrain it. Only anger and embarrassment kept her from laughing, from rolling her eyes at her own self-indulgence. Could she be any more selfish or self-absorbed? Why was Claire even still there, asking her questions?

And then, she wasn't. Claire stormed past Austin back into the studio. As Austin started to follow, Claire looked behind her and said quietly, "Don't."

***

Austin had just opened the door to her car when she heard the back door open. She stepped back and looked, hoping to see Claire. Instead, Brian was bounding down the steps, stopping inches in front of her. "What the hell, Austin?"

"What the what, Brian?" Austin crossed her arms.

"Claire just came in, all sorts of ticked off. What you'd do?"

Austin shrugged. "None of your business, Brian."

"The hell it isn't, not when it affects my employees."

"So, you're saying Claire's incapable of separating her personal life from work?"

Brian shook his head, puzzled. "What? Of course not."

"So, she'll be fine for customers. The rest is none of your

business." Austin turned away to walk to her car.

Brian grabbed her elbow. "I don't want you involved with Claire." He seemed to hear how that came across and quickly added, "Any of my employees."

"A little FYI, Brian. Not your decision to make." Austin yanked her elbow from Brian's grip. "We're not seeing each other. We're friends. I really fucked up this week and hurt her feelings, okay? Leave it alone."

"That's what I'm talking about, Austin. You live in this little bubble and don't know how you impact people. You can't just go screwing around with people's lives."

"You talking about Claire? Or our family?"

"Both."

"Fuck you, Brian."

"Austin."

"That's what you really think of me. I screwed up with Claire. I screwed up with our family. I'm trying to screw up another family. It's all my fault. You're saying maybe I should have just accepted everything and moved on." Austin scoffed. "No wonder Claire thinks I'm passive. My family actively encourages it. Tell me, Brian. Why are you so angry?"

He didn't respond.

"Is it really because I'm so self-absorbed I don't even know I'm hurting people? Or is it because of you. That you're afraid my being adopted will change your perception of me, of our relationship."

Brian blinked. "Of course not! You're my little sister. Nothing could ever change that, Austin."

Austin released her breath. She needed that answer.

Brian stepped toward her, voice softer as he spoke, "All I meant was consider other people's feelings. Look at things from others' point of view sometimes."

"Trust me, Brian, I do, actually. A lot. Who's looking at it from my point of view, Brian? Who's walking in my shoes?

Or is that too much to ask?"

"It's not all about you, Austin."

"Actually, Brian," Austin again turned from him to walk to her car, "on this subject, it kinda is."

~

17

After starting to call Claire four times in the three minutes she'd been home, Austin briefly considered deleting Claire from her contacts list just to end the temptation. What purpose would it serve? So they could argue more? So Austin could defend herself even though Claire wasn't attacking her, simply pointing out something that was true?

Austin had been letting her calls go to voicemail, been vague in her texts over the last week. The problem was, she couldn't tell Claire why. What could she really explain to Claire without sounding even more pathetic? That, when faced with complex emotions that rendered her incapable of maintaining her stoic facade, she fled her feelings like a deer in flight from wildfire? Rationally, she knew she had cause to be in pain, not from Claire, of course, but there were other, indistinguishable sources of the hurt that sloshed around within her, attaching itself in thin layers to the inner lining of her skin so that her skin prickled with every breath.

But an unwillingness to show or share her pain wasn't what kept her from responding to Claire. She knew this. Knew Claire didn't turn away from the sight of pain laid bare. Hadn't she borne witness to her own mother's death, a slow-growing pain measured in months, then days, then hours and finally minutes?

No, what had stopped her was the knowledge of Claire's capability to withstand the pain of others, her willingness to be present for it. With strength such as that, what could Austin possibly offer in return? She couldn't even face her own pain. All she could do was withhold her pain, prevent Claire from knowing it, from sharing it. It wasn't forever. These wounds would heal and then she could be present again. On equal footing. Level ground. If Claire was willing to give her a second chance once she'd had a chance to stabilize her world.

She plopped on the couch and watched tv for a couple of hours before feeling immeasurably bored. She wandered across the living room, into her bedroom, then into the kitchen. She opened the cupboard below the kitchen sink. Lauren had left a bottle of bourbon here. She set it on the counter. Lauren had mixed it with Coke. Austin hadn't tried it, but it tasted good on Lauren's lips. She peered in the fridge. No Coke.

She unscrewed the top and sniffed. It smelled good. Strong, maybe. She took a short swig. It burned a little, but the taste was tolerable. She took a longer drink, then set the bottle down. Was this a healthy thing to do, drinking out of a bottle, at home, alone? Probably not. She screwed the top back on the bottle and tucked it beneath the sink.

Her phone buzzed on the coffee table. A text from Monica, asking if she wanted to go out to The Village. *You bet,* she texted back. She didn't feel like pacing the floor and crawling the walls in here tonight. Why not go out and pretend she knew how to have fun.

***

"That's so creepy." Monica handed Austin her phone. "Creepy cool, I guess, but how does a record player play a tree stump?"

Austin laughed. "It's not an actual record player. He uses a special camera and assigns a specific music scale to each particular tree."

"You're such a geek."

Austin shut off her phone. "I know."

"I mean that in a good way."

"I know."

Linda appeared, holding a full tray of liquor shots. Austin's eyes widened as she turned to Monica. "You didn't order a whole tray…"

Monica laughed. "No. Two at a time." She maneuvered two glasses in front of Austin, and then slid two in front of herself. "Thanks, Linda."

"Yep." Linda turned and deposited the remaining shot glasses from her tray on the booth across from them, before hustling down the aisle toward the bar.

"God, how long has she been working here?" Monica asked.

"Twenty-five years," Austin answered. "I asked one of the bartenders. He said she never lets them forget it either. Rules the place with an iron spatula."

"Ouch!" Monica nudged the shot glasses toward Austin. "Drink."

"Still Fireball whiskey?"

"Why fix what isn't broken."

"Right." Austin picked up the glass. "You know, I really don't drink."

"Yeah. You've mentioned. Multiple times."

"But this is easy to drink. Think I'm just gonna sip it though."

"Whatever you want." Monica slid out of the booth and motioned for Austin to slide over. "I'll lose my voice if I have to keep shouting over all this noise."

"I'd rather sit on the outside, if you don't mind." Austin

stood up to let her in.

Monica smiled up at her. "Well, you do have long legs."

"I guess." Austin realized she wasn't as steady on her feet as she was used to being. She slid into the booth. "How many shots have we had? Just the two each, right?"

"And these make four. But really it's not that much." Monica downed one of her shots. She looked at Austin, apparently waiting for Austin to do the same. Monica stretched other elbow on the table, leaning her head against her hand. "So, what's up with you and Claire?"

"Nothing. What do you mean?" Austin slid the empty shot glass between her hands, eyeing the full one.

"Really? You guys seemed like you're getting pretty close."

Austin shrugged. "First Lauren. Now Claire. If you're interested in these women, Monica, why don't you ask them out?"

Monica laughed. "I'm not. You're adorably dense, Austin."

Austin wasn't quite sure what to make of that. Adorable sounded like a compliment. Dense did not. She shrugged again and tossed back her remaining shot. It hardly burned this time.

A couple of hours and more than a few more shots later, Austin was trying to listen to the music Monica wanted to share with her, but the noise in the diner was too loud. She handed Monica's earbuds back to her. "I think I like her, but I can't really hear," she said. She might have shouted. Everything was so loud. Austin looked around. The diner had completely filled up. People were sitting in each other's laps, spilling out of the booths, drinking, laughing. She wished it wasn't so bright. The overhead lights, though dimmed, bled into every corner.

The water stains on the ceiling swam across the tiles, making her dizzy. She looked down at the table. She felt a light pressure on her knee. She looked down and saw

Monica's hand.

"I'm glad you came out with me," Monica said.

"Yeah? Why?" Austin wasn't fishing for anything. She had been surprised to get Monica's invite. She'd just figured Monica had run down a list of people and Austin was the first available.

Monica's lips brushed Austin's cheek as she leaned to speak in her ear. "I've been wanting to get to know you better."

Austin felt the cheap thrill of a woman's breath close to her skin. She turned her head toward Monica, finding herself a few inches from her face. "I could've saved you some time."

"How so?" Monica moved an inch closer.

"I would've let you know I'm not worth much effort."

Monica bridged the gap and kissed her lightly on the lips. "That's not how I see it."

Austin leaned forward and kissed Monica this time. Longer. Long enough to taste the whiskey on her tongue. Long enough to realize she was kissing the wrong lips.

She pulled back. "I have to go."

Monica slid away from her. Smiling, maybe sadly.

Austin dug in her pocket and pulled out a couple of twenty-dollar bills. "My treat." She dropped the money on the table.

"It's Claire, isn't it?"

"Claire? I'll be lucky if she ever speaks to me again."

"Because of this?" Monica looked perplexed.

Austin shook her head, wished she hadn't. "No. Anyway, sorry 'bout this. I didn't mean to…give the wrong impression."

Monica gathered the money and lightly tucked it back into Austin's pocket. "My treat. I think maybe you've had a rough couple of months."

"Stop being nice to me, Monica. Everybody has been so

fucking nice to me and I've really been nothing but an asshole. Just ask Claire."

Austin stood abruptly. The room spun. She clutched the table's edge until she felt her feet beneath her. She glanced toward the exit. Five feet.

"Girl, seriously, chill." Monica slid out of the booth and stood next to her. "You can't blame a girl for trying, but it's cool. C'mon, I'll take you home."

Austin scoffed. Monica had at least a few more shots than Austin, and Austin had lost count after six. "No way you can drive."

Monica held up her phone. "Uber."

"Oh. Good."

"I'll call one for us. Don't move." Monica took some bills out of her purse and made her way toward the cash register at the front of the diner. Austin watched until her head disappeared within the crowd up front. She turned and lurched toward the back exit and stumbled through the door.

***

Austin was halfway down the block when she heard Monica calling after her. She swung around but couldn't hear what Monica was saying. She took out her phone and texted her. *I'm good. Walking home. Thanks. Sorry.*

She saw Monica look at her phone and got a text from her a second later. *Okay. Text when you get home.*

Austin waved and turned back around. The street lights blurred together, coating the street in hazy yellow light. Just a couple of months ago, she had joked with her mom on the phone about going out with friends. Now, everything was so different. She turned down the alley she usually walked. She really wished she could call her mom.

It felt satisfying, hearing the crunch as gravel compressed beneath her feet. For a moment, it was the only sound she heard as she walked. Then, a car honked in the distance.

Crickets chirped in unison, rising to a crescendo before falling to a whisper. A breeze rustled the new leaves of the trees lining the alley. Poplars overshadowed dogwoods, flowers just starting their bloom.

Austin squinted to see the shapes of the branches overhead, but everything slipped into haze. She glanced down the alley. Everything was shrouded in shimmering mist. Moisture prickled along her skin and the breeze lifted the hair on her arms. Heat released from the ground rose and condensed into the fog drifting around her as the evening temperature dropped. As it thickened, the air stilled and silence returned.

She stood a moment, though she swayed forward. Inertia working with inebriation. Time stretched. Minute particles of mist swirled around her, whirling eddies of chaos belied the apparent calm enveloping her.

Austin took a deep breath, which brought a chill into her lungs. She forced one foot in front of the other. She wanted to call her mom. Her fingers reached for the reassurance of her phone tucked in her back pocket. What would she say?

Her mom had broken her heart. She didn't know that was possible, but that's how she felt now, trudging along this gray-shadowed alleyway. What comfort could her mom offer her right now?

She couldn't call Rivka. God knew that poor woman deserved a break from her. She had a baby, and a husband. A whole life that Austin had no right to invade, over and over again like she did. And Claire, better not to think about that one at all.

She felt wetness on her cheek. When had she started crying? She shook her head and wiped her face with her sleeve. Great time for a pity party, walking home alone in the middle of the night. Drunk. Brilliantly safe, too.

She kicked at the gravel. It felt like kicking air.

Unsatisfying. She tried to kick the larger pebbles, only to stub her toe and lose her balance. She landed hard on her hands and knees. Sharp edges dug into her palms. Fitting, she supposed, struggling back to her feet by using a garage wall to keep her balance.

It was then she spotted the cardboard box sitting next to a recycling bin, filled with empty beer bottles. Across the alley was another garage, this one with a brick siding. She looked back at the box of bottles and gave into temptation. She grabbed one, turned and threw it hard against the brick wall. It shattered, tiny shards of glass splintering out in all directions, dimly sparkling. Her shoulder twanged. She'd never played a throwing sport. Soccer in middle school, and then swimming in high school. For a year.

Austin picked up a second bottle. This time, her throw was high and to the left, sailing past the garage wall, over a fence, and landing with a soft thump onto someone's backyard grass. Bummer. She threw a third and watched with satisfaction as it exploded against the wall. She reached for another bottle as a screen door squeaked open somewhere nearby and a man hollered, "I'm calling the police!"

Well, that was enough of that, it seemed. She crouched by the box, hidden (she hoped) in the shadows along the side of the garage. Several minutes passed without further threats. No one stepped out into the alley to look for her. She glanced at the ground. Glass shards glittered among the gravel. Pretty damn irresponsible of her. Felt pretty damn good, too. She wished she could throw more. Maybe she should take advantage of Rivka's punching bag. She didn't know how to punch anything, though. Probably would bruise the hell outta her knuckles. She started to walk away, then looked back at the mess she'd made. After far too many attempts, she succeeded ripping off a top flap from the box, and scooped up glass mixed with gravel, dumping it into the box.

Satisfied, she lurched away from the garage, and tottered down the alleyway, only slowing down when she'd doglegged her way to the alleyway on the next block.

After another couple of blocks, she found herself wishing she had thought through the idea of walking the two miles home. She couldn't quite feel her legs. Her feet, too, weren't quite landing where she'd intended, causing her to stumble more than once. Great. She was a blundering drunk. Whose bright idea was it for her to walk home anyway?

Her phone felt like a stone in her pocket, weighted with numbers for people she wanted to call but couldn't, or wouldn't. Dim headlights diffused through the mist behind her, enshrouding her in faint luminescence. Whoever it was had their brights on. Didn't they know that made it harder to see in fog? That's why there were fog lights. Obviously.

She looked behind her, but the car was in the alley on the previous block. Ahead, she noticed a small break in the shrubs planted along the row of backyard privacy fences. She needed rest. Ducking into a space between two bushes, Austin sat and leaned back against the fence. The soil, slightly damp, chilled her but only momentarily. She could still hear the car crunching along the distant gravel. Didn't matter. She was tucked away.

She closed her eyes and tilted her head back. She missed her mom. A lot. Not that she really would call her right this minute. Or even this weekend. Nothing was stopping her but her own…everything. What would happen if she let it go with her parents? Was their trust, their relationship, really irrevocably broken? She could choose to believe that they did what they thought was best, whether it was could remain up for debate. But she knew they did nothing with the intention of hurting her. She trusted that. Could she forgive and move on, without resentment percolating within her, ready to burst out at some random unexpected passive-aggressive way?

This option sounded like the mature one, like the one she should make. But could she actually do it? She wasn't sure.

Maybe she could just let her anger run its course while keeping her relationship with them intact. She didn't have to avoid them, as long as they let her be angry. They would have moments, days or weeks probably, of testy talks and ignored voice mails. But maybe, too, she could have some times again when she could call her mom, and joke about the proper times for beer and dinner and coffee. Could that even work? Maybe she should call her mom and ask.

A familiar voice called out to her. "Austin. What are you doing?"

Austin flicked open her eyes and saw Claire standing a foot away, bathed in the headlights of her idling car. "Claire?"

"Yeah."

She didn't sound happy. Why would she? Why was she here? Austin scrambled to her feet, using the fence for balance. "I was just thinking about calling my mom." Because that made sense, given the current scenario.

"Which mom?"

Wow, snarky much, Claire? Austin glared at the ground, not risking doing it to Claire. She wanted a ride home. "My mom."

"Right." Claire crossed her arms.

Austin squinted at her. "What're you doing here?"

"Monica called. Said you wandered off toward home, drunk as a skunk."

Austin stiffened with indignity but refrained from offering a flippant response. "Not completely wasted, thank you. I did manage to make it this far. I just needed to rest a sec."

Claire grabbed her wrists, not hard. She looked at Austin's palms. "Jesus, Austin. Your hands are chewed up."

"I fell. Guess I scraped them on the gravel." Austin pulled her hands back. "I might be a little drunk, I guess. I'm not sure. I've never been drunk before."

Claire stared at her a minute, then led her by the elbow to the passenger door. "Are you able to get in the car?"

Austin opened the door and fell into the seat. "Looks like it."

Claire put the car in gear and edged slowly out of the alley toward Austin's neighborhood.

***

"You've never been drunk?"

Austin shook her head, then immediately wished she hadn't. Her third attempt to unlock her apartment door failed. She tiredly dropped her keys into Claire's outstretched hand.

Claire pushed the door open. Austin stumbled into the front room, then lurched toward the work table. She swung around and used it to remain standing as she addressed Claire. "Thanks for the ride. I didn't ask Monica to call, you know."

"She was concerned." Claire stood in the doorway, backlit by the entryway light, face hidden in shadow.

Austin looked back at her. Her vision was blurry. She couldn't tell what Claire's face looked like. "What're you thinking?"

Claire edged into the room, leaving the door open. She shifted to the side, leaning back against the wall. She said nothing.

Austin tried to focus her eyes. The lighting wasn't helpful, but she finally noticed Claire wore a dress. A really sleek—and short—cocktail dress. She walked carefully toward Claire, squinting at her face. Did Claire wear make-up? She was this evening, apparently. And she smelled good. Subtle. Not floral. Not too sweet. Nice. Why was Claire dressed so nicely? "Oh my god, Monica didn't pull you away from a date, did she?"

"A date? Austin. Really?" Claire shook her head. "Not exactly."

Not a date. Austin barely had a chance to feel relief before she remembered what the day was. Saturday. Claire's opening photography exhibit at the gallery. "Your exhibit," she whispered. She pushed at Claire's shoulder. "You need to get back there. You gotta go. You shouldn't have come!"

Claire sighed, then shut the front door. "You're a pain in the ass, sometimes, Austin."

"Only sometimes?" Austin asked, hopefully.

Claire guided her by her elbow to the bedroom and set her down on the bed. Austin fell back on her elbows and struggled to get back upright. "I don't like this, Claire. Drinking sucks."

She felt Claire's cool hands on her burning face. She lifted her eyes. Claire gazed at her, but Austin couldn't read her at all. She could see, though, that Claire wasn't angry. Why wasn't she angry? She pulled her head from Claire's hands. "You back to the gallery. Monica shouldn't have called." Austin realized she was slurring, but the gist came through.

"I didn't have to come," Claire said softly. She stood and moved to the doorway.

Austin pushed off her sneakers. No, she didn't. Why had Claire come?

As if to answer, Claire said, "I have a savior complex, right? How could I resist a call in need?"

Her tone was only gently mocking.

"That's not what I said," Austin protested. Caretaker, not savior, big difference, she thought. "Claire."

"No. Not tonight, Austin." Claire left the room.

Austin sat slumped, waiting to hear the front door open and close. It didn't. She heard sounds coming from the kitchen. She wondered what words she could say to Claire to make things right. The floor was spinning. She looked at her bed covers. She felt like she was on a boat on the ocean, swells swaying her side to side. Not sure if she was actually moving, Austin grabbed the edge of the mattress. Her knuckles were white. She couldn't think outside of how her body felt. Her stomach lurched and acid erupted up her throat. She swallowed, throat burning.

Claire appeared, holding two bottles of water and the bag-lined trash bin from the kitchen. She handed one bottle to Austin, who clutched it with both hands like it was priceless. "That one's for now. Drink up. All of it." She put the second bottle and the trash bin on the floor near the head of the bed. "For later. Now, let me out so you can lock the deadbolt behind me."

Austin stood and wobbled her way behind Claire. Claire opened the front door and walked through to the entryway door. "Helpful tip. When you lie down, the ceiling is going to spin. Put a leg off the side of the bed. Make sure your foot's touching the floor. Doesn't have to be flat, but make sure it's solid on the floor. It'll help. Don't forget the water. Got it?"

Austin nodded. "Thanks."

She hoped Claire might say something else, might suggest they meet up for coffee or something. But Claire exited the building without a backward glance or even a goodbye. Austin probably deserved that.

~

18

Austin awoke the next morning, thirsty, sore, and unsure why she was wrapped in her comforter on the cold hardwood floor. She vaguely remembered thinking her bed was too soft. Every time she moved, she felt like she was trying to sleep on a boat in the middle of a hurricane.

She sat up, groaning. She grabbed the water bottle Claire had left out. Empty but for a few unsatisfactory drops. At least she followed instruction at some point last night. Her head didn't hurt as much as she'd been led to expect. At some point during the night, she'd also managed to shed her jeans, but not her t-shirt and bra, which now dug painfully into her ribcage. Her stomach was a bit queasy, she noticed while struggling to her feet. A little toast and jam would probably fix that. Great, now she was channeling her Mom from the last time Austin had the flu, which was her junior year in high school. All she needed was some ginger ale to top it off. Too bad she didn't have any.

She stood at the kitchen counter to eat, not waiting to bother with a plate. She tried to review the previous night's events in detail. So many wrong things happened. A few not-so-bright decisions, including the stellar idea to go out drinking in the first place.

If she hadn't ruined everything with Claire yesterday afternoon, she definitely sealed the doom with the follow-up last night. Getting drunk. Kissing Monica. Dozing in an alley. Had she actually dozed? More like meditated. Oh man, she had kissed Monica. Was that a big deal? Seemed more like a thoughtless mistake. Monica had a go-with-the-flow vibe. Frankly, Austin was surprised by the pass. She'd never gotten the impression Monica was interested in her before. Probably just an opportunity that presented itself. Austin blushed thinking about it. It was so not her. Monica was probably chill about it. But would Claire be? Did it even matter now? What if she was able to fix things somehow with Claire? Would it matter then? Austin rubbed her temple. Whatever. Bridge to cross later.

Her head throbbed. She gulped down a glass of water, then another. Looking out the kitchen window, she noticed the misty haze from the night before had transformed into a thick fog this morning. She could see sunlight brightening the top layers, struggling to break through. It was supposed to be near eighty today. Fog should mix out by noon. Which was good because she had some reparation to do today, starting with seeing Claire's show in the gallery. But not tell Claire. Not to try to make up for her lack of awareness over the past week, up through last night. She wanted to get to know Claire, not try to score some kind of forgiveness brownie points.

She opted to walk the two-plus miles to the gallery. By the time she'd showered and dressed, the morning fog had lifted. The walk would hopefully clear her brain fog out as well. That last night was such a huge night for Claire, and that Austin had forgotten all about it made her face flush with shame. It struck her as rather unforgivable. Even worse that Claire had been called away from it to once again clean up the mess that was Austin.

Yeah, she didn't have to do it, but she did. Austin's stomach roiled violently as she thought about it. Not thinking about it wasn't an option as Austin couldn't get the situation out of her mind. She considered the ways in which she'd abused Claire's empathy. Her willingness to be kind. Even if Claire lacked the ability or interest to say no, that didn't mean Austin had to take advantage of her. She felt a growing sense of embarrassment at how easily, and thoughtlessly, she had availed herself to Claire's generosity.

She thought through the last couple of months, all of their interactions. There had been far too much self-absorption on her part, way too much to simply offer up an apology. She couldn't really see a clear path for starting over with Claire, but maybe something would occur to her.

Austin had clearly underestimated her well-being at the time she'd left her apartment. She had to rest for a few minutes at each of the three neighborhood parks she passed as she walked through the Fan district. The gallery opened at one. Austin arrived a few minutes after the hour, surprising the proprietor, who was still turning on the lights. Austin quickly explained she was a friend of Claire's and wanted to look at her exhibit, if it wasn't too much trouble. The owner, Linda, led her to the far wall, happily chatting about artful contrasts, deliberate compositions, cohesive narrative threads, and a whole jumble of other comments that were completely over Austin's head. She nodded thoughtfully at each exclamation, inexplicably proud that Claire had impressed this art connoisseur to such an extent. She did understand when Linda talked about Claire's uncanny ability to capture her subjects' authenticity. After all, that was the first thing Austin had noticed. Linda then went on to make comparisons to some famous photographer, Joyce Tenneson. Linda clearly had expected Austin to know who that was, so Austin nodded, smiled, and agreed. She also made a mental note to look her up when she got home.

At last, another patron entered the gallery. Linda, perhaps bored with talking to someone who didn't talk back or simply eager to actually help a potential customer, hastily exited their one-sided conversation. Austin was grateful to have the opportunity to appreciate Claire's work in solitude. Claire had included the series of her mother, displayed backwards by starting with the ones taken in the hospice, to better days at home, and ending with happier, healthier days of her mother working in a garden. They were marked as not for sale. Austin's heart ached.

Despite all their talk of Austin's mothers, Austin had never asked about Claire's mother, aside from their initial conversation when Claire shared the works-in-progress pictures. Why hadn't they gotten along? Had it always been that way, or did something happen between them? Austin wished, for the thousandth time that day, that she'd been brave enough to let Claire know she was interested in getting to know her.

There were other portraits in the exhibit, as well, all for sale. None of Lauren, which Austin felt grateful for despite recognizing it as a pretty bit of pettiness. Both Gil and Monica had texted her that they'd heard Lauren was out of the hospital, which made Austin feel relieved. Beyond that, she didn't want to know what Lauren was doing with her life. She had her own life she needed to put back on the rails.

She noticed some photographs were already marked as 'sold', for which Austin felt another absurd swell of pride. To know someone of such talent, with courage enough to share it with the world. She slipped out of the gallery, with a quiet 'thank you' called out to Linda, who waved. It looked more like a dismissal, but Austin took no offense.

She stopped down the road at a convenience store, picking up water and a granola bar to sustain her for the arduous trek back to her apartment.

She'd opted to keep going past the first park, but gave in at the second one, sinking gratefully onto the metal bench. She'd preferred the old wooden ones, but they'd recently replaced them. Easier upkeep, she supposed, given the mercurial weather. The park was the center of a traffic roundabout, connecting two one-way residential streets. Quite a few people were passing through, many walking their dogs. One dog sniffed her leg with such intent, she worried he was about to pee on her. Fortunately, the owner—talking on his phone, oblivious to his pet—continued walking. As soon as the leash grew taut, the dog reluctantly dawdled after the man.

A voice from behind startled her. "Austin! Fancy meeting you here." Rivka came around to the front of the bench. "Mind if I join you a minute?"

Austin scooted over. "Sit. I'm happy to see you." She hadn't spoken to Rivka since their tense exchange in the synagogue library. She wasn't too surprised to see her, given that Rivka lived a few blocks away. She occasionally went for walks, but 'not often enough,' she'd often comment, patting her belly. Today, though, she was wearing slip-on shoes designed for comfort not exercise.

Rivka sat, tucking her hair behind her ears. Austin tried, and failed, to hide a smirk. Rivka's hair was super-curly, and always sprung out, no matter how vigorously Rivka tucked it.

"What brings you out?" Austin asked.

"I was gonna ask you the same thing," Rivka responded. "I'm on the way to the grocery store. David gave me a list." She scrunched up her face in disapproval. "He can't leave the house. Waiting for a client to call and he needs to be by his computer."

"On a Sunday?"

"The cost of being self-employed. Anyway, I was driving by when I saw you."

"And you parked just to come over to say hi? Aww. By the way, did David make you swear not to deviate from the grocery list? I can't believe he's straight up trusting you on this. Last time, didn't you go a little overboard on ad-libbing groceries?"

"I had good cause. I was pregnant. Anyway, I did promise to do my best to stick to the list. What more could he ask for? So, what are you up to?"

Austin filled her in on her gallery visit, which she highly recommended Rivka check out. Then, before she could stop herself, she shared the sorry tale of the previous night. She left out the part about kissing Monica. Rivka didn't need to know everything.

Rivka thought a moment before responding. "I suppose you don't need a lecture from me on the dangers of walking home, drunk, alone, in the middle of the night?"

"Not really, no."

"No. I didn't think so. Because you already know what I'd say."

"Yeah. It was dumb. Got it. And for the record, being drunk sucks."

"Drinking in moderation is fine."

"Yes, I know. But I don't think I'm a fan right now. I probably should have just taken you up on the punching bag thing." Austin had also left out the throwing of beer bottles in her retelling. Rivka definitely didn't need to know about that. Although she might have at least been pleased that Austin had cleaned it up afterward.

"Offer still stands. Still, if the worst you do at rock bottom is drink a little too much one night, that's pretty good, I'd say."

"Have I? Hit rock bottom?"

Rivka smiled. "I meant it more figuratively, sorry. I don't think there's a rock bottom here. Just complicated situations that require a little more attention from you as it pertains to your feelings, which you're not really used to giving."

Austin wanted to argue, but when Rivka was right, she was right. Austin did not like to dwell in the murkiness of emotions. Obviously. Maybe she should have warned Claire about that. "Things are a mess, Rivka. And I've made them worse. I don't know how, or even if, I can fix things with Claire, for one thing."

"You may not be able to."

That's Rivka, always honest. "Right."

"But, given what little I know about Claire, and the tremendous amount I know about you, I'm willing to bet she'll give you another chance. At least, to re-establish a friendship."

Austin didn't bother replying she wanted more than friendship. Rivka had known that before Austin did. "Hopefully. You know, I've had a lot of people telling me recently that I need to think about other people. I mean, consider things from their point of view, as you well know because you were one of the ones telling me. Put myself in my parents' shoes. Jeremy tells me to put myself in my birthmother's shoes. Try to consider things from Brian's point of view. Well, he basically told me that one himself. And I've tried. I really have. My point is, Claire really is one person who deserved that effort, that kind of consideration, and it never even occurred to me to try."

"I'm not quite following. What didn't occur to you?"

"Well, basically what you said to me on Mitzvah day, right? Try to see where's she's coming from, and be mindful of my own actions, I guess."

"All I meant was that the two of you should talk. It seemed like maybe you were waiting for her to do something, or she was waiting for you to give her a sign. Honestly, I probably should've stayed out of it. I thought I saw potential."

"And you were being a Jewish matchmaker?"

Rivka laughed. "Something like that. I should stick to what I'm good at, huh? Anyway, I was encouraging you to talk to her about how you feel."

Austin slumped into the bench. "Yeah. I'm not really good at that. Plus, with everything going on, I wasn't sure what I felt. Stupid, huh? Seems like it would be black and white."

"It's pretty much never black and white," Rivka responded. "Anyway, it seems to me that both of you are responsible for the myriad of misunderstandings that has occurred. The onus isn't entirely on you to fix it. Claire likely knows that too. But speaking of other things going on, how are the other things going?"

"I miss talking to Mom. I know I can call her, but I don't want to pretend none of this happened. I'm not sure what to do, with graduation coming up in a couple of weeks. Not a solicitation for advice, by the way. Not that I don't appreciate your advice. I need to think about it on my own."

"Sure."

"David's gonna wonder what's taking you so long."

"You're right. Let me text him."

While Rivka was doing that, Austin glanced at her own phone and noticed it was quarter to four. Four. Didn't she have something planned at four? She jumped to her feet. "Shit, Rivka. I totally forgot!"

"What?"

"My mom. My other mom, I mean. I told her I'd call her at four today. Obviously not gonna make it home in time."

"Wait, you're talking to your birth mom?" Rivka gawked at her. "I didn't even know you found her."

Austin stared at her. How long had it been since they talked about this? "Yeah. I sent her an email last week. She wrote back and told me I had the wrong person. Then she wrote back Friday and apologized and admitted she was the right person. And we agreed to talk today."

"Wow. That's a lot." Rivka forcefully exhaled a breath and leaned back, hands rubbing her thighs.

"I know, right? Wow. What am I going to say to her? I can't believe I forgot."

Rivka stood, digging her car keys from her pocket. "Come on. I'll give you a lift home."

"Thanks." Austin opened her messages, debating whether she should push off the call. Finally, she texted a request to Elise whether they could push the call back to five. Elise must've been staring at her phone because her agreement was instant. She trotted to catch up with Rivka.

~

19

Rivka got her home a couple of minutes before four, but Austin was glad she'd pushed back the call. She needed to get her head on straight, shake the panic that engulfed her when she realized the enormity of speaking to her birthmother for the first time. With each step she had taken to find and contact Elise, Austin focused on the logistics of how to do it and getting it done, of biding the angst of Elise's denial, then the relief at her admittance. At no stage had she actually considered the end game of having an actual conversation.

She filled a glass of water from the kitchen sink and sat down heavily on the sofa. She had so many questions pop in her head over the last three months, yet her mind currently drew up generalized, broad questions that would make this conversation sounds like an inquisition. Why? How? Should she try to write down more specific questions before making the call? She didn't want to sound scripted. That would come across as awkward.

Elise had to be nervous, too. It also hardly seemed likely they were going to engage in some kind of brusque Q & A session. She was overthinking this. As usual. She'd call. They'd talk. It'd be fine.

She refilled her glass and started to drink. No, what if she had to go the bathroom in the middle of their conversation? She wasn't one of those that could keep yapping while on the toilet. She set the glass down on the table, careful not to let it drop from her sweaty hands. She was going to need a sweatband if she couldn't get her nerves under control. She glanced at her phone. Twenty minutes to go.

She needed to find her bluetooth earpiece. Last she saw it was on her change bowl. She trotted into her bedroom and looked. It was there, thank God. No doubt she'd drop her phone if she tried to hold it while talking and if she used speakerphone, she couldn't pace.

Fifteen minutes to go.

Austin sat on the couch. Stood. Walked over to the front porch doors, then back again. She took a small sip of water that turned into a slosh of liquid cascading over her chin, shirt, and floor, as well as down her windpipe, leading to a spasmodic coughing fit. She managed to get the glass safely on the table.

It was five o'clock by the time she got things cleaned up. She hardly had time to take a zen moment before dialing Elise. Her hands were still shaking.

Elise picked up on the first ring. "Hello?"

At the sound of her mother's voice, whatever fledgeling thoughts Austin had in her mind fled, leaving her to simply introduce herself, leading to an awkward silence.

"I'm sorry if I sound awkward." Austin finally said. "I'm not that comfortable with phones." The trembling that started in her hand when she dialed the phone worked its way through her arms, across her chest, down into her gut, flowing through her legs. Her body felt frail, weak, as she heard what sounded like a stifled laugh on the other end of the call.

"I'm not a fan either, to tell the truth. For something meant to connect people, it really seems to," Elise paused, clearing her throat. She chuckled slightly again. "Oh, I don't know."

"Emphasize the distance?" Austin supplied.

"Yes, exactly."

Standing in the kitchen, listening to the soft lilt of her stranger mother's voice, Austin felt the distance, not just in miles, but in years and memories not shared, a thousand moments spent unaware. Of course, Elise had not been unaware. What must it have been like, living each day, with that knowingness of her being out there? Could she feel the presence of her? Austin's thoughts were a knotted handful of partially formed ideas, wonderings, questions. She thought of the ever-questioning internal voice haunting her, a constant companion all these years, always seeking answers, never satisfied. Even when she gave it the whole damn universe to peek into and study and explore, that voice still questioned, still wanted more to fill the deeper void within her, undefined, unexplained until Jeremy shone a light on it. Was that her own unknown awareness of Elise?

"Are you still there?" Elise's voice cut through her ribbons of thought.

"Yes, sorry."

"What are you thinking?"

Austin searched her tone for impatience, but found only concern. Elise sounded like a mother. Not her mother, though. Her mother was quick to fill silences, anxious for the forward movement of conversation, the accomplishment of words exchanged, plans made, purposes met. Austin wiped at her watering eyes with the back of her free hand. To her own ear, her voice sounded compressed, "I wouldn't know where to start."

"Are you angry? I understand if you are."

"I'm not..." but Austin wanted to be honest and honestly, she was angry. She just wasn't sure about what or who or even why. "I guess I'm angry. Angry at this whole system, this business of adoption, maybe at you, definitely at my parents, and at the circumstances, but it's not, it doesn't..." Austin couldn't figure out what she was trying to say. The funny thing was Austin didn't feel angry, thinking about it now, perhaps because it was working out. Elise was on the phone with her, not denying her, not abandoning her to the unknowing void again.

"Austin? Are you alright?"

"No. I mean, I'm thinking. I'm fine."

Elise sighed. It felt like a caress along the side of Austin's head, as if Elise's hand were running through her hair. Austin pressed the phone harder to her ear, wishing Elise stood with her in the room so she could rest her head on her shoulder. Which was such an odd thought. She never did that with her own mom. Why would she feel that with a total stranger? Was it always going to be like this? Having an ongoing, internal comparison between her moms each time they talked? Suddenly, she felt exhausted, the weight of this conversation too much to bear on these wobbly legs. She made her way to the couch and sank down. As the physical weight lifted, another weight scarcely more bearable replaced it within her chest. Not anger, but ache, an ache so deep she felt gutted.

"Are you sure?"

Elise's voice made the ache bearable. Austin breathed deeply. "I just need a minute. I wasn't expecting, when I heard your voice, what I feel."

What did Elise feel, hearing her voice? Austin could still only detect concern, but what else was there? Did she feel this ache, too, that only shifted into abeyance when Austin spoke? What was that saying, only the ones who caused your pain have the power to heal you? Something like that, probably meant for lovers and broken hearts. But what's more heartbreaking than a mother and child separated? Would talking together bring healing, even if Austin wasn't sure exactly what hurt and where? Austin could not imagine the ache within her subsiding entirely; its immensity seemed, in fact, to grow as she imagined Elise with a phone to her ear, standing in a kitchen or living room or some unknown place 500 miles away. Whatever broke from their separation might heal, but there were missing pieces, gaps formed by that distance, those years and moments so that even in healing, the pain might diminish but never disappear. Austin felt her anger then, at that thought, but it was a vague anger at an even vaguer target.

"Why are you angry with your parents?"

Austin caught her breath. Jesus, of course Elise didn't know about how Austin found out about her. They haven't told each other anything. She needed to tell her, but felt strangely protective of her parents now. She didn't want Elise to think poorly of them. "I wasn't told I was adopted. I found out when I accidentally got," (she was sticking with that lie), "my original birth certificate instead of the amended one."

"Oh. I see." It sounded like Elise, too, was attempting to be careful with her tone. "I imagine that must have been very difficult for you."

"It's been difficult for all of us, honestly."

"When did you find out?"

"Two months ago."

Another sharp intake of breath. "Wow."

"Yeah." Austin straightened her posture. She was strong enough for this, strong enough to be truthful and hear the truth. "I have a question. Why did you lie in your first email? Why did you say I had the wrong person?"

Another sigh, this one felt to Austin like a hand withdrawn, a back turned to her. "I suppose you've discovered, since you found me on Facebook, that I'm married. I met Steve two years after you were born. We married a year after that. I didn't tell him. I never told him anything about it, until a few days ago."

"Why? Were you ashamed? Afraid to tell him?" Should Austin be spewing out assumptions? Probably not.

"No, I wasn't afraid. I wasn't ashamed either," Elise added fiercely, as if to impress it upon her. Austin waited silently until Elise continued, "I just couldn't think on it, couldn't bear it. If I told him, it would be this real thing I had done. It would exist outside of me because he would know and might want to talk about it. I didn't want to talk about it. I wanted to move on."

Austin took in her words, rolled them over in her mind, and wondered about her being 'a real thing.' What did that mean? And why didn't she do an open adoption, if it pained her so much. From what she read, weren't they pretty common starting in the early nineties? She didn't ask that, though, caught instead by Elise's last words. "And did you? Move on?"

She knew Elise would detect her undercurrent of anger there and she did, answering in a calm, measured voice. "No. It's a ridiculous notion, don't you think?"

"I don't know." Austin could hear petulance in her voice yet didn't restrain it. "I'm not the one who said it."

When Elise spoke next, she sounded almost relieved, as if manners could now give way to honesty. "Well, I said it, wanted it even, but couldn't do it. I doubt such a thing is possible. As the years went by, I thought of you often. At first, I tried not to. I would keep myself busy, going back to school, doing volunteer work. There were days, one day in particular, your birthday, that every year I would plan on being busy from dawn until I couldn't keep my eyes open at night. Those were the hardest days."

Austin could not respond, remembering how she had

spent those days, images of cupcakes and party hats, ice cream cakes and brightly wrapped presents flooding her mind. Even now, knowing what she knew about the secrets and lies surrounding the day she was born, she could not feel the deceit in those celebrations, in her parents' genuine delight at her six-year old self eagerly unwrapping her first real pair of ice skates, her nine-year old little girl squeal of excitement over going to the big ice skating rink that took an hour to get to from their home, or even her 19-year old teen-self hugging her mom in gratitude for the tickets to a Paramore Concert. On all of those birthdays, every single one, three states away, there was this woman—Elise—hurrying through the day, wanting it to be over and done with so she didn't have to think, didn't have to feel. "How awful," she finally said.

"I didn't tell you to make you feel bad. I wanted you to know you were, are, always in my thoughts."

It was a strange notion to think about, that she had been in Elise's mind all these years without Austin even knowing she existed. It made Austin feel like she had let Elise down, not being able to tell her the same. "Was he mad?"

"Who?"

"Steve."

"He was, is still, upset. I don't blame him, of course. I should have told him."

"It seems like it would've been a hard thing." Feeling more stable, Austin stood and started pacing along the living room wall, tracing a finger along the cracking paint.

"I had just done something much harder."

"My parents should have told me," Austin said abruptly.

Elise said nothing for a moment. When she spoke, Austin could hear, in her slow response, how carefully she was choosing her tone, her words. "I suppose they were doing what they thought best."

Austin echoed what she said to her mom at lunch. "Best for who? Whom. Whatever."

"I can't answer that."

"Well, I asked them and their answer, it wasn't good enough. I should've been told. Do you know what it's like suddenly finding out that everything you've ever known about your life is a goddamn lie?"

Elise didn't admonish her for cursing, only said softly, "They love you."

"Don't defend them! For God's sake." Austin leaned her forehead against the cool wall. "I'm sorry. I'm still dealing with...that stuff, I guess."

"I know." She sounded tired. Almost as tired as Austin felt.

"I'm sorry. You're being all mature and I'm throwing tantrums. I know you're dealing with this too. I know that. I'm trying."

"Yes, I am. But, you can stop saying you're sorry. Of all the people involved, you're the only one who had no voice, no choice in what was done. You have some right to be angry. Also," here she sounded a little more cautious, "while I don't want to come between you and your parents, I want you to know, that's not what I would've chosen for you, keeping your adoption a secret."

Again, Austin thought of how open adoption would have solved all of these problems. But she had another pressing curiosity. "Can you tell me about my birthfather?"

There was a long silence. "I will, but not today," she said finally.

"That's a pretty odd answer."

"It's complicated."

"All of this is complicated. I can handle it. No offense, but that's a bullshit excuse." Austin scuffed her toe against the base of the wall, scraping off little flakes of white paint.

"Yeah? Well, it's honest." Elise paused for a moment.

Austin wondered if she was waiting for permission from her dad. Then, she spoke again, "You're right. It is, but it's just not something I'm prepared to discuss right now. We'll table that conversation for another time, I promise. Can you accept that for now?"

"Yeah." Austin really needed to temper herself.

"So, we can talk again? Soon, I hope?"

For the first time, Austin heard uncertainty creep into Elise's voice. It almost made her smile with relief. "Yeah, that'd be great."

"And, Austin, you can call me anytime. I mean it. Anytime."

"Okay."

"I was also wondering, and it's okay if you don't want to, if you would send me some pictures?"

Until hearing the nervousness in her voice as she said those words, Austin hadn't realized that Elise was just as off-kilter during their conversation as she was. She supposed the additional twenty years of living allowed Elise to cover it better, but it made Austin feel better, knowing the anxiety of this impacted them both. "I don't have very many, but I'm sure I have some. Did you want current or old ones?"

"Any," Elise answered quickly. "Although I would love to see some pictures of you when you were young."

"I'll see what I can find."

"Thanks."

They chatted another minute or so before hanging up with promises to talk again soon.

~

20

Austin replayed the conversation with Elise over and over again as she went through the motions of finishing the final week of classes before final exams began. Rivka had called and they met for coffee on Tuesday. Austin recounted the bulk of the conversation to her, with the caveat of Rivka not repeating any of it to her mom. At some point, she hoped she'd get to the point where they could discuss Austin's birthfamily, but right now, she figured her mom would probably respond to anything she heard with a big dose of defensiveness. She didn't want to rub it in her face. She could at least be sensitive to that.

Gil called her Friday afternoon in an absolute panic. Austin couldn't understand most of what he said, but she got the gist of it. He had forgotten to get a key shot with the rover. Could she and Claire save his ass by meeting him in the morning to shoot it. She told him it was fine with her, but he needed to call Claire to check with her. He hung up in the middle of his own 'thank you' in his haste. He texted her three minutes later to tell her it was on for eight the following morning at the river.

Austin would've loved to call Claire herself, but wasn't sure she'd pick up if she saw Austin's name. They hadn't communicated at all in the week since Claire left her apartment Saturday night. Not that Austin didn't consider calling at least once a day. She wasn't sure she owed an apology for anything she said, exactly. She still felt an insecurity that Claire had focused her attention on her mostly because Austin was a flailing fish on a carpet, and Claire couldn't resist a rescue. She did owe an apology for how she treated her over the last couple of weeks though. She had no excuse for ignoring her, for shutting down and shutting her out. It wasn't that she was too proud to apologize. She just wasn't sure how to do it so that Claire knew she meant it.

True, too, she felt nervous. Now that she willingly acknowledged that there was a depth of feeling involved with Claire, she wasn't sure she wanted to expose herself. She still had no clear idea of what Claire felt toward her, if anything, after all this. It seemed remarkable that this might mark the first time she ever actually felt the fear of rejection. She longed for her laissez-faire attitude back. But that was cowardly, evidence of being passive, exactly what Claire had accused her of.

Claire hadn't reached out to her either, though. Was she waiting for Austin to do it, to prove some kind of commitment to save their friendship, or whatever it was, or could be? Or was Claire just done?

She didn't have to call Rivka to know the advice she'd give. Clean your own house, she'd say. You can't do anything about what's in hers. It was good advice. She'd have to thank her for it later.

***

Saturday morning had gone as well as Austin thought it might, which was somewhere between an uncomfortable mess and complete disaster. Of course, she might be over-angsting on it, she thought as she drove home. Claire had been in a terrible rush from the moment she'd arrived, but whether it was to minimize time spent with Austin or to ensure she could get to work on time, Austin wasn't clear.

They spoke little as Gil directed them on the shots he needed. Then, as they were wrapping up, Gil mentioned he was hosting a showing for cast and crew Friday night at eight. Austin glanced at Claire to see if she was interested in going but, much to her disappointment, Claire apologetically declined, mentioning she would be out of town all week.

That news was both a surprise and a let-down. Austin only had one final exam on Wednesday. Her other final grades were predicated on papers and projects that were culminations of a semester's worth of work. She'd hoped to ask Claire for dinner that night to try and repair the rift between them.

She waited for a chance to speak with Claire alone, but when they finished, Gil walked her to her car. She tagged behind and finally spoke up as Claire was starting her car, asking Gil to give them a moment. He trotted to his car, perhaps perplexed but happy to have his footage. Claire had sat there, engine idling, waiting for Austin to speak. Everything Austin had rehearsed in her head over the last twenty-four hours flew from her mind. Finally, Austin simply said, "I'm sorry, Claire. I've behaved badly. I miss you. What can I do?"

Claire said nothing for a moment. Austin waited, resisting the temptation to fill the space with words. She'd said exactly what she meant. The moment stretched on.

Then, Claire said, "I need a favor, if you can do it."

Elated, Austin nodded. "Sure. You bet."

"You don't even know what it is." Claire offered a genuine laugh, flooding Austin with warmth. "I'll swing by Monday morning at eight, if you'll be there?"

"Yes," Austin answered.

Claire said nothing more. She waved and pulled out of the

lot, leaving Austin full of dissatisfaction and hope. Austin's trip to Paris at the end of June now felt like a deadline, like she had a few scant weeks to repair their relationship, or the opportunity would be lost.

She arrived home at the same time the postman arrived. He was a stickler, though, so she didn't bother asking for her mail, though she saw him fold a tantalizing manila envelope in half and slip into her box. Last time she'd asked, he'd looked at her like she had two heads, and then mumbled that she'd have to wait. This time, she said hello (no answer) as she entered her apartment, only to pop out again the moment she heard the lobby door shut.

The envelope was from Elise. A carefully placed sticker to the right of her address read 'Do Not Bend.' Evidently more of a quaint suggestion to the mailman than a firm instruction. True, it wouldn't have fit unfolded but, really, he could've just handed it to her. She sliced open the top with her penknife and slid out several sheets of handwritten stationery, along with a thin stack of photographs. Excited, she settled onto the couch to read.

The first thing she noticed was how different Elise's handwriting was from her own. Unless she put great care into it, Austin's handwriting slanted across the page like wind-driven rain surrounding a tornado, lines angled in every direction. Rarely would a word of more than one syllable be written in its entirety, making pretty much everything she wrote illegible to anyone but herself, and sometimes not even then.

Then again, Elise likely put some thought and effort into ensuring her letter would be legible, make a good impression as it were. Her script was even along the unlined paper, with a consistent slant to the right. Every letter was clearly constructed, as if Elise wanted to make each word and its intended meaning as clear as possible.

The enclosed pictures were mostly of Elise at various ages, including one where she was eight years old that made Austin catch her breath, so similar did Austin look like her at that age. There was one photograph of a young man, wearing jeans, blazer, and an off-white button-down. He sported his sandy blond hair long enough to brush the top of his collar. Austin wondered if he was perhaps Elise's brother, but couldn't spot any familial resemblance, either to Elise or herself, so she was shocked when she saw the name Elise had written on the back of the picture. Bill Hargrave.

This man was her father? She studied the man in the picture, wishing it was digital so she could zoom in. She couldn't be sure, but his eyes looked green, light-colored in any case, and much more almond-shaped than her own. His face was round, despite a well-defined jawline. Fairly good-looking, she supposed, though he'd look better smiling. He didn't look unhappy either, more like a deer in headlights. He held a soft, brown leather briefcase in his left hand. She flipped the picture over again. Elise had provided some context: First day as PhD candidate of Mathematics at GMU!! 8/21/1995.

Math, huh? Well, she may not have gotten his looks, but she must've inherited his love, or at least his ability, with numbers. Elise had mentioned his name when they talked the other day. She could've looked it up, searched for more information on him. Truthfully, though, he'd only been a passing thought. Now, faced with his reality, she wondered had he known Elise was pregnant? If not, did he know now? Was that why Elise needed a few days before sharing more details about him?

Stupid to speculate, Austin realized. She returned to Elise's letter, ignoring the graceful curves of handwriting to better focus on the content. It was apparent, after Austin read the first few paragraphs, that Elise needed the extra time not to contact her birthfather, but to gather the courage to tell the tale of a clearly disastrous and dangerous marriage. She read through the whole letter quickly, then again, more slowly.

Her father was an alcoholic and hid it well the first few years. They met when Elise was in her second year of grad school, and he was a few months shy of getting his PhD. His drinking worsened as he was promoted to full professor and trying to meet the standards that would allow him to get tenure. Elise learned not to confront him when he'd been drinking, as he was quick to anger and, on occasion, violence, though it had not yet been directed at her. He was contrite when not drinking, but that became fewer and far between. By the time Elise realized she was pregnant (and here, Austin couldn't help but wonder if the circumstances leading to her being pregnant were actually consensual), Bill had entered, and been kicked out of, rehab twice. He'd lost his position at GMU and was teaching part-time at a local community college, all of which naturally spurred his drinking more.

Elise had already made the decision to leave him when the police called her late one night. Bill had been in a car accident. No, not been in, caused an accident, caused the death of a mother and her daughter. He'd not only been drunk, he was drinking from a bottle of whiskey at the time of the accident. Elise filed for divorce while he was in jail, awaiting trial for aggravated vehicular manslaughter. She didn't look back as he was convicted and sentenced to fifteen years in prison. She never bothered to find out what prison he was in, communicating with him only through her lawyer to have the divorce finalized. He had her lawyer deliver a handwritten letter to her, along with the finalized divorce papers. She'd burned it. As a result of her success in cleaving the past from her (and Austin had some questions over whether her own removal from Elise's body and life was a part of that), she had no idea where he might be now, and no intention of finding out. She said she'd understand if Austin wanted to find him, but he did not know about her.

In short, Elise seemed to be telling her to proceed with extreme caution. Point taken. She placed the letter on the coffee table and dropped back on the couch. It was a lot to take in, a lot more of a story than what she was expecting, not that she had pondered it in depth. She'd assumed a broken marriage, perhaps an acrimonious divorce, a single mother who couldn't afford to raise a child. She'd thought her father might be just a guy who married too young, or wasn't a fan of monogamy. She'd also considered her father might be an asshole, or a deadbeat. She hadn't considered her father might be a criminal and, if not a murderer legally speaking, someone still responsible for killing two human beings.

Austin didn't know much about alcoholism, no reason she would, given both her parents' ascetic drinking habits. She'd never seen the appeal of drinking and, after the events of last Saturday night, that was unlikely to change. The thought of alcohol still made her feel queasy. She did, however, recall reading about a possible genetic predisposition toward alcoholism, or was it addiction in general? She couldn't remember. In any case, something to bear in mind but not dwell on, she decided.

More importantly, given what Elise wrote, did she really want to track down her birthfather? Invite him into her life by finding him, communicating with him? If she did find him, he'd likely be significantly changed from when Elise knew him, but changed in what way? She felt his actions to be despicable, couldn't shake the disgust even when she tried to mitigate it by reasoning that alcoholism was a disease. She hadn't grown up with him as her father. There was no love lost. She could choose to learn about him, but not contact him. Not let him know she existed.

Then, she felt guilty for judging him without even trying to learn about him. She was curious about him, his past, his story. Maybe she could try to find out about him before making a decision. She had his name and, with Elise's story, knew the approximate time period of his accident. There might be a news story, something to shed light on him.

Her search skills had improved exponentially over the last couple of months. It didn't take long to find references to a few articles of the accident. Unfortunately, all of the articles were gated behind the paywall for a newspaper archive service. She really didn't want to pay for each article, and it wasn't worth signing up for a monthly subscription. The picture Elise sent also made it easier to eliminate most of the social media accounts that popped up as well.

On the fourth page of the Google search results, she saw a header for an obituary that made her heart stop. Again, the piece was hidden behind a paywall and what little preview she could see didn't make it clear if the obituary was for her father, or that he was just mentioned in the text. Damn it, his being dead was another outcome she forgot to think about. For all the musing she had done about Elise, she had spared no thought for her father. The idea he could be dead, however, didn't generate the same lurch in her stomach or ache in her chest when she'd considered the possibility for her mother. Was it unfair, this greater interest in birthmothers? It hadn't escaped her notice that, on the registry boards, almost all the adoptees posted search requests for birthmothers. On occasion, she saw requests for birth families, but she couldn't recall more than a few instances of someone specifically seeking out a birthfather, and those likely were because the adoptee had already found their birthmother.

It made sense, she thought. Women were the ones who carried the baby within them for nine months. Even Austin, not given to sentimentality, believed that time had to have forged some type of bond, some form of relationship, between baby and mother that the father simply wasn't privy to. There were tons of articles on that sort of thing, but what she was trying to put her finger on was a little more ethereal, ineffable. There were studies done on the psychological impacts of infants being separated from their mothers. She had seen references to them on some of the book flaps when she was searching out books on the adoption experience. She hadn't read any of them, though, thinking it might be too depressing. Now that she'd found Elise, though, and it had been a positive experience, so far, maybe she would read up on it. It was that bond, she reasoned, that adoptees cared more about finding their mothers than fathers.

She may not feel that same depth of anxiety and fear over the fate of her father, but somehow that lack made her curiosity all the stronger. She took another look at the search results. Although she couldn't access the articles, she did get the name of the newspaper that had published them. A little more digging and she was able to find a library in Falls Church that kept archived copies of the newspaper. She checked out the library's website, excited to discover they had digitized much of their local history reference materials. Thrill turned to disappointment when the items she searched for were unavailable online. They were, however, available at the library, and it was free. The library opened at one o'clock on Sundays. It looked like she'd be taking a road trip tomorrow to her hometown.

***

It rained for the entire two-hour drive up to Northern Virginia. Austin spent the trip, chastising herself the entire time for procrastinating on replacing her windshield wipers. The car, her mom's 2010 Honda Accord, was convenient to have, but Austin so often preferred to walk that she frequently neglected the minor maintenance issues as they arose. The car was due for an oil change in a few weeks, and she'd put off replacing the wipers until then. She regretted it now as she squinted to see through the thin layer of water smeared across the windshield.

The rain tapered off, of course, as she pulled into the library parking lot. She had a few minutes before the library opened, so she flipped through her emails. Her mom had written to confirm plans for graduation day. That reminded her that even though Brian said he'd join them for lunch, the two of them hadn't spoken at all since their argument the previous Saturday. They'd rarely fought, given their significant age difference, and he wasn't one to hold a grudge, so it was unusual, this avoidance. She'd always felt Brian was the best brother in the world when she was growing up, and not much had changed since then. The silence between them gnawed at her.

She also couldn't help realizing she was twenty minutes from her mom's house. She could stop by for a few minutes. Not long enough for an argument to break out. Just a quick hello, something to thaw the ice. Going cold turkey on shutting her mom out really sucked. Maybe that's how healing could happen. Not through a lengthy avoidance but with well-spaced touchpoints. She didn't want to remain estranged from her parents, no matter how angry she might still be.

She quickly texted her mom before she lost her nerve, mentioning she could stop by around three if her mom was going to be home.

Her mom agreed, following up with a tricky question. What was Austin doing in town? Austin had walked right into that landmine. What could she say that wouldn't make her mom immediately feel defensive? It was after one and Austin was eager to get into the library. She glanced around her car and saw a bag that held some extra sensors and

Roomba pieces she had collected for her rover. She texted her mom that she was in town for emergency parts for her robotics final projects. Her mom probably wouldn't ask for specifics, but if she did, Austin had the bag for proof. Yeah, it was a lie, but for the greater goal of peace and it just didn't bother her much at all.

The library was a beautiful stone building, with several arches over the entryway. She made her way to the reference room, where she asked a librarian about the local history room. Much to her dismay, the room was available on an appointment-only basis as it was run by local historian volunteers. She lucked out though, as a volunteer arrived just as Austin was asking about the room. The volunteer, who introduced herself as Bhavna, agreed to let her use the room, but only for an hour because she had to leave right at two.

Austin gratefully followed her into the room. She admitted, apologetically, that she'd never been to this library before so she had no idea where to start. She pulled up the webpage that held the references for the articles she wanted to read. Bhavna had a stack of newspapers in front of her within five minutes.

"I can only narrow it down to the month for each of the articles," she explained. "The first two articles will be in the left stack. The third one in the right stack. And I'm fairly certain we have the obituary on microfiche. I can pull up the week, but you'll have to search through it."

"Thank you so much," Austin exclaimed. She watched Bhavna pull open a drawer and pluck out what looked like several translucent sheets of paper. That must be microfiche. Bhavna set the sheets next to a small machine that looked like a combo screen-projector-slash-monitor. Austin wanted to see the obituary first, so she stepped over to the machine. She sat and picked up a sheet. There was a thick glass plate and a knob handle on the side. Clearly, the sheet was supposed to go between the two plates, but Austin couldn't quite figure out how to open them.

Bhavna stepped over and pulled the knob toward Austin. The glass plates opened in a 'v'. Austin slid the sheet in. "Thanks. I've never used one of these before."

"They are a bit old school. We're trying to digitize these as well, but it takes significant time." Bhavna turned on the machine and demonstrated how to move the plate around so Austin could read everything on the sheet.

"Thanks again."

The obituary wasn't on the first two sheets, but Austin hit pay dirt on the third one. She zoomed in as the print was somewhat grainy.

Richard Hargrave

Birth: June 7, 1970
Death: Nov. 16, 2018

Mr. Richard Hargrave, age 48 of Pueblo, Colorado, passed away Wednesday, November 16, 2018 in the Spruce Community Hospice Home in Colorado Springs, after a brief illness. He hailed originally from Falls Church, Virginia, but had made Pueblo his home for the past 11 years.

Mr. Hargrave was a Finance teacher with the Pueblo Adult Continuing Education Services (PACES) program, as well as a senior consultant for Vestas Blades Americas. He was preceded in death by his father, Edward Hargrave Sr.

Mr. Hargrave was survived by his wife, Donna Hargrave (née Pinter); one daughter, Anne Marie Hargrave; brother, Edward, all of Pueblo; and his mother, Janice. A memorial service will be held this Saturday, at the New Hope Baptist church in Pueblo. In lieu of flowers, memorial contributions may be made to the American Cancer Society.

She read through it once. So, her father had passed away. That took one hard decision away from her, leaving her with several others. She needed to print this. So much information to take in from a few short paragraphs. She found a little print icon and clicked it. She listened, but didn't hear the whir of any printer, couldn't actually spot a printer anywhere in the room. "Is there a way to print off these?"

Bhavna nodded and turned, flipping on a printer behind her. "It's ten cents a copy," she mentioned, almost apologetically.

Austin nodded as Bhavna handed her the page the printer just spit out. The obit was off-center, with several words of each sentence cut off along the right edge. She looked at the screen again and repositioned the slide, hitting print again. This time, the copy looked legible.

She glanced over it again. Colorado. What made him decide to move there? His brother? Had he been there first? He had remarried, which made her feel oddly relieved. And she had a sister! A half-sister, but still. How old was she? The article didn't say. Austin tried to calculate it, but there were a lot of missing variables. She needed more information. She checked her phone. One-thirty. She'd have to ponder all of these questions later and just stick to tracking down the information right now.

It took another laborious twenty minutes to go through the daily newspapers and find the other three articles. She made copies of all of these articles, as well, noting the print date on the back of each one before sliding them into an empty folder she brought. With five minutes to spare, Austin thanked Bhavna profusely and donated ten dollars to the cause and for the print copies.

She hurried to her car, clutching the folder, fingers white

and aching as she pinched the open side tightly shut. Irrational fears of the slight breeze blowing the sheets away consumed her until she was safely in the car with the folder. Immediately, she used her scanner app to secure digital copies of the articles, and only then did she relax. She found a paperclip in her console and used it to clip shut the folder before setting it on the floor in front of the back seat.

She really wanted to read the articles, of which she'd only seen the headlines and the first couple of sentences to ensure they were what she thought. She had no time, though. She'd told her mom she'd be over between two-thirty and three, and it was a solid twenty-minute drive if traffic was light. It'd be better to wait, anyway, she reasoned, pulling out of the lot. She should read them tonight, in the privacy of her home, with plenty of time and space to consider whatever information she learned. If she thought about it too much now, she'd probably feel distracted, impatient to get back to it, when with her mom and her mom would know, would ask questions.

The gloomy morning had given way to sunshine while she was in the library, but Austin grumpily realized she'd left her sunglasses at home. There was a drugstore on the way to her mom's. She'd have to stop to pick up a pair of cheapies. Her mom had always kept an extra pair in the car. Austin ought to do the same.

~

21

It felt odd, like it did every time she drove through her childhood neighborhood. It had changed so much she would hardly recognize it were it not for the street names that remained the same. Small, one- or two-story mom-and-pop shops had slowly given way to multi-story corporate buildings. The kind with a few upscale retail shops on the mezzanine level, along with a food court with trendy fast food that sold spinach wraps and couscous veggie bowls. Traffic lights had popped up on every other corner, turning ten-minute drives into 25-minute exercises of frustration.

The residential streets had also transformed grotesquely, Austin thought, as she took a right into a residential area. The once-modest, two-story (three if you counted the attic) homes now boasted three or four stories, not including the attic or basement. With little space to expand sideways or backwards (though people did that too), they built up, the extra height creating disproportionate monstrosities. Even the unattached garages at the end of each driveway were built up into mini-houses. The tall maple, magnolia, and oak trees had been removed, replaced by smaller, aesthetically pleasing dogwoods and birch trees.

Her parents had bought their home in the late eighties,

when the area was solidly middle-class. Over the years, as D.C. spread its fingers into Northern Virginia and the surrounding Maryland suburbs, these neighborhoods had shifted to affluent, to now verging on the edge of obscenely wealthy. Or at least obscene expression of wealth, as her mom recently described it. They'd paid off their mortgage early, which was the only reason her mom could still afford to live here. She'd kept the house in meticulous condition over the years, so much so after Austin left for college that the house hardly looked lived in at all. Her mom told her she was hoping for a tidy windfall when she sold it after her eventual retirement. Austin couldn't imagine her mom retired, though. The woman was a tireless workaholic. How in the world would she fill her time?

Austin came to a complete stop before turning right onto her mother's street. Her neighborhood was an incorporated township and made most of its revenue through traffic stops. She smiled as she passed the playground next to the Adler Jewish Community Center. She'd spent a great deal of time there growing up, with it being just a half-mile from her house. They had after-school programs, as well as summer day camp. She'd been a camper for several years, then a counselor while in high school. That was her first real job. If she never drank that godawful bug juice again, it would be too soon.

On a whim, Austin pulled into the parking lot of the center, which sat on a corner lot, with the front doors facing the intersection. The community center wasn't just for children. It also housed a work-out room, a small library with internet access, and hosted senior dances and bingo night. It opened at ten daily, but there were only two cars in the lot this afternoon. She parked the car, intending to take a quick walk-through of the place to indulge her nostalgic hankering for the familiar.

She first noticed an older man, with a thick shock of gray hair, standing in front of the brick wall to the right of the doors, a cleaning bucket at his feet. He was scrubbing the wall vigorously. At first, Austin couldn't see what he was trying to clean, but as she stepped from the car and walked closer, it became clear. What she'd assumed was a benign design motif along the wall she'd noticed out of the corner of her eye was, in fact, a line of white spray-painted swastikas. There were four to the right of the doors, and four to the left. The sight, once recognized, compressed her chest, robbing her lungs of air. Her skin felt set afire, burning from her face to her fingertips while a high-pitched ringing grew in her ears. She put her hands on hips, leaning over a bit to capture a breath, which finally came in as a gulp only to leave as a gasp.

The man at the wall turned around as Austin straightened. He took an uncertain step toward her. "Can I help you?"

"Shalom Aleichem," Austin replied, and what she really meant by it was 'don't fear me' and 'I'm one of you' and 'you're not alone.' She noticed the man relax as she resumed walking toward him, hand outstretched.

"Aleichem shalom," he responded, shaking her hand. "I'm Daniel, the center's director."

"Austin." She gestured at the building. "This is appalling." An insufficient word, but short of letting loose a stream of expletives, another word didn't come quickly to mind.

"Are you new to the area? I don't think I've seen you before."

"I grew up here. Visiting from college down in Richmond. I spent a lot of time here when I was younger." She couldn't stop staring at the swastikas. "Let me help you clean this up."

"That'd be great. I'd appreciate it tremendously."

Daniel directed her to find Martha, who could provide her with a brush and can of graffiti cleaner spray. He'd gone out and bought quite a few cans, just in case this happened again.

Martha, a plump tiny lady with obviously dyed blonde hair, teared up and dabbed at her eyes with a tissue when Austin appeared in the office doorway, asking after cleaning supplies. She was recently retired, she told Austin as she led her down the hallway to a small supply room. She'd thought it'd be nice to work part-time and see the children every day. Her own daughter's family had relocated to Arizona the previous fall, and Martha missed her grandchildren something awful.

Austin filled the cleaning bucket with water from the deep basin in the room, while Martha continued talking. "After today, I'm thinking to move to Arizona myself. When I came in the morning and saw those awful things, I had half a mind to go right back home and start packing. But it doesn't matter where we are, does it? They find us just the same. They hate us just the same. It's so frightening."

Austin thought Martha might burst into tears, but she merely wiped again at her eyes. She took the scrub brush from Martha's shaking hand. The poor woman was still afraid. Austin dropped the brush in the bucket and set it on the ground. She placed a light hand on Martha's arm. "It'll be alright, Martha. The ones who did this were cowards. You know that. They did this to make us afraid."

"I know you're right. But still, what's next? A coward with a gun when all the kids are here after school?"

Austin didn't know what else to say. Rivka would know, but she was no Rivka. Instead, she said nothing but patted her arm again and thanked her for the supplies.

She stopped in the hallway to text her mom about where she was and why she was going to be arriving late. She waited a couple of minutes but didn't receive a response.

Daniel had moved on to the first of the four swastikas on the left wall, so she started on the farthest one. She didn't feel up to making small talk. Daniel obviously wasn't much for talking either so they worked in silence. The brush and spray worked well enough, though Austin's forearms and shoulders ached with the effort. A pressure washer would have made the task easier but by the time she located a place to rent one and bring it back, they could probably have this mostly cleaned.

The assholes didn't even draw the damn things correctly. The one she was working on had left-oriented arms, while the one to her right better resembled a mutated spider. The hard work of cleaning paint from brick distracted her from the harder task of pondering the intent and impact of the hateful symbol itself. She didn't want to dwell on the who and why of it. Jewish people were often targets in America, just as they had been for centuries everywhere else in the world. These days, any member of any minority seemed to be a potential target for hate, for violence, and God help you if you were a member of more than one group. Of course, she never thought of herself as a victim. The lingering, lurking hate and fear harbored by others were simply facts of life, one she'd become as accustomed to as being the only girl in an engineering class.

This wasn't the first time Austin had seen the expression of raw anti-Semitism. Even Beth Israel had gotten a bomb threat the previous year. Rivka had actually fielded the phoned-in threat. The idiot had assumed there were services on a Sunday morning, not knowing that most synagogues held shabbat services on Saturday morning once the six-day workweek ended. Rivka had been the only one there. She'd told Austin she thought the likelihood of an actual bomb being planted seemed unlikely, but she didn't want to take chances. She'd hurried to her car, drove down the street, then called the police. No bomb had been found and, while police had pulled phone records, nothing had come of it. A couple of local news stations covered it, which was followed by another bomb threat the following weekend, again on Sunday. This time, Rivka had been prepared, using her cellphone to record the conversation. A couple of the TV news and radio stations played the audio and provided a hotline for tips for anyone who may have recognized the voice. Nothing panned out though. Then, a couple of months after that, someone shot the stained glass above the front door with a BB gun, leaving it peppered with tiny holes. On the surface, it could feel like no big deal. Hoaxes, pranks, no real harm done. You could also look at it, though, as someone who was testing the boundaries of police follow-up, of community reaction and protection, and working up the courage to do something bigger and much worse. Not knowing whether that could be the case could keep you up at night. Rivka said she didn't worry about it, so Austin worried about it for her.

A surge of anger went through her. She used it to scrub harder. The bristles buckled. The brush tumbled from her hands and her knuckles scraped along the bricks. "Damn it," she muttered, wiping away the loose skin and trickles of blood on her jeans. She heard a car pull into the lot. She turned around, astonished to see her mother getting out of the car, holding both a scrub brush and a pair of long bright green rubber cleaning gloves.

"I got your message, Austin, and thought I might help." She walked toward Austin, but turned her head to call out to Daniel. "Hello, Daniel. I see you've met my daughter. She told me you had some garbage to clean up."

Daniel glanced over and smiled broadly. "Kathy!"

Austin raised her eyebrows as he hurried over. Much to her surprise, Daniel gathered her mom in a quick hug, complete with a peck on the cheek. He then looked over at Austin. "I should've known. How many Austins can there be around here, right?"

Her mother gestured at the wall. "I think you had other things on your mind. This is a terrible thing, Daniel. Did you take pictures? Call the police?"

"Yes, and yes. As soon as I arrived." Daniel looked at the wall and took a deep breath. "Fortunately, it's coming off fairly easily. Martha's inside. She's just beside herself."

"I'm sure," her mother responded. "Why didn't you call me, Daniel?"

"I didn't want to trouble you."

Austin glanced between them as they talked. Something was going on here. How did her mom know Daniel? More intriguingly, how well did she know him? The easy camaraderie suggested it might be rather well.

After Daniel returned to his portion of the wall, Austin handed the can of cleaner to her mom and whispered, "How do you know him?"

Her mom sprayed the wall and started scrubbing. "My treadmill gave up the ghost in January. I started coming after work to use the one here."

"Oh. Well, you seem to be very comfortable with him." Austin didn't care if she sounded like she was fishing for information because that's absolutely what she was doing.

Her mom bent down to retrieve Austin's fallen brush. "Clean now. We'll chat later."

***

Austin readily agreed to her mother's suggestion that they have an early dinner at Taste of Rome, her family's go-to restaurant for every possible occasion—birthdays, graduations, promotions— as well as the once-monthly family dinner out. Her mom had suggested Austin park her car at the house and she could drive them to the restaurant, but Austin preferred the security of having her own getaway car. Austin also turned down sharing a bottle of wine. The idea of it made her stomach lurch and bile fill her mouth, not that she'd mention that to her mom. Plus, she needed to stay awake for the two-hour drive home. It was five-thirty now and she hoped to be on the road by seven.

"Why don't you spend the night," her mother asked, seemingly able to glean her intentions. "It won't take but a minute to put clean sheets on the spare bed."

Her mother sounded so hopeful it tempted Austin to say yes to make her happy. But Claire was coming over the next morning at eight. Austin planned to be there, come hell or high water. She wasn't going to tell her mom that either. Instead, she referenced her previous lie. "Can't, Mom. Emergency repair on my finals project, remember? The reason I'm up here? It's due Tuesday."

"Oh, right. What is the project? I so rarely hear the specifics."

"Because you say it makes your eyes cross," Austin responded. She explained her rover was a Mars' Curiosity replica and briefly described how she built it. "It's all on my Instagram account, Mom. If you ever want to see the step-by-step."

Her mom waved a hand. "Ugh. Being on Facebook is bad enough. Don't get me wrong, I love new technology, but social media is, to put it mildly, an utter waste of time."

Austin didn't bother arguing. She often felt the same way. The waiter came by to take their orders. Austin turned down an appetizer, mindful of the time and the dangers of a food coma impeding her drive. Both of them had ordered house salads with their entrees. As had always been their custom, Austin exchanged the olives in her salad for the tomatoes from her mother's plate. They spoke little until they finished the salads.

Her mother sipped from a glass of red wine. "It's so hard to make a glass last through a meal," she commented, smiling. "I wish you'd shared a bottle with me."

"Encouraging your child to drink before hitting the road. Nice." Austin knew her mother was trying hard to re-establish some of what they'd lost over the past couple of months. To her surprise, she didn't mind. In fact, she welcomed it. Anger drained her of so much energy and she wasn't up for being angry anymore today.

"It's rotten, what was done to the community center," her mother remarked, buttering a piece of sourdough bread.

"That's one word for it," Austin responded. "It shocked me. I'd never actually seen swastikas, you know, outside of newspaper articles and history books. I mean, I know these things happen. I'm not naive. It's so hard to understand. What drives a person, people, to do that? Is it a joke, some immature way for a stupid teenager to get a rise? Or is it exactly as it looks, a symbol to embody the hate someone feels for us, just being Jewish? I can't really wrap my mind around how it is to live that way."

"It reminds me of a poem by Adrienne Rich. I can't remember the name, or the title, but I remember this one stanza." Her mom took a sip of water. *"What grownups can't teach, children must learn. How do you teach a child what you won't believe? How do you say unfold, my flower, shine, my star, and we are hated, being what we are?"*

Austin felt her eyes water up. She quickly looked down at the table, cleared her throat. "Yeah. That pretty much sums it up. Bummer, though, isn't it?"

"Yes." Her mother snapped her fingers. "That does make me remember the title though. 'Eastern War Time.'"

Austin typed the name and title into her phone to look up later. "I don't remember anything like that happening while growing up here. Do you?"

Her mother thought a moment, then nodded. "I remember in the early nineties, maybe it was the mid-nineties, before your time, there were a series of vandalisms and arsons, but not just of synagogues. A number of predominantly Black churches, too. It was across the South, as I recall. Virginia, North and South Carolina, Georgia, Alabama, maybe Tennessee, I don't quite remember. I do remember it was talked about quite a bit in the community."

"The community? You mean the neighborhood?"

"The local Jewish community. We all tended to know each other, from synagogue or the Rosen deli or the community center."

Austin couldn't disguise her surprise. "I didn't think you were really part of the Jewish community."

"Because I don't go to synagogue? Austin, the Jewish community is much more than those who engage in public religious expression."

"I know that. We never talk about it, is all." Austin shrugged.

"True. And it's also true that I often don't give it much thought."

"Until something like this happens?"

"We do tend to band together when threatened." Her mom finished the last of her wine. The waiter came with their dishes. Her mom ordered another glass of wine and winked at Austin. "I don't have a two-hour drive home."

"No, you don't, Mom. Have at it. And, since we're kind of on the subject, how about you tell me about Daniel."

***

Austin awoke Monday morning, full of anticipation. She'd arrived home a little after nine the previous night, too tired to do anything but strip off her clothes and tumble into bed. She had felt more calm, more at peace with herself, than she had in weeks. She enjoyed being with her mom so much.

Claire had texted her during her drive home to confirm she could still stop by this morning about eight. Austin had pulled over to respond swiftly, lest Claire change her mind about asking Austin this favor, whatever it might be. Claire still had provided no hint as to what she needed from Austin.

Austin showered, dressed, snacked on a banana, and still had fifteen minutes to spare. She paced the front room, checking her phone every so often. Time flowed like molasses in winter. She remembered she'd left her folder with the articles in her car and decided to retrieve it. That would eat three minutes, at least.

It had rained the previous night, though the sky was now clear. Water droplets glistened on the leaves of oak trees and dogwoods. The pale morning sunlight cast long shadows in front of her apartment building. The birds were relentlessly loud. It was, Austin thought, a morning of promise. She rolled her eyes at her own sappiness, but the optimism remained.

She tossed the folder on the coffee table and resumed pacing. She thought she heard a car door shut. Then, another car door shut. Would Claire have brought someone? Austin resisted peeking out the curtains covering her porch doors. Just as she'd decided she imagined hearing the car doors, Austin finally heard the lobby door open, then a rustling and clanging before a knock on her door.

She waited several seconds, then called out, "Coming!" She took her time to walk to the door. "Hey."

Claire, dressed in a familiar faded gray t-shirt and blue jeans, hair pulled back in one of her messy, scraggily ponytails, smiled at her and Austin caught her breath. She gestured for Claire to enter, opened her mouth to speak, but heard a tiny 'mew' sound that silenced her. She glanced down. A small dark blue pet carrier sat at Claire's feet. She looked at Claire.

"Are you allergic to cats?" Claire asked. "I thought it'd be fun to surprise you, but I didn't even consider allergies. Let me know and I'll put him right back in the car."

Austin shook her head. "Not that I know of. You need me to kitten-sit?"

"If you can."

Austin opened the door wider. Claire picked up the carrier and came into the room. She set the carrier on Austin's work table, then stepped back into the lobby and returned with a stuffed plastic bag. Claire began unpacking items from the bag.

Austin bent down to look through the gate of the carrier. All she could see was a blanket, maybe two, bunched up and filling two-thirds of the interior space. She moved closer until her nose touched the metal. Two shiny eyes peered back at her from within the folds of fabric. "Oh. There you are."

She pulled back as the kitten emerged and pressed its impossibly tiny, black, fuzzy body lengthwise along the gate, emitting a rumbling purr. "Hello, little tiny," Austin whispered, instantly delighted. She pressed her index finger against the gate. The kitten turned and rubbed its cheek against it. She was just about to open the gate to pick it up when Claire cleared her throat.

"There's stuff I need to show you and you won't hear a thing if you're holding him."

"True enough." Austin straightened up. She glanced over the items on the table. There was an awful lot of stuff. "He? Name?"

"Bailey. He's three and a half weeks old." Claire held up a can with the letters KMR. "He's still eating milk-replacement formula. Now, he's learning how to lap it out of his saucer," Claire tapped the shallow dish, "But, he still gets it mostly over his face, chest and paws, rather than his stomach so you'll still need to bottle-feed him twice a day."

"Okay."

Austin must have looked terrified, because Claire patted

her shoulder. "No worries. I'll show you everything you need to know."

For the next half hour, standing over the kitchen sink, Claire did show her everything about feeding Bailey, including having Austin do each of the steps. There wasn't actually a bottle involved. Claire said she had an easier time using a plunger syringe with something called a miracle nipple.

"Fortunately," Claire said as she took the syringe from Austin and rinsed it out, "Bailey does know how to use the litter box, so you don't have to help him out with that."

Austin wasn't sure what helping Bailey out with that would actually entail, but she was certainly glad she didn't need to know. "Ok, so twice a day with the syringe, and when with the saucer?"

"Morning and night for the feedings. And I'd leave a saucer in with him in between feedings."

"So, in between the syringe feedings." Austin closed the Tupperware that held the formula they'd just mixed up and put it in the fridge. "Needs to be refrigerated, right?"

"Yep. Powder, too." Claire handed her the KMR can. "Also, I wrote everything down, times, amounts, heating." With a flourish, Claire pulled a folded sheet of paper from her back pocket. "It's typed. Take a look, see if you have questions."

Austin took the sheet of paper and glanced through it. It was pretty straightforward, but she lingered on it to buy a moment to think. Claire's mood was…interesting. Austin couldn't quite put her finger on it, but Claire seemed an odd cross between a seeming eagerness to re-establish their comfort level, offering up her usual easygoing approach, but combined with an uncertainty, as if she worried she was asking too much. All of this, of course, without any acknowledgment of the awkwardness that should, and did exist, between them. Austin couldn't quite bring herself to thank Claire for her help the previous Saturday, did not want to make any reference at all to her drunkenness. She could scarcely bring herself to think of that night, even when alone, so embarrassed was she at how Claire found her, squished between two bushes, basically passed out against the fence. Though she'd argue to this day that she was merely resting her eyes, and thinking about things. What things, she couldn't quite remember any more.

If they were to ignore this awkwardness, left it all unspoken to resume an easy rapport, they would likely never be more than friendly acquaintances in the long run. Of this, Austin was certain. However, she reasoned as she clipped Claire's instruction notes on the fridge, that didn't mean she had to jump into it right now. She needed to take it slow, take care of Bailey as requested—and honestly that didn't seem like much of a hardship—and maybe things would move organically toward a resolution. Great, she was channeling her mom again. She looked over at Claire, who was busy wiping at Bailey's face and paws.

"About the litter box, where? He's way too small to be running loose, right? Should I keep him in the bathroom? I can't keep him in that carrier. It's tiny!"

"No, yes, right! I forgot his crate. It's in my car. I'll go get it."

Austin followed behind her to the door. "Need help?"

"Nope. It's collapsible. Be right back." Claire handed Bailey to Austin and hurried off.

Austin held Bailey in one hand and rubbed her eyes with the other. Claire was a whirlwind. Austin couldn't get a handle on her at all. At least she could keep a grip on this tiny one, she thought, nuzzling Bailey's head. How had she never considered getting a kitten before?

Claire had everything ready in minutes, setting up the crate beneath her bedroom window, across from her bed.

Claire had laid out a towel first, so the metal wouldn't scratch the hardwood. The litter box went in, then a blanket, a round fluffy bed, and hand towel on the side for the saucer. Claire set a small bag of litter, a scoop, and a stack of small pine-green bags down to the side. "Biodegradable poop bags."

"Awesome." Austin nuzzled the kitten again, then set him on his pillow. He looked even tinier inside the cage. "I didn't even know they came that small."

"It's a crate for small dogs."

"Not the crate, silly. The kitten." Austin smiled. "I've never been around kittens or cats. My mom's a neat freak."

Austin walked Claire, who now seemed rather calm, back to the front door. Standing in the open doorway, Claire squinted at her and asked, "You really don't mind? It's a big ask. I shouldn't have sprung it on you."

"It's fine. I'm happy to do it. I think I might already be in love."

"Wait until a few feedings and poop cleanings, then decide on that." Claire turned to step out, hesitated, then turned back to face her. For a second, Austin thought she was going to hug her, but she seemed to reconsider. Austin opened the lobby door for her, grasping Claire's shoulder briefly. "So, Saturday?"

Claire grinned. "Yeah. I know you have graduation, so late Saturday. And I'll call you mid-week or so, to check in."

"Great."

"And, congrats, you know, on the graduation, too."

"Thanks." Austin wished she knew what to say to make this less awkward, even though it wasn't awkward in a horrible way. Nothing came to her. But Claire honked as she pulled away from the curb, which warmed Austin as she waved. Awkward, yeah. Promising, though, too.

~

22

The first time she fed Bailey on Monday evening, it took over an hour. Austin was surprised by the strength of his tiny body squirming and writhing to get closer to the suction syringe, little paws grasping and clawing to grip the slippery tube, more often hooking into the skin of her fingers, flaying the top layer off in bits and strips. Thin red lines filled in for the missing skin. Austin gritted her teeth and mind-over-mattered the pain. She focused on keeping the nipple in the kitten's mouth, gently pushing the plunger until it was empty. She repeated the process a second time after seeing how much formula was splashed on her hand, face, jeans, even her shoes.

By Thursday, Austin had both cleared her plate of her remaining school obligations and become an absolute expert in feeding Bailey without harm to her skin. As Claire warned, he was still working on the skill of lapping up formula into his mouth rather than smearing it all over his face. She'd spent a good fifteen minutes this morning, washing his face with a warm cloth to remove the formula that had dried on his face overnight, his stiff spiky fur making him look more like a porcupine than kitten.

Now, she was on the couch and he was stretched across her

lap, sleeping in what looked like implausible comfort. His head was on her knee, his body stretched along her thigh, and his back paws were resting against the cushion. She gazed at him, wondering how she made it this far in life without a kitten. She found it difficult to resist petting him, but that would wake him. At four weeks, his whiskers were already in serious form, strong thick white wires stretching out from his cheeks, standing in contrast to his thick, black fur. Even his eyebrows were eager to take on cat form, spreading out above his eyes in long curves. She gave in to temptation, lightly stroking Bailey's head between his too-large ears. A slow rumbling purr emerged, delighting her.

With effort, she turned her attention back to her tablet. She'd scanned in the articles she'd gotten from the library but hadn't had much time to think or do anything about the information as she prepared for her last exams. She wished she could feel more excited over graduation. Knowing she had at least five more years, between getting her master's and PhD, rather put a damper on it.

Now, she read through the articles several times. Repetition didn't help settle the conflicting emotions that flowed within her. She read about the thirty-five-year-old woman who was driving her eight-year-old daughter home from a ballet recital, hit by a wrong-way driver two miles from home. They both died on scene. The article didn't say much about her father, beyond providing his name, age, and that he had been literally drinking while driving. The second article was centered on the funeral for his victims, while briefly mentioning her father's trial and plea deal. The last article was a couple of paragraphs, obviously buried in the back of the paper, on her father's early release from prison, with a recap of his crime.

It felt crazy that her birthparents lived in Falls Church, just a few miles from where she grew up. Falls Church may have been close to D.C., but, like her own home town, it very much had a small-town feel. No wonder her mother had moved. No wonder he had too, once released. Her heart ached for her father's victims, their lost lives, their grieving families. Their whole future denied them because of her father. It hardly seemed forgivable and, yet, she also felt relieved to some extent that he had managed to turn his life around. He'd started over in Colorado, married, had a child. He clearly spent a lot of time giving back to his community, as evidenced by his obituary.

Beyond the moral muddle her father and his actions had made of her feelings, Austin also had to consider his daughter. Austin had to battle her initial instinct to reach out to Anne Marie. Her first thought was how exciting! She could be an older sister. But Anne Marie had to still be a minor, which made things iffy. Austin would need to go through Anne Marie's mother, Donna. Austin was way too aware of how crappy it was to be blindsided. There were so many dynamics to consider in these new relationships. Austin barely held her footing in her new world with her mother. Perhaps it would be better to wait until time had tamped down the uncharacteristic impulsive urges all this newness seemed to bring out in her.

She printed out a copy of the obituary so she could add it to her adoption binder. The final question remained on whether she should pass along this information to Elise. Not the articles, of course. Elise didn't need to be dragged back into that nightmare. She might appreciate knowing Bill had died, though. Maybe it would bring closure, if she needed that. Or maybe it would open old wounds.

Her phone rang. She answered as soon as she saw Claire's name on the screen. "Hey."

"Hey. It's Claire."

"Yeah. Austin here."

Claire laughed and Austin's shoulders inched down from her ears, where they'd been residing for much of the past week. "Photoshoot's done for the day. Thought I'd check in with you."

"Thanks. I'm doing okay." As soon as the words were out of her mouth, Austin did a mental facepalm. "Right, you meant checking in on Bailey, of course."

"Well, I'm glad to know you're good, too."

"Thanks. You?"

Claire sighed. "Busy. Exhausting. Great experience. Exhausting. I owe Brian so much for the opportunity."

"Do you need to check in with him every day? He can be such a control freak."

"Every other day."

"Nice."

"I'll tell him you said so. How's Bailey?"

Austin looked down at the ball of fluff curled up on her thigh. "He's awesome. Doing great, well mostly."

"Mostly?"

As if on cue, Bailey lifted his head and sneezed. Austin yanked a Kleenex out of her pocket and attempted to wipe at his nose and whiskers. "Did you hear that?"

"Maybe. A sneeze?"

"He started this morning. It's gotten more frequent through the day."

"How do his eyes look? Any watering?"

"A little, not much. Do you know how hard it is to wipe a kitten's nose?"

"Austin!" Claire laughed. "He's not a kid. You don't have to wipe his nose. He'll learn how to clean his face."

"Yeah. In the meantime, snot everywhere."

"Deal with it. How's his eating?"

"Normal, as far as I can tell. He's still drinking about 6 CCs, I guess. Anyway, he eats every five, six hours. Why?

Will he stop eating if something's wrong?"

"Well, if it's an upper respiratory infection and impacts his ability to smell, that'll impact his interest in eating."

"Oh, I see." Austin frowned at Bailey. He yawned. "I just fed him an hour ago and all was good."

"Good. Lemme check... Oh good, so it's four-thirty. I'm gonna call Dr. Kuntz and call you right back, 'kay?"

"Yup."

Austin set the phone down by her side and scratched Bailey's head. He stood, stretched, then padded his way up to her shoulder. "You're ridiculous," she whispered into his fur. His purr tickled her skin. Then, her phone lit up.

"Okay, so Dr. Kuntz said to bring him by in the morning, if you can. Before nine, preferably, after eight, though. Can you?"

"I got it. Between 8 and 9. I told you I'd take care of this little snot volcano. I meant it."

"He'll probably give you amoxicillin. It's super easy to give with an eyedropper."

"It's fine, Claire. Don't worry. Me and Bailey got this." It bothered Austin, how anxious Claire sounded, like she wasn't sure Austin could handle it. "I'm not going to wake up to you knocking on my front door, demanding to see Bailey, am I?"

"Oh, God, do I sound like I'd do that? I do, don't I?" Claire laughed. "I trust you, Austin. I wouldn't have left him with you if I didn't."

"How you could let him out of your sight for a week is beyond me, though." Austin picked Bailey up, rubbing his head with her chin. "These big eyes. And so fuzzy! Everything about him is just so cute."

"Sounds like a potential foster fail to me."

"Definition?"

"I'll tell you when I see you. I don't want to give you any ideas."

Austin had hoped to have gathered the courage to ask Claire to stay for dinner when she came Saturday for Bailey, but now that she had the opportunity, she hesitated.

Claire cleared her throat. "I better get going. Some of the crew invited me out to dinner."

"Sounds fun. I guess I'll text you after I go to the vet tomorrow,"

"That'd be great, thanks."

"Sure. Listen, would you be willing," she paused. That wasn't the right approach. She needed to be direct, for once. "Will you have dinner with me Saturday night here, when you come to pick up Bailey?"

To her surprise, Claire asked, "Are you asking me on a date?"

"Yes."

"Okay. I'll be there at five, give or take a few."

Austin had been prepped for disappointment, resignation that she'd blown a chance. Claire's quick response made her pulse thrum so that she could feel it down through her fingertips. "Great. See you then."

She waited until she heard Claire hang up before turning off her phone. Bailey sneezed again. She needed to move around but worried too much about tripping over him to leave him unattended. She had put his carrier on the coffee table, so he could be out in the living room with her, though. Reluctantly, she settled him in the carrier, on a blanket and with a tiny stuffed tiger for company.

He laid in his round fluffy bed, curled on his side, the tiger at his back and a blanket half-covering him, almost disappearing into shadows as Austin marveled at his amazingness. Somewhere deep in her gut, an ache rose up and filled her, pushing up through her chest, her throat and spilled out of her eyes as tears. She wiped the back of her hand across each cheek, but the tears kept spilling out. She didn't know why, but didn't mind, either. It felt okay, maybe even good. The tracks they made sliding down her cheeks tickled her skin and she smiled. The sensations thickened her throat. "You're making me sentimental, furball," she grumbled.

~

23

Austin expected to find Rivka hunched over her desk as usual, creating her next sermon masterpiece with a pencil nub. However, as she approached Rivka's office, the smell of fresh paint assaulted her. She set Bailey's carrier on the hallway floor, a few feet from the doorway. The evaporating solvents permeating the air couldn't possibly be good for tiny kitten with a cold. In fact, she probably shouldn't leave him in the hallway. She carried him down to the kitchen and set the carrier on the table.

She returned to Rivka's office and peered into the room. Rivka had pushed all the furniture into the center of the room, with plastic tarps covering the pile and floor. Blue tape stretched around the base boards and trim along the ceiling.

Rivka, clad in those cheap paper-like painter coveralls, stood at the far right corner, using a long-handled roller to paint the wall near the ceiling. Without missing a stroke, she said, "There's an extra pair of coveralls on my chair if you wanna help."

"How do you always know I'm here?" Austin strode over to the chair and worked the overalls up over her clothes. She plucked a paintbrush out of a Home Depot bucket and set up a tray. Rivka had finished the whole center of the left wall near the ceiling with the roller. Austin started on that side, using long, smooth brushstrokes to cover the lower portion of the wall down to the tape at the base. "There's a kitten in a carrier on the table in the kitchen."

Rivka stopped mid-roll. "Really? On the table?"

"I'll use a Clorox wipe. He has a respiratory infection. Very snotty. Just came from the vet. I was worried about setting him on the floor."

"How did you come to possess a kitten?"

"I think he's come to possess me. His name is Bailey and Claire asked me to watch him this week while she's out of town." Austin filled Rivka in on the latest with Claire, trying to contain her own agitated elation at the possibility of working things out with her.

"Finally. A real date. That you initiated." Rivka resumed painting. "Clear communication. See how that works? Good times."

Austin resisted the urge to thwack the smug look off Rivka's face with her paintbrush. "Gloating is not a good look on you." She stepped back and looked at the wall. "What color is this anyway?"

"Periwinkle."

"I like it. It's thought-provoking. Is it a light blue, a shadowed purple? I mean, it's really indeterminate."

"I can't tell if you're making fun of me, or offering approval. I'll take the latter." Rivka exchanged her roller for a brush to start on the lower portion of the right wall. "Have you spoken with your mother recently?"

"Do you have to ask me that every time we talk?" When Rivka didn't answer, Austin said, "Which one?"

Rivka gave her a look that could flay at least her outer epidermis.

Austin hurriedly said, "Not being facetious. I've recently talked to both."

"Tell me."

Austin started with Elise, giving a rundown on their conversation. Austin remembered it almost verbatim, having replayed it in her head every night before going to bed. "You can't imagine how awkward I felt, Rivka. But it was also cool. She was pretty straightforward after the first bumbling minutes. Anyway, it was much better than letting my imagination fill in all the blanks on why she gave me up."

Rivka nodded. "Did you ask about your birthfather? Are you interested in learning about him?"

"He passed away a few years ago. I did find out more about him, but it's a bit of a longer story than I think there's time for today." Austin concentrated on making smooth strokes to create an even texture on the wall. Doing this reminded her of scrubbing the bricks of the community center. She really wanted to talk to Rivka about that, so when Rivka started to speak, Austin interrupted her. "I really wanted to talk to you about something else that happened."

Rivka stopped painting. "Do you want to sit?"

"It's easier to think through it if I'm busy." The repetitive task also helped to keep her emotions in check as she told Rivka about deciding to visit her mom and seeing the disturbing graffiti on the walls of the community center. "The thing is, I realized these assholes, these haters, they don't care how anybody came to be Jewish, do they? Born Jewish, converted to being Jewish. It's not like they ask when they pick a Jewish place to deface, to terrorize. When they go into a synagogue with an AR-15, it's not like they're checking these little details before shooting people."

"No. They don't care." Rivka faced her. "What did this realization mean for you?"

"I've decided to convert. Officially."

Rivka set her paintbrush in the tray. "And you want to do this. For you."

"I know who I am now. I mean, I'm still figuring some of it out, but I know I'm Jewish. I know I belong in our community, my community, but I want to do this for me."

Rivka suddenly embraced her. Austin looked down between them. "Um."

She'd been holding her brush. Thanks to Rivka's impulsiveness, now they both had a large splotch of paint on the front of their overalls. Rivka shrugged. Austin caught herself before she leaned against the wall out of habit. She wanted to get one more thing off her chest.

"It really sucked, Rivka, thinking through all this and finding out I have this stupid prejudice."

"What'd you mean?"

"I found myself thinking people who are born Jewish are somehow more Jewish than those who convert. I mean, I don't know that I feel that way anymore, but it did go through my mind. I feel appalled by it."

Rivka didn't look appalled, or even surprised. She thought for several minutes before saying, "It's so important to question all aspects of your relationship to being Jewish, and to God. These challenges you face strengthen your understanding and affirms your commitment to your faith. It is a lifelong discovery process to understand what Judaism means to you. I'm so proud of you"

Austin laughed softly. "You're such a rabbi."

"Yes, yes I am."

Austin looked at the wall. They had covered a surprising amount of it, given their distractions. She dropped her brush in a bucket filled a third of the way with water. "I hate to say it, but I gotta bail."

"Bailey?"

"Bailey."

Rivka walked with her toward the kitchen. "Send me the dates you'll be in Paris. I'll set up a study schedule for the conversion. That is, if you want to study with me for it."

"Of course I do."

Rivka insisted on cuddling with Bailey for five full minutes, despite his squirms of protest. Reluctantly, she set him back in his carrier. "Kittens are so hard to resist," she muttered.

"So I've learned. I may be addicted to him now."

"Can you come to shabbat service tomorrow night?" Rivka asked, peering into Bailey's crate.

Austin considered it. Gil invited her to his viewing party tomorrow, but she couldn't do both because of Bailey's feeding and medications. She decided she could just do a drop by with Gil. "Definitely. I can't stay for the supper, but service I can do. Why? Is there something important?"

"It will be a special service, I think. I hope. For you, too, maybe."

"Alright. I'll be there." Austin hugged Rivka for a long time. "Thank you. Thank you so much. I know I've been a pain in the ass lately."

Rivka handed her Bailey's carrier. "Don't worry about the table. I'll wipe it down."

***

On Friday, Austin got to the synagogue with time to spare, though she didn't see Rivka anywhere in the pockets of people milling about in the lobby. She didn't see her in the sanctuary either. She slid into the second-row pew. She looked around and waved with delight at Mrs. Wolfson, who was cradling an itty-bitty new Wolfson. Rabbi Adler came up the side steps to the front, followed by a nervous-looking Rivka. Rabbi Adler started service by announcing both his retirement and Rivka's ascendancy to the senior rabbi position. Austin refrained from throwing a fist in the air. It was about time.

After service, Austin made her way through the crowd of

well-wishers surrounding both rabbis after the service. She hugged Rabbi Adler and barely contained a squeal as she threw her arms around Rivka. "You're amazing! You did it."

Rivka gave a squeeze then stepped back. "Yeah, can't let you be the only one showing some guts around here."

"You deserve it, Rivka." Austin gave her another quick hug. "I have to run, but I'm so glad I was here for the announcement."

"I was hoping you could stay. I have something for you. For graduation, since I can't be there tomorrow."

"I'll swing by Sunday, okay?"

Rivka nodded and Austin waved and got out of the way as another small group of well-wishers moved forward.

She left the synagogue and hurried to make it to Gil's apartment by eight. She wouldn't be able to stay, not with Bailey waiting to be fed, but she wanted to at least say hi.

It didn't occur to her, until after she walked through Gil's door, that showing up meant she'd run into Monica. She willed herself not to blush when Monica spotted her from the other side of the room and made her way over. "Hey, stranger." Monica bumped her arm with her shoulder. "How're ya doing?"

"Fine. Good." She sighed and looked at Monica. "Better."

"It's been a tough couple of months, huh? With Lauren, and the family stuff. Claire, too."

"Yeah, I guess." Austin had never really paid attention to Monica before, even though they'd run in the same loose circle of friends since her sophomore year. Monica had always appeared checked out with her music, never really present. Austin had no idea whether Monica actually liked her or was simply bored when she'd called her to go out. No excuse for how she acted, though. "Monica, I'm sorry. I was a total ass to you."

"Hey, it's cool. We're cool." Monica shrugged. "We were

just having a good time."

Austin grimaced. "Yeah, well, I'm not so good at that. Thanks for looking out for me, though. I probably would've fallen asleep under the bushes if Claire hadn't come along."

"If I'd been there, I would've had it up on snapchat in three seconds, too." Monica laughed.

"Oh, God." Austin glanced over Monica's shoulder and spotted Gil. "I gotta chat with Gil for a sec and then bail."

"Sure."

Austin focused on her. "It was nice, though. Spending time with you. Maybe next time, not so many drinks."

"See ya around, Austin. Have fun in France."

Austin smiled and moved to catch Gil as he started to speak to the crowd. "Hey. I can't stay, but wanted to say it was awesome, helping you out, seeing what you did and stuff. It's a swirl of confusion to me, but it was great."

Gil clapped her on the shoulder. "Man, you really need to stay and watch!"

"I really want to, but I got a thing."

Gil nodded and reached into his pocket. "Claire couldn't make it either. She asked for a copy, so I have it on a drive." He handed her a thumb drive. "Can you pass that along to her?"

Austin agreed. Maybe they'd watch it over dinner tomorrow night. She said goodbye to Gil and waved to a few others she recognized, then slipped out the door. It was after eight. Bailey was going to give her an earful when she got home.

~

24

It was quarter to five by the time Austin had everything set up for her dinner with Claire. She'd gotten home from lunch much later than anticipated. She hadn't wanted to rush things with Mom and Brian. It had almost seemed like old times, Brian being a goof, teasing her, and her mom gushing about how proud she was of her. Austin caught her mother's eye a few times, and there was a hint of sadness, of seriousness there that she had never previously noticed in her mother. It wasn't about something lost, though, more like camaraderie over a shared experience. Austin had wondered if her mom was thinking about the community center. It had not been far from Austin's own thoughts in the days since.

So, she hadn't rushed through lunch. She had, in fact, been sorry when it ended. But, then there was the anticipation building in her, the shakiness invading her as the time drew closer for her dinner date with Claire.

She'd swung by the grocery store on her way home to pick up their food. She went for simple—a roasted chicken, with sides of potato salad and green beans—all of which were currently neatly packed with a wicker picnic basket sitting on the coffee table she had removed from in front of the couch and pushed against the wall in the front room.

She drew the blackout curtain around its track. Inside the oval space, she double-checked the connection between her laptop and projector. When she first arrived home and tried to access the video she'd had in mind for their dinner, there'd been a glitch on the website. Trying to get that to work took a good half hour as her anxiety slowly increased.

Finally satisfied that it would work as planned, she then shook out the cheesy, plastic red-and-white checkered picnic mat and spread it across the floor. She retrieved the basket and placed it in the middle of the spread, setting a couple of paper plates and plastic utensils on top. She then double-checked the small camping lantern she'd dug up out of a trunk. It should give them enough light to see each other. Austin was no expert in romance, but if this set-up lacked in ambiance, she hoped to make up for it in uniqueness. Mostly, she wanted to offer Claire thoughtfulness, without distraction or expectation.

The doorbell rang. Austin hurried to the door to let Claire in, slightly out of breath. "Hi."

"Hi yourself." Claire smiled and stepped into the apartment as Austin shut the door behind her. Claire gestured to the curtains. "Are we watching something?"

Austin pulled back the curtain, waiting for Claire to step through before saying, "I thought we might have an indoor picnic."

Claire looked at the set-up and laughed. "That's cute, Austin. Very cute."

Claire set cross-legged next to the basket. "Any particular direction I should be facing?"

Austin shook her head. Suddenly, she felt ridiculously shy. She set the video loop to play on her laptop, then draped a towel over it to block the screen light. "Can you turn on that lantern?" After Claire did, Austin flipped off the light. Austin watched Claire as she looked up at the curtains. "Wow! A meteor shower?"

"Perseids. One of the most active showers we can see here in North America." Austin opened the basket and set out the plates. "I hope you like roasted chicken. And green beans. And potato salad. I wasn't sure. I should've asked you before getting the food, but then it was today and, well, I hope you like it." She was aware she was babbling. It was oddly surprising, how nervous she was.

Claire opened containers with the sides. "It's fine, Austin. It sounds good."

Austin handed over the roasted chicken. "You gotta be starving. How long was the drive?"

"Four hours. Not too bad."

They didn't talk much while they ate. Claire seemed fascinated by the meteors streaking by, while Austin kept reviewing in her head the things she wanted to say to her. When it looked like Claire was done, Austin pushed the basket and plates to the side and pointed to the small pillows she'd placed on the floor. She waited until Claire stretched out on the floor before lying down beside her. She shut off the lantern so there was just the dim light of the stars and meteor streaks.

"Do I have to give Bailey back?"

"No." Claire turned her head toward her. "Not if you really want him. I've been fostering him for the shelter, but he's not even on their books yet, so there aren't any applications for him."

"I really want him. Thanks for trusting me to take care of him." Austin turned her head as well. "Honestly, I can't remember how I spent my time before he came along. Aside from being a pain in the ass for you, I mean." Stupid way to apologize.

"You weren't that bad."

"Yeah, I was. You've been nothing but awesome to me, and

I've been someone that doesn't bear even the slightest resemblance to who I am, normally. I'm glad you're giving me a second chance."

Claire turned on her side, lifting herself up on her elbow. Austin could see she was smiling. "Is that what I'm doing?"

"I hope so."

Claire leaned down and kissed her on the lips. Austin had barely closed her eyes when the kiss was over, and Claire had returned to lying on her back. "So, tell me about your birth family. I have a lot to catch up on."

For once, the subject was the furthest thing from Austin's mind. Looking over at Claire, though, she figured some things didn't need to be rushed. She thought back to the last bit she'd told Claire, and started sharing.

~

Epilogue

It was unfamiliar territory, Austin thought, standing on a terra cotta tiled porch she'd never cracked with four-wheel roller skates. A porch bench-swing she never swung on swayed in the breeze. Potted begonias lined the concrete stoop she never sat on at three am, trying a forbidden cigarette. Behind her, pachysandras she never planted fill out one side of the yard, while a tree she never sat under filled the other side. She was from…not here, but somewhere else, and yet the space within contained her point of origin.

With a deep breath, she took a step forward to knock on the wide maple door with only a peephole, no window. Without reason or logic, Austin leapt back after knocking, as if the door would burn her. After a few seconds, she acknowledged a feather hitting the door would have made more noise than her knock. She knocked again, strong, firm, loud. She was expected. Welcomed. This shouldn't be so hard.

She waited, looking at both sides of the house, checking out the Honda Accord in the driveway (sensible) and the weeds growing just this side of out-of-control along the side fence (not something she'd lose sleep over.)

A disembodied voice descended from somewhere above the porch roof, asking for an extra minute. Austin recognized

Elise's voice, released a breath she hadn't know she was holding. Elise really did live here, really had meant for them to meet.

Austin heard footsteps on the stairwell, steady but not careless taps, then solid steps toward the door. She hadn't known she would need to remind herself of the necessity of breathing, an important part of everyday living, usually automatic but sometimes voluntary.

Then, Elise was standing before her, framed in the wooden doorway. Austin stood before her, too, a stranger bearing her eyes, her hair, and what else? For better or worse, older and younger, she was facing her mother for the first time. Elise opened her arms and Austin stepped into her embrace.

FINIS

Acknowledgements

First, I must thank my good friend Parv, Keeper of Gestalt (her words), for her never-ending patience in dealing with me during the course of making this book fit to read. Her comments, both humorous and insightful, were instrumental in pushing this book forward.

I have to thank my trio of amazing friends and colleagues—Evelyn, Lib, and Jamie—whose enthusiasm and support were always present, no matter how many times I crawled into work, declaring "I have to make changes. It's terrible." May I never take such steadfast support for granted.

One might be forgiven for thinking I'm thanking my parents here because it's simply what one does. Not so. My parents, Phil and Helene, have always encouraged my writing and never failed to read a single sheet of paper I sent them over the years. True, I'd often receive those sheets back covered in red detailed marks noting all of the grammatical errors (thanks, Mom!), but it only ever served to make me a better writer.

Finally, and certainly most importantly, I'd like to thank my wife for kicking my butt every time I felt like giving up. I look forward to you doing the same for the next 20 years.

About the Author

REBECCA TUCKER splits her time between writing fiction and working as a global marketing director for a research and consulting firm. When she's not at her desk, she is busy pursuing numerous geeky hobbies (that she rotates every few months to fit them in), such as meteorology, rockhounding, and fossil hunting. She lives in Texas with her wife of 20 years, two dogs, and a few cats, the true number of which she will never reveal.

SECRETS MY MOTHERS KEPT is her debut novel. To sign up for her mailing list, visit the author online at www.rebeccatuckerbooks.com. You can also reach her by writing rtucker@rebeccatuckerbooks.com.

Book Club Questions and Topics for Discussion

Book club members, if you'd like to invite the author to virtually join your next book club meeting, or if you'd like more book club discussion topics, please contact the author at rtucker@rebeccatuckerbooks.com.

1. What do you think of the book's title? How does it relate to the book's contents? What other title might you have chosen?

2. What do you think the author's purpose was in writing this book? What ideas were she trying to get across?

3. Did the characters seem realistic to you? Did they remind you of anyone?

4. Which character did you like most? Which character would you want to sit down to dinner with?

5. Did any symbolism used by the author stick out for you? What and why? (Consider the use of

astronomy, physical space, and/or the concept of abandonment, to get you started.)

6. Share a favorite scene from this book. Why did this scene stand out to you?

7. Do you think Austin's anger at her parents was justified? Who did you find yourself empathizing with the most?

8. What do you think about Austin's feelings around how being born Jewish may somehow be "better" or "more Jewish" than converting to Judaism?

9. What type of relationship did the Austin-Rivka pairing remind you of and why?

10. What do you think about Austin's decision to find her birthmother? Did you understand Austin's desire to search?

11. What, if anything, jumps out at you with Austin and Claire's burgeoning relationship?

12. Did you notice the ways in which these two women interact with each other non-verbally? What about the non-verbal ways they inhabited the same

space? Did it influence your reading of their relationship?

13. Did you like the author's narrative tone and style?

14. Would you read another book by this author? Why or why not?

Manufactured by Amazon.ca
Bolton, ON